BROKEN VOW

THE PHOENIX RISING INFINITOLOGY

Angela JK Timms

ISBN: 1522932259
ISBN-13: 978-1522932253

DEDICATION

FOR MY PARENTS JOYCE & GEORGE TIMMS
THEY WILL NEVER BE FORGOTTEN AND
ALWAYS LOVED.

1

Joniel laughed as Kyla splashed him with a spray of water. His muscular frame glistened in the sunlight, his blonde curls now dripping with salt water. His eyes flashed with mischief.

The sea around them was a radiant blue and the white sand below the waves and occasional shell was visible through the crystal clear water. The sun beat down from a cloudless sky, its bright blue hue reflected in the gently lapping waves. Joniel dived at Kyla, catching her around the waist and pushing her under the water before lifting her up and throwing her so that she landed in the gentle waves with a splash.

On the beach two beautiful young women, one blonde, one brunette, were sunbathing. They heard their father laugh and looked up in time to see their mother fall flailing into the water. The blonde haired sibling laughed, sat up and turned to her sister. "Aliniel, I love to see them together. We have been very lucky. I love it here but I heard them talking last night. They were talking about taking us back to where they came from."

Aliniel smiled and lay back down on her reed mat. Her dark brown hair almost tumbled off the mat onto the fine white sand. "You shouldn't have been listening into their conversation my sister. If they decide that is the right things to do, they decide. I wouldn't question either of them. Arla, well, what do you think? Do you want to leave here? You must have an opinion or you wouldn't have mentioned it now when they are not able to hear what we are saying."

Arla was picking up handfuls of sand and letting the grains and minute shells run between her fingers before falling back onto the beach. Her body was well toned and muscular which was quite a contrast to the more delicate physique of her sister. "We'll do what we have to, we aren't children any more. That is probably why they are thinking that it is time we saw the real world. I have loved it here but I can't help feeling that there is more to life."

Aliniel closed her eyes and felt the warmth of the sun on her face. "This is our real world. Why can't it go on forever? You know we can never come back if we leave here."

Arla laid back and closed her eyes too. "I know, but some things aren't meant to last forever."

Joniel and Kyla ran out of the water and up the beach until they disappeared into the green leafy undergrowth of the thick jungle. They emerged an hour later dressed and a lot drier. Joniel ran over to the two girls, Kyla following. He laughed and shouted. "It is time for your training. You will hunt us today." He grabbed Kyla's hand and ran back into the Jungle.

Once in the jungle they split up. Both shinned up a tree with great ease and ran along the branches, jumped to the next tree and the next. Then they ducked down and hid.

Arla and Aliniel counted the usual amount they had done hundreds of times before at the start of their hunt and kill game and then set off after their parents. They ran up the beach leaving a trail of disturbed sand. They entered the jungle carefully and followed the tracks that had been left. They both found a tree that had tracks leading to it though those tracks to most people would have most likely have been undetectable, particularly Joniel's. They moved along the ground carefully, hiding in the undergrowth. They then scampered up a tree each. They crouched in the branches, balancing unaided as they smelt the air and listened. The animals were disturbed. Birds squarked and twittered their annoyance at the disturbance in their territory. Somewhere a long tailed Ekalan squeaked its shrill cry and they heard it crashing through the greenery as it swung off using its amazing striped prehensile tail and long gripping arms. Its long nose would be sniffing out the best place to go, its long tongue flicking out to scent the air in order to avoid danger.

Both sisters remained motionless until they were certain of where they thought their prey was hidden and the animals had calmed down. Then they moved fast, jumping from branch to branch.

Kyla heard Aliniel coming as she darted through the trees and swung down from her branch and climbed down the tree. Aliniel was faster, she climbed down the other side of the tree and by the time her mother was at the bottom she had her dagger at Kyla's throat." They both laughed and hugged each other.

Arla knew where Joniel was but she also knew that in speed and dexterity he was much faster than she was. She cursed not finding her mother, someone she was much more evenly matched with. She didn't head directly for him but jumped to the tree to the side and climbed into the upper branches. She could feel him watching her. She climbed and then leapt from the branch. She thought she had caught him completely by surprise as she landed on the branch where he was crouching. One arm wrapped around the tree, the other around him and she suspended him off of the branch.

Joniel laughed and she looked down, he had his dagger pointed at her heart and his other hand had a firm grip on the tree. "Sorry, Arla, but that was close, really close. You are getting better." Arla laughed and they climbed down the tree together and ran back to the beach where Aliniel and Kyla were laying on the mats.

That night was stormy outside the cave system they called home. The wind lashed the trees and drove the sea onto the shore with a ferocious power. It howled in the entrance tunnel and water pooled on the rocky floor. The family had retreated to their caves, used to the regular storms, and the girls were in their room. Arla sat on the bed, Aliniel was standing beside an ornate dressing table with a huge mirror which reached almost to the top of the cave. Around them they had an impressive array of make-up and dresses. Arla looked up at Aliniel who had just finished dressing up in a fine ball gown. "It was good of Uncle Nai to bring these for us. He always brings such wonderful presents." She picked up the ornate lacquered box that he had brought them the new makeup colours in and put a few things back in it. "Do you think he'll take us to his realm one day?"

Aliniel smiled and unzipped her dress. "I'm sure he will. He told me he would years ago. Now that we are older perhaps we will meet a Fey Prince and live happily ever after?"

Arla laughed. "You are such a dreamer. I think what Nai has told us of his people should be enough to put you off. They are dark, dangerous and eternal. Forget those story books that he brought us as well. The human's view of them is so different but I find it amusing, don't you?"

Aliniel smiled mysteriously. "Yes, I do. Well we can be dark, dangerous and eternal too. Are you going to accept father's bite when you are old enough? Would you claim that immortality that is your birth right?"

Arla looked thoughtful. "I don't know yet. I don't have to decide for five years, you six so I wouldn't worry about it. It depends who I fall in love with. If it is one of our kind then yes, I suppose I would. If I love a human or other race then perhaps I would choose to grow old and die with him. I really don't know."

Aliniel looked thoughtful. "I am worried about going back with our parents. They haven't said anything yet and I think that is more worrying than actually having to face the prospect. I know we've been trained to deal with the politics and I really can't wait to see my first state ball but life is simple here. That I could meet someone, settle down here and be happy to the end of my days, why should I want for more? I can't see why they want to leave. They have everything here and they are so happy."

Arla looked down at the makeup she was putting away in her box. "For us, so that we can find the love that they have. Where are we going to meet anyone here? Also I would think that it is because there are people dying out there and people suffering when they think that they can help. We might be able to make a difference."

Aliniel slipped her dress back onto its hanger and back into the zip up wardrobe. "I don't think we have a choice anyway. I've seen it in their eyes, both of them. They feel guilty for their happiness here. I know that a lifetime here is but a minute there but it weighs on them sometimes. I've seen them in the evenings when they sit outside beside the bonfire on the beach. They talk about life back there and they go over and over plans of what they can do to help. I've seen that dark shadow come over father's face."

Arla closed the lid. "They can go back any time, they don't have to go back now. Father has told me that he is different there. Here he is happy and with the woman he truly loves. They are not threatened and they don't need to be the people they are back there. Back there he has to be a commander, a warrior and by what I can work out one of the most feared assassins on many galaxies. Here he is just father, we love him and he loves us. I can't imagine him being anything else than that."

Aliniel shrugged. "But what would we be if we went back? We've been trained. You could be a great warrior. Both mother and father have said so. They are training us so I've always known that we'd go back one day. Didn't you? So is that what you are going to be? Will you be a freedom fighter for Mission Command and fight against the religious controls of the evil Followers?"

Arla laughed. "If I had a choice then that is probably what I'd do, join mother and father and try to help them. No, that won't be possible, we know that. When we return we will have to be presented at Father's home court. One or other of us will be married off to someone there or for some political alliance."

Aliniel smiled. "We don't have to be. I spoke to mother about that subject ages ago. Father has seventeen children, six of them are women and they have already been married into the Court. We may well be free to love who we want to and do what we want to."

Arla smiled at her sister. "Oh sister, you have such romantic ideas. We carry mother's royal bloodline. Don't you think that is going to be a bargaining point? From what I've heard about the family our great grandmother will want to make as much of that as she can."

Aliniel looked thoughtful. "But it does mean that they will accept mother and that she may be with father when he is back on his ship even though she was not born into his family. The rules are complex but I've spoken to her. She's worried about going back obviously. She has always said that it is years in the future and not to worry about it. I know that she does though."

Arla also looked thoughtful. "I suppose so. But what if they don't accept her? I know that father is important but there are older members of his family. I can't imagine anyone choosing not to love mother but then I've only seen her here. It will be strange to actually have to put into practice what we have learnt. Deep down I suppose I can't wait. I'm of course terrified about the idea."

Aliniel smiled. "I could wait forever to avoid all that in fighting and watching my back though. I really can't imagine what that will be like. I love the idea of the grand balls on father's ship and the elegance of living in such a gracious way. They will probably think us complete barbarians if we cannot meet their high standard of manners and etiquette."

Arla smiled back. "We will cope won't we sister? We are going to take that Court by storm. We knew we were going to be presented one day, that day may well be sooner than we thought."

Aliniel looked serious. "That is unless great grandmother takes a dislike to us."

Kyla stood at the cave entrance. They hadn't heard her arrive and had no idea how long she had been there listening to their conversation. She was dressed casually in a long deep blue velvet robe, her hair was loose and wavy after being braided since she got back from the beach. "What isn't there to like? You are two beautiful girls and we have taught you etiquette, manners and I would put my money on either of you in a fight. Do not worry your heads about it and has someone been listening at cave entrances again?"

Arla looked down at her box as Kyla came to sit beside her on the bed. "You and father have everything you want here. Why leave?"

Kyla looked down, initially with a knowing look but then they saw the sadness on her face. "We do have what for us is a perfect life here. But life can't be like that, not for people like us. Your father has a duty and I will follow him. I too have a duty and your father will support me. Even if we can have forever here before going back, we would forget what we were fighting for. Time will erase the anger of what the Followers are doing and the sadness of losing our friends. That is what makes us strong when we have to fight the radicals. They have their passion, we have to have ours. Anyway, it is time you two experienced life and found yourselves loves of your own. You are eighteen and nineteen now. You must choose your futures and whether to accept your father's gift or not. That is another choice you must one day make. If you stayed here then you could have an eternity of happiness but it would be lonely. There is more to life than our little family group."

Aliniel looked down at her mother while tying the belt on her silken robe she had slipped on after taking the ballgown off and carefully hanging it with the others on a rail suspended from the ceiling. "Why can't you give us the gift? Why can't you bite us if we want to take on the immortality?"

Kyla smiled. "I am an immortal because I followed the path of the White Lady and trained for many years to accept her gift. I am of Joniel's race now because I accepted his blood. I cannot pass my blood on to anyone else because it carries the markers of the White Lady which prevents that. I have given you the royal bloodline as you are my daughters. That is all I can do for you. If you wish to choose Joniel's gift or curse you must accept his bite, if you would follow mine you must train for years and then be accepted by the White Lady as a true believer. Now I think it is time for you both to get some sleep. Joniel is going to put you through two days of intensive training and testing before we have to leave and he does not tire. If you don't get your sleep he is going to really make you suffer for it. As you have already overhead what we were saying there is no point in us discussing this. It is your father's decision and I have to say that I agree with him. It is time you had a wider experience than this island." Kyla kissed her daughters goodnight and left the room.

In their room Joniel was sitting on the bed. He had his head in his hands and he was thinking. He looked up when she came in. "Are they happy with our decision?"

Kyla smiled and kissed him. "I didn't have to tell them. They had already overhead what we were talking about. I think so. I overheard a fair bit of their conversation before they noticed I was there. It is time that they made their own way and found their own lives before it's too late. We can't keep them sheltered here forever. I just hope we have trained them well enough."

Joniel kissed her passionately. "I just hope I've trained you well enough to survive the family. That is my greatest fear. I trust you to know what to do and I have complete faith in you that you will take them by storm. You have elegance and I know you can play politics or at least keep out of it. I don't trust them, not in the slightest and neither must you. What I do trust is that you are bright enough to deal with them.

I am myself here, we can love and laugh and I have been truly happy. There I must be the person I have to be. Whatever I have to do and however I have to appear, never for one moment doubt that I love you."

Kyla smiled. "If we could stay here I would but we must return with our daughters. I'll keep saying it and then it may seem real. It doesn't at the moment. I did think through sending them with Nai for a while first to get used to bloodthirsty politics." There was a flicker of hope on her face.

Joniel looked down at his hands. "I would not send my two beautiful daughters into that pit of vipers without my protection. You still do not grasp the true darkness of that place. Under the elegant beauty beats a heart of true blackness. Well not all of them but some, and it is hard to tell the difference. Our family's code of ethics is built up on strength, manipulation and status. In those things you can trust in a way. Nai's people can be and do anything, the chaos and randomness makes that place very, very dangerous. I believe our girls can survive going back but I wouldn't want them to do it alone. You haven't met grandmother but you will have to. She scares me totally. If I am going to be able to have you with me on the ship she is going to have to accept you. She is a master political strategist and a purist. You are of the blood now but you weren't born that way. She will want to speak with you and on that conversation will hang our future together and possibly our lives. I will not live without you. They may not let me live with you and their solution will be swift and if we are lucky painless. So now you know why I have doubt about going back."

Kyla smiled at him. "I am going to be positive here and say that I can handle your grandmother. Are you going to tell her we're already married?"

Joneil smiled and looked up at her. "I'm not that brave. We'll leave that one unsaid as she would probably not accept a marriage performed by two of the Old Ones. She must see our laws carried out. It is the only thing that has held the Enclaves together through the millennia. Now my love, I suggest that we set worries aside and enjoy the last of our time here. I have summoned Nai."

Two days of intensive training later Nai arrived. He was expected and knew exactly when to make his entrance. He did this with his usual style, a blue flash, a little smoke and his long robes shimmering in the sunlight. He'd left it until they had done their packing and what possessions they wanted to keep and take with them were neatly put away in boxes ready for the move. This packing had been done in silence and they now waited with their boxes. The girls had packed up what they wanted to take with them which was pretty much everything that Nai had given them. Joniel and Kyla had very little to take.

The two girls were elegantly dressed which looked totally out of place in the clearing outside a cave on a deserted island stepped out of time. Their jewels glittered in the sun, the tiny elegant tiaras crowned immaculately dressed locks, pulled up into a bun at the back with neat twirls hanging down either side.

Joniel was feeling far too hot in his black velvet tail coat. He nervously fingered his cravat which sat amidst the ruffles of his white wing collar frilled shirt. He cast a nervous look at Kyla who looked elegant in a body hugging evening dress. She self-consciously smoothed down the fabric and looked hopefully at Joniel who smiled. In the sunlight his pantaloons were immaculate. His polished boots had taken him a long time. He'd been polishing the buckles on them all morning. Kyla wasn't allowed to touch him and he'd moved all the boxes before changing. Now he fidgeted and couldn't stand still as he felt totally uncomfortable.

Nai was sombre, the full weight of what he was doing showed on his face. "Are you sure about this? Do you really want to go back?"

Joniel smiled ironically. "No I do not want to go back." He smiled at Kyla. "But I must go back. It is the only choice really as the girls are getting older."

Nai tried to smile. "I really don't understand why you have to do this yet. You could have many more years here and then go. If you gave them the gift then you could pretty much have forever."

Kyla put a hand on his arm and he looked down at her gently. "If we stay here we could have a wonderful life, I agree. The memories of the pain and the loss fade daily in all this beauty and I blessed that to start with. But, nothing changes back there if we go back the moment after we left. For us it has been years and holding onto the memories and the information that we need is getting harder every day."

Nai sighed. "That I can well understand and I do realise why you want to go back now. I have enough trouble remembering the password for my computer if I don't log on for a few days. I can't imagine what it must be like to try to remember all those details for nearly twenty years."

Kyla smiled and raised an eyebrow. "I expect I have forgotten a lot. But I will remember. I've got to."

Joniel was watching them as he stood between his two girls. He looked from one to the other approvingly. "I think we had better go straight to my ship. There would be no forgiveness from my family if we didn't. I don't want that mistake hanging over them, or me, sorry, or us. It is time to go."

Nai took them directly to Joniel's flagship and they arrived in the middle of the empty ballroom. Nai bowed to them all. "Well, that's my task done. I have to get back to the Prince. If I've got it right they have just arrived back at the new building they are using as Headquarters and I have to inform him that you have returned. He has the MacJoniel so you don't need to hurry. I wish you luck and I must bid you farewell." He turned and hugged Kyla. "Farewell my friend, we will meet again soon." He touched his wrist and disappeared.

The two girls were looking about the room in wonder. They felt the solid wood floor under their feet and the warmth of the room. They were itching to dance on the smoothly polished floor and all the gloriously elegant balls they had been told about seemed to play out in their memory. It was real now, they were here after hearing about it all those years. They heard a sound. They all turned as they heard the footsteps behind them coming across the floor from the doorway. A young woman dressed in a long black velvet evening gown approached and Joniel stepped to meet her. "Ralissa, my sister in law, it is a pleasure to see you again. May I introduce Kyla and my two daughters by her Aliniel my eldest and Arla. I will explain later but I have had twenty years of life in the last few minutes here."

Ralissa smiled at Joniel and then looked around the assembled group. "So it would appear. I am very well and so is your bother. I didn't know we were to expect guests. Jaz is overseeing the ship powering down and we're off of battle stations now. I will see that someone arranges rooms for your guests." She was casting a critical eye over Kyla who looked very uncomfortable. She was thankful that they had dressed appropriately before returning. She, like her two daughters, was also now dressed in a long black evening gown and their hair had been dressed and curled. It had felt so out of place on the island but it was so right now. She could feel the stiffness on her face caused by the makeup that was layered on in a similar way to Ralissa's and she felt very uncomfortable wearing the high heeled stiletto shoes. She was good at balancing but to walk in them and do much more was proving difficult. The floor was well polished and it looked like an impossibly slippery challenge to even walk to the door.

Joniel looked serious. "I need you to arrange a meeting for us with grandmother. It is important."

She smiled and walked briskly away on impossibly high heels without even a wobble. "I bet you do. It has been nice knowing you. She arrived just after we came off of battle stations."

Joniel turned to Kyla and looked visibly nervous. "I just can't get my head around it being twenty years since I walked out of this place and to them only a matter of days. Still, it will be easier when we have explained it and I must speak with grandmother first.

She must not hear any of this from someone else or my life will be forfeit. She must be the first to know."

A tinkling bell sounded and a man's voice filled the air. "Would Lord Joniel come to Matriarch Jerissa's rooms immediately."

Joniel looked worried. "Oh well, if I don't make it back it was a pleasure." He kissed Kyla's hand and hugged his two daughters. "I'll have to leave you here and I am hoping that someone will come for you soon to bring you to grandmother or I will return and take you to our rooms. If they don't then you will know that you are in trouble, get yourself to the shuttle bay and steal any ship you fancy, Kyla you have my code, and get out of here quick."

Joniel strode off out of the room, he could hardly breathe, and ascended the sweeping red carpeted stairway. Once at the top he strode along the right hand corridor and stopped outside an ornate gold filigree door. He knocked and a stern voice inside called. "Enter."

He opened the door and stepped smartly inside. He took a deep breath as he did so. His grandmother was sitting on a high backed, black carved chair. Her long blonde locks flowed around her immaculately white shoulders. Her black lace ball gown filled the chair and accentuated her impossibly slim waist. She looked up at Joniel and smiled, her eyes sparkling blue, her alabaster skin flawless. "Joniel, I hear you have guests with you?"

Joniel looked stunned. "I wish to present Kyla and your granddaughters to you at your bidding. They are my two daughters and their mother. I am here to tell you the full story and I have much to explain to you."

Jerissa smiled. "You do not. I have been speaking with Nailindris who visited me on my ship on the way here. He is the reason that I am here to make sure that this matter is handled appropriately."

Joniel gasped and tried not to let his emotions show. His grandmother allowed a slight flicker of a smile to cross her lips. "King Nailindris has explained the situation to me and I am extremely proud of you. I would not have imagined you could have made such an impressive political move but now that you have, rest assured that I will be seeing you in a totally new light from now on. It was an amazing stroke of genius that you managed to get a child of the bloodline to love you. That you could master the manipulation of those emotions is testimony to your discipline and study. Not least one of the High Priestesses of the White Lady. We will surely benefit from having a priestess of the only Order that can heal us under our control. A very valuable pawn in the years to come I hope. Your assistance to the Prince will certainly bring us advancement in status. I have seen your daughters on screen, they are indeed most magnificent. I will be able to achieve much with them. I trust you have trained them?"

Joniel took a deep breath and let it out slowly. "I am pleased that you approve. Both of my daughters are trained in etiquette, dancing, assassination and combat. They have had the benefit of two very attentive teachers."

Jerissa gave him a strangely wicked smile. "Good so one or the other would make an excellent bodyguard for the Prince. Should that arrangement become a union then we would have one of our own on the throne. I will arrange a welcome ball where you may present your daughters and their mother and I will of course welcome the Prince and your other friends should you wish to invite them. I seriously suggest that you do.

It is wholly appropriate and proper that your daughters be presented to the Enclave in such a fashion. I would also insist that you make your union with the woman known as Kyla more permanent. She must also be presented to the Enclave tonight. I will inform the elders that they are to vote on her acceptance as your wife. I have been informed that she has already taken your blood. That is good. Her daughters will be accepted as part of the family and once you have given them the blood as well there can be no challenge to their rank and position. I realise that they are not yet old enough."

Joniel looked at his grandmother wide eyed. "I thought you couldn't stand the sight of her and wanted me to keep away from her? How many arguments have we had about this?"

Jerissa smiled. "Yes, but then I thought she was unworthy of you. I am sure she is absolutely charming and I look forward to meeting her at the ball when she is presented to me. I will hear no refusals. She no doubt has nothing appropriate to wear. I have taken the liberty of choosing something appropriate for all three of them. I have had the dresses laid out in your room and in the two rooms I have suggested for your daughters. She smiled. Nai did me the good service of returning to me shortly after you left and explaining all this to me. He knew I would want to know this news immediately."

Joniel glared moodily at his grandmother. "I didn't know that you knew Nai so well?"

Jerissa smiled. "In my position I have to know a great many people. Now, leave me, I have plans to make. Which of your daughters have you chosen for the Prince?"

Joniel gave her a very wicked glare. "I would let my daughters decide." He turned and left.

Jerissa smiled. "It is of no matter, either would do." Her eyes twinkled as she said the words, her mind racing as she made plans.

Joniel returned to the ballroom and found Kyla sitting on the window sill. His daughters were looking out of the window at the stars. He walked slowly over to Kyla and held out his hand. "Come with me now, all of you, we will talk in my private rooms."

He led them to his private sitting room and showed them inside. Kyla gasped as she saw the room. It was every bit as ornate and elegant as the main room downstairs had been and had the same deep red décor and drapes which adorned the windows and the carpet was a similar deep pile. Joniel stepped inside and they followed. He shut the door and took out a device which caused little popping sounds around the room. Wisps of smoke emerged from the bugging devices that he had destroyed.

Joniel smiled to himself. "When will they ever learn?"

His daughters were looking around the room. They smiled and were about to open drawers when Joniel coughed. They froze and went to stand beside their mother. Joniel half smiled. "Good, well now that I have your attention it seems that grandmother now likes you Kyla. She is delighted with our two daughters as well. She is arranging a welcome ball for us which will also be a celebration of what was a successful mission. This will be your chance to be introduced to everyone."

Kyla had just spotted the black velvet and lace ball gown hanging on a stand by another door to the room. Joniel spotted it as well and picked it up gently and held it to his face, smelling the fabric. He looked wistful for a moment then laid it over a chair back. "You will look beautiful in this, as beautiful as my mother did when she wore it. I think that dresses have been laid out for you in your rooms. I am guessing that you have the two empty rooms on this floor. I designed them so I hope you'll like them. Would you like to go and have a look?" They both bowed and ran out of the room.

Joniel turned to Kyla. "I know this is a lot to take in. It is a lot for me to take in too. I left here thinking that I could never be with you, I've returned and suddenly you are accepted, we are together, we have the daughters. It is so much to come to terms with."

Kyla smiled. "I am just happy that we can be together. It would be good to see the others again soon and to have time to adjust before we go back to active service. We haven't discussed that. What are your plans?"

Joniel looked down. "In all these years I'm surprised we haven't discussed it. I don't have to go back as the Prince's bodyguard. He has the body double and I was thinking of suggesting that one of our daughters takes my place. That would leave me free to come with you and we can then join up with Kel and the others. Is that acceptable?"

Kyla took his hand. "Why wouldn't it be? That sounds perfect."

Joniel looked a little sad. "No, perfect was the island. This is probably going to be a mix of hell, wild excitement and a little piece of heaven occasionally. I think that grandmother has her mind set on a wedding as well. How do you feel about that?"

Kyla smiled. "Are you asking or telling?" She looked serious. "I don't know what a wedding here would entail."

Joniel's smile fell from his face. "I'm saying we've both been told. I don't think that a choice comes into it."

Kyla looked serious as well. "We can't let your grandmother rule our lives."

Joniel smiled again. "She won't. Well, she will try but she does not hold sway here although you may think she does and she certainly thinks she does. She has her own ship and she will be returning to it shortly. If she feels as though she does rule our life she won't fight us. We just have to make sure that her decisions for us are the ones we would make for ourselves."

Kyla smiled. "But are you asking and am I forced to accept?"

Joniel grabbed her around the waist. "I would be very, very disappointed if you refused after nearly twenty happy years of marriage on the island. What difference does it make to us anyway? It would also ensure your safety if something were to happen to me. A wedding would be a fantastic affair and our anniversaries would be magnificent."

Kyla gasped in horror. "Don't you ever talk about something happening."

Joniel grabbed her arm. "It is always a possibility. We have dangerous lives and one day something could happen. Now I have something to show you."

He led her to the first of two other doors in the room. He opened the ornately carved wooden box on the wall and put his hand on the lit up panel. It did an identity check and the red light also in the box flicked over to green and they heard the slight click as the lock opened. "This is a room I have never used before. I hope you like it. I designed it in the hope that one day we would be able to live here." The door swung open to reveal a large room. In the centre was a heavily carved ebony wood four poster bed with black velvet drapes. Dragons climbed up the posts, watched by faerie creatures who sat in the carved trees at the top of the poles. Walls and ceiling were painted with rich dark oil murals depicting country, woodland and the seashore. The artwork was superior quality and seemed to take on a life of its own. All the furniture looked antique but it was all in immaculate condition and obviously handmade, carved with intricate detail and magnificently finished off. Joniel smiled. "I have collected furniture from some of the most elegant houses on the planets. Some have been gifts for services rendered, some I bought. I have never slept in this room. I created it for us. Do you like it?" He stood in silence, looking slightly nervous.

Kyla looked around in wonder, trying to take it all in. "I love it. It is truly beautiful and an absolute work of art."

Joniel smiled. "For now we must attend to business though. This is a dangerous day still. Grandmother may be on side but that will bring us enemies just because she is. There are some who would seek to advance their position by what they see as an opportunity. We must be seen to take our position here without any lack of confidence. I must get to the deck and take command again. It has after all only been moments and the people here do not know we've had so long. I need to remember what was happening before we went. Later you can take a closer look at this room, it is ours, nobody else goes in here and I can have some time off duty to actually enjoy it. I will also have to contact the Prince. He'll know by now that I'm healed and back but we should visit him and see what we can do to fit into their general plan. I would rather that our friends met our girls privately than at a state affair. Particularly knowing what our soirees can be like. I've told you enough about them and I have no reason to believe that this one is going to be any less deadly. The number of people around will make any direct attack impossible. There will of course be political manoeuvring and we'll have to be careful that none of us fall into any traps. I think we should see the Prince sooner rather than later. Grandmother wants the Prince to come here. I'm not altogether sure that is a good idea but I will leave that to him."

Kyla nodded, Joniel found the girls and brought them back to the room and they all stepped closer together and grabbed Joniel's arm as he programmed in the location and touched his wrist device.

Prince Anathorn was seated in his new meeting room in Kilaniak Palace on Althaeus Minor on the edge of the Selaron Nebula. The palace had been commandeered at high cost from a noble who had at least four other palaces, didn't need it and who was more than happy with the monetary reward he had got from relocating to another one of them. He'd been more than happy to leave enough furniture behind for the Prince and his entourage and he had left quickly enough for everything to be carefully checked out for more than woodworm. Kel sat on his left hand side, his feet on the table, expensive gold leaf carved chair tipped back onto its back legs. The Prince scowled at him but Kel shrugged. Rennon was seated on the other side of the table. He sat neatly, feet on the floor, papers neatly placed around him. He had his laptop laid out on a place mat and was clicking away on the keyboard. The body double Joniel stood silently behind Anathorn but Intendi was nowhere to be seen. Kel was dressed in his tribal tunic and loose fitting trousers. Rennon was dressed in a casual suit, no tie and the top button of the shirt was undone.

They all jumped as there was a slight clap of thunder and the four arrived. The Prince jumped up and Kel drew his blaster. Joniel acted swiftly and put his hand up to stop Kel from firing. "It is only us."

The Prince looked stunned. "I thought you were staying on the island? You are walking. How are you?" He rushed to get Joniel a chair.

Joniel laughed. "It was twenty years ago that we parted company even though it has only been a few hours for you."

The Prince looked stunned. "Only twenty years, why are you back so soon? You haven't fallen out? Has something happened?"

Kel looked up hopefully.

Kyla smiled. "No, we haven't fallen out. We just felt that if we stayed any longer in that island paradise we'd forget what is important. It was getting harder and harder to even think of coming back. Also, we would like to introduce you to Aliniel, our eldest daughter and Arla, our youngest. We came back as they are of age and although there was much the planet could offer there were other things that it could not."

The Prince stood up and walked over to the two girls who smiled nervously at each other as he approached. He took Aliniel's hand and kissed it and bowed his head. He then took Arla's hand and similarly kissed it and bowed his head. "It is an absolute pleasure to be introduced to two such beautiful young ladies. Your parents must be very proud of you. I am delighted that they chose to bring you back to our world and time rather than to have allowed Nai to choose any of his people for them to meet. I am deeply honoured." He looked meaningfully at Joneil who shifted his feet slightly. Joniel smiled and the Prince visibly relaxed.

Joniel sat down at the table, Kyla joined him and the Prince escorted the two girls to the table and pulled their chairs out for them. They were awkward, nervous and slightly clumsy until Kyla glared at them and they looked away from Anathorn and concentrated on what they were supposed to be doing. They then were able to recover their composure, their dignity and their elegance.

When they were seated Anathorn poured them all a glass of a blue liquid from the decanter on the table. He hesitated before pouring the first of the girls' drinks and looked up at Joniel who nodded, so he poured them each a glass. "Well, here we are. I cannot say how glad I am to see all of you, old friends and new. We've just got back and I'm reviewing information. So you haven't missed anything but I'm guessing you have forgotten a few things. Sorry Kel, this is not going to be a lot of fun for you as it is likely to be a very political time as I've just had my Council of Elders wiped out in that terrorist attack. I need to organise their state funeral and to oversee the appointment of new members. As you can imagine after the brutal way in which they were removed takers for those positions are not going to be as easy to find. If they are then I will have to be naturally suspicious of them.

Joniel, I trust I can count on your support and I am going to make an unprecedented move. I would like to offer a seat on the Council to you for one of your chosen elders. Similarly Kyla I intend to invite Maran to sit on the Council. I value their opinion and if we are to hold all the galaxies together we need to have a Council of Elders that is representative of as many of the planets and galaxies as possible."

Joniel smiled. "I am sure that competition for that position will be enthusiastic and deadly. I will propose it to the Enclave."

The Prince smiled. "As you are still alive I assume that introducing your family to the Enclave has been successful? Or have things changed since we last spoke about it?"

Joniel looked down. "They haven't changed at all. My grandmother says that she has accepted the situation and that we have her blessing. That means she is either happy with the political power Kyla's bloodline offers or she will arrange Kyla's death as soon as she can. There is a possibility that she will use the situation to unbalance the other matriarchs. Whatever ideas she has, she will be using it to her advantage. I really need to consolidate my position within the Enclave though. I've made a few moves lately that are against tradition or just plain frowned upon and my position isn't that strong if some of the political players start sticking the knife in. I think I am giving my elders severe worry lines over some of the things that I am doing. I ought to make an effort to appease them. If I can do that I'll be free to join you. I think it is going to be a busy few days."

The Prince raised an eyebrow. "I had assumed that you would have matters to deal with there. May I ask what your plans are?"

Joniel looked at Kyla who smiled at him reassuringly. "Initially I plan to return to my Flagship and to establish Kyla and my daughters within the hierarchy of the Enclave. Then I intend to leave the Flagship in the able command of Jaz, my son, and return here. Kyla and I have discussed this. You have the Unit here for your protection and we would like to propose that you accept one of our daughters as a bodyguard. We have personally trained both of them in all aspects of civic duty and protection. One excels in her mother's fighting skills as her prime talent. The other has excelled in my skills."

The Prince looked at the two girls and smiled broadly. "I would be delighted to accept either one of you as my bodyguard. I am happy for the choice to be yours. I would suggest that we get to know each other a little better before we make such an important decision. I also want to know that you would accept the position of your own free will." He smiled at the girls and they both looked captivated. Joniel caught their gaze and glared at them. They both looked chastised and chose a more sedate and aloof expression.

Arla looked directly at the Prince. "I am sure we are both very able to undertake whatever duties you would ask us to perform."

Joniel coughed. "That would be in your protection, not in undertaking the sort of missions you used to send me on. My daughters are not going to be following me into my chosen profession."

Kel grinned. "I'm sure they won't. Well why doesn't one of them stay with the Prince and the other be assigned to our missions?" His interest in Arla was obvious, he couldn't take his eyes off of her.

Joniel smiled knowingly at him. "That may well be the final solution. It is a good idea Kel." Kel grinned widely. "My grandmother is organising a ball to welcome Kyla and the girls into the family and so that they can be presented to the Enclave. You are all most welcome. It would be an opportunity for us to open diplomatic channels between yourself and the rest of my people. I speak for only a small proportion, those in my fleet. Our nation is vast and there are many commanders. But grandmother commands them all and few would speak against her, and live. So I don't need to tell you what forming an alliance with her would mean."

The Prince ran his fingers through his hair. "I would be delighted to accept although I am guessing it is one of the most dangerous things I've agreed to do this year. I realise now how much my days are likely to be taken up with politics and meetings. But a ball might at least be pleasurable and the chance to accompany such beautiful ladies should never be passed up. As you say I do have the body double to take on my duties here and I would be delighted to have one of your beautiful daughters by my side. So, Joniel and Kyla what are you going to do?"

Kel was looking intently at Kyla. She noticed his gaze and smiled at him. He looked away. Kyla then turned to the Prince. "I would like to re-join my unit. Specifically I would like to be able to join up with you, Kel and Rennon again." She smiled at Kel and Rennon. "I would also like to propose that Joniel be permitted to join us too. We have discussed this and we do not want to be apart anymore. Is it likely that we can return to the Argo and continue with our quest?"

The Prince looked stunned. "Joniel, you! Take orders! Become part of an official organisation? What is going on? I would of course be delighted to have you with the team. If it is your wish, consider it done."

Joniel smiled. "It is my wish."

The Prince smiled and looked around the assembled crew. "Well, it looks like we will have one last mission together before I bury myself totally in politics. Joniel I for one would be delighted to attend the ball that your grandmother is proposing. As to the Argo, we'll have to work out what is happening there. It was sent on a deep cover mission with a new crew. Many of the old ones are still there and the last I heard they were being extremely successful in wreaking havoc in Follower territory."

In the darkness of space two ships were still docked. Their immense bulk blotted out whole star systems from view from the planets many light years away. Osiris handed the command console position over to his second in command, a dog headed creature in black body armour and stepped from his ship and strode down the connecting corridor to where he knew his queen would be. He threw open the door and marched over to her, grabbed her and pushed her up against the console. "So you got your way in the end."

Isis smiled. "Is it not your way as well? Have you not fought against yourself on this matter for years? It was the way life would always be. Eventually we had to be together. That is an impossible force to resist. It would destroy us if we didn't accept that. Our battle is outmoded. The reason for us to be apart is no longer relevant. I have had too many years without you that I've even forgotten what our original argument was about. I think it is time to put all that aside and be together."

Osiris glared at her. "That is all very well but will you release the wandering one? Will you let her lead her own life? We still cannot directly intervene, would you leave her free to make her own decisions?"

Isis glared at him. "I cannot. She was born of a deal that was struck. I cannot break it as her mother kept her side of the bargain. Her mother has however now told the woman part of the story as much as she knows it. Then again, why should I?"

Osiris gripped her even more tightly. "Because of the confusion you have caused by it. Your political playing and convoluted plots have caused many great distress. I won't say you haven't been remarkably successful in intervening without directly taking a hand but it all could be simpler."

Isis tried to pull away. "You are quick to blame me but you were swift enough to create your own wandering one. Would you release your essence as well? Would you let your servant be free? You trapped part of my essence, I trapped part of yours. Isn't it time that we let those entities live out their own lives?"

Osiris smiled. "No. But why did you bring my incarnated earthbound essence back as a woman to force me to bring yours back as a man?"

Isis' expression softened. "Do I have to spell it out to you my brother, lover. Have you enjoyed an eternal lifetime of being able to touch but not enjoy that one act that makes us one. I brought your wandering one back as a woman so that was again possible for them. Even if it is denied to us."

Osiris released his grip and hugged her. "One day they might find each other. We may be denied some things but I will always love you. They will come together. Every time they come close there seems that some act or circumstance makes sure they don't meet."

Isis smiled. "I've played my cards to try to bring them together, the path is laid out but it keeps getting muddied. It is romantic that they will only feel a passion for each other, time with anyone else will pale into insignificance and when they find each other they will be a force to be reckoned with."

Osiris looked at her gently. "Or they will find the peace they have both been looking for. They have got a lot done for us though haven't they? It was worth it. Then they might just fight like we do and find what happiness they can in the times that they do not."

2

Kel was just leaving the training room in basement of the Prince's new palace on Centra Lakural. He carried his sword rolled up in a towel and he was heading for the shower room. His loose fitting fighting robes were stained with blood from cuts on himself and his opponents. He was soaked in sweat and there was a fairly deep cut on his right hand. He was deep in thought and he didn't see Joniel coming until he was right next to him.

Joniel smiled a little nervously and struggled to think of something to say. "Been sparring?"

Kel jumped slightly and grunted. "Yes." He glared at Joniel.

Joniel looked at him sincerely, evaluating his face and body language. "Kel, we need to talk."

Kel pushed past him even though the corridor was wide enough to easily pass without touching. "No we don't."

Joniel fixed him in a moody stare. "If I have offended you I am sorry."

Kel matched him with an equally moody stare. "I have nothing to say to you." He looked down and walked past.

Joniel caught his arm and pulled him back. Kel spun around and aimed at punch at Joniel's face. Joniel nimbly dodged. He turned on Kel. "Well that said volumes. Perhaps this is something we need to take in to the training room to work out. I don't know what I've done to offend you but tell me and I'll put it right if I can. I can assure you I have done nothing intentionally."

Kel grunted. "You can't put anything right, so leave it unless you want trouble. Don't push me." There was a lost look in his eyes that turned to hatred as he looked at Joniel.

Joniel glared at him. "It is Kyla isn't it? Do you feel I've wronged you in some way?"

Kel grunted and turned away. Then he turned back. "You turn up here and any chance I had with her went out of the window. She is my race, not your race, we could be the last of our kind. Doesn't that bother you at all? She is mine by right. Then you go and turn her head with your pretty boy looks and moody stares."

Joniel viewed Kel with complete contempt, sufficient to actively make Kel jump. His glare was icy. "She is not anyone's by right. Kyla has made her own decisions."

Kel laughed. "That is easy for you to say, you won! You wouldn't be saying that if she had chosen me. So she was a healer who healed you. You owed her a debt of honour, you came back and then you helped to heal her. That should have been an end to it and I was happy for you to do that. I didn't see your slithery plan until it was too late. Your debt was paid so why didn't you just walk away? Why did you want more? You were released from your life debt. You had to carry on and take what should have been mine."

Joniel's voice was flat and cold. "I could not walk away for the same reason as you can't accept the truth now and maybe you won't. You certainly haven't seen the truth for yourself. You are talking about things you know nothing about. For your comments to me you don't deserve the truth but as you are Kyla's friend I will tell you. I met Kyla when she healed me. To heal me was against her creed and she risked being banished from her Order for doing it. It was a very difficult decision for her to make and I trust you respect her enough to realise that it wasn't something she undertook lightly. She took pity on me when I was dying."

Kel shook his head. "Big deal, she's a kind person, so what? You paid her back, surely that should be the end of it."

Joniel smiled coldly. "She healed me and she looked after me. I was arrogant and made her life difficult even though she did her best to make me comfortable while I was healing. That was despite knowing what I was and who I was. That was despite the fact that I had taken her as a slave. She had seen me kill in cold blood but she still took pity on me. That takes a very special woman."

Kel laughed. "Yes she is and that was all that it was, pity. You won her over because you were an arrogant pitiful creature. You are evil Joniel, you are a cold blooded killer. Why do you think that you deserve her?"

Joniel caught Kel by surprise as he caught his arm and pushed him up against the wall with strength that Kel had not expected. "I do not deserve her, I never have. Our union was forbidden and we had to live with that. My wife had died and I defied our law by refusing to take another all these years as there was only one woman who could ever fill that gaping hole in my life and she was denied to me by my own people. So if we want to claim ownership, and I never would, she was mine before you met her."

Kel spat at him. "A few years of lost romance and you think you can take the last chance of rebuilding my race from me. Look at yourself? What can you offer her? It was pity again wasn't it. It was just pity for a poor broken creature laying there paralysed in the cave. Look at yourself Joniel. Cold hearted, political, untrustworthy. You'll find something else that takes your fancy soon, someone with more power and you'll be off. If you hurt her I will kill you."

Joniel released Kel and he took another swing at him. Joniel grabbed his fist and used the power behind it to unbalance Kel and throw him to the ground. "No you won't and I find your words offensive. I'm telling you this as the alternative would be to kill you where you lay. I should have killed you already for your insolence. You are going to have to accept this. Our union was not on a mere whim and it is you who is the shallow one. If you call nearly seventy years "a few years" then you are a fool. I suggest that you look at yourself. Was it guilt for having nearly killed her? Was it that she was something pretty? Was it that she was of your race? What you are feeling is an infatuation. It is lust. You are definitely not the last of your kind, you'll find others. You are going to have to get over this or it will become a problem."

Kel struggled. "You only got to be with her because I had been drugged and controlled to attack her again."

Joniel released Kel and let him get up. "I want you to stand in front of me like a man when I tell you this. There is no point trying to attack me and that will solve nothing. I will tell you our story. Yes I was dying when she met me and we spent many months in that cave while she nursed me back to health. In that time we talked and we came to realise that there was something between us. That was something lasting. Not built on any physical lust although I would never deny that I have always been attracted to her. We had to wait all those years and that is a long time to wait when you love someone that much. Yes we were together that night when you were injured. It was the first time after so many years of waiting but only because we found out that we could. You cannot help who you love Kel and you certainly cannot make someone love you. You can make them notice you. You can give them time to get to know you. But you can't force the river. If they are going to love you they will. If you are going to love that person then you cannot stop it, however hard you try."

Kel made a lunge at Joniel who jumped aside.

Joniel spoke softly but there was a certain menace in his tone. "Alright pal if you can't stand and hear this like a man." He grabbed him and threw him on the floor and held him down. "I got to be with Kyla that night because it was the first time I could. You were acting without knowing the information and that is your problem Kel, you don't look and you don't listen. When you don't want to hear something you completely ignore it. Kyla and I have been lovers for more than eighty years, unable to see each other more than fleeting moments when we happened to be in the same place at the same time. We often had to ignore each other on purpose just to keep each other safe. Can't you get the message Kel? It was forbidden by her order for her to be with a man until she attained her first mastery, it was forbidden by my family for me to be with her. Even when she had attained her first mastery it was impossible for me to physically join with her. This is hard Kel, you really are making me put this into words. If I made love to her I would kill her as I would not be able to control myself at that moment of euphoria. I cannot explain what it meant to find out that I could finally touch her after all those years. I have just had twenty years of total happiness with her and I've given that up to come back here because what we are doing here is important. So don't you dare to judge me. Don't you dare put your petty wants and needs above what is really important. We have to work as a team. Can we do that?"

Kel looked stunned. "I didn't know. You seriously had to wait all that time?"

Joniel managed a smile as he felt Kel relax. He stepped back and offered the big man a hand up. He took it and stood in front of Joniel. Kel looked down. "I feel really stupid now. And you really don't know how much respect I have for you now that I know."

Joniel shook his head. "You were defending something you believed in and on the face of it perhaps it did look like I walked in and ruined your chances. We had to keep our love a secret. There is no need now. My family have accepted her and she is a Master of her healing arts and can make her own choices."

Kel looked up. "For what it's worth, I'm sorry."

Joniel smiled. "You needed to say it and I needed to tell you. You need to work on that aggression my friend. I would suggest that you try sparring with Arla."

Kel smiled back. "So you think she's good?"

Joniel smiled and rubbed his side where a bruise was still hurting. "I know she's good."

Kel looked down. "Thank you."

Joniel smiled. "I see a lot of Kyla in her. I wouldn't kill you if you wanted to try your luck with her. She is still mortal. She hasn't taken the blood. She doesn't have to if she doesn't want to. So you could have a whole lifetime of happiness together. That is if she doesn't break you first."

Kel thought for a moment. "What would she want with someone like me?"

Joniel laughed. "If you are asking that question then you might just deserve to find out. You'll have to bear this in mind though. If you ever upset her, she will kill you."

Both Joniel and Kel's pagers went off at once. They looked down, then at each other, then checked the screen. Then they ran together to the Prince's meeting room.

The Prince was sitting at the head of the table. He had paperwork laid out in front of him and he looked worried. Kyla was sitting beside him looking at one of the sheets of paper. She looked up when they came in and smiled. Kel went to sit opposite her, letting Joniel take the seat next to her.

Rennon came in about ten minutes later. "Sorry it took me so long. I was in the middle of amending something and I had to save it and I had an experiment running. So, what's up?"

The Prince picked up the papers, put them together and tapped them so that they were neat. "It seems that the Followers have perfected the drug we found at the Research Establishment and they have infected

Selurious Nine. Reports have come in of an almost total population infestation. We have a base there where they are researching the pods and looking for a serum to counteract the Follower drug. I need you to go in on an extraction mission to rescue Dr Eli Colt's team. They are sealed in a chamber in the Caverns of Ek'la'nadeem. We received a communiqué from Dr Colt earlier this week that he had developed a drug that can counteract the one the Followers are using. He has now activated his emergency beacon and reported the outbreak. The base is in lockdown but the beacon is still transmitting and will do so until all in his group are dead. While we hear the beacon we know there is still hope. Also one of the pods we found was en route to him. I have lost contact with the courier but I have to assume that it arrived. I need you to find out what happened to him and retrieve the scientists and the pod. If that falls into the wrong hands the results could be devastating.

Rennon, I want you piloting and to stay on the ship. Under no circumstances are you to go down onto the planet. Kel you are going to have to stay on ship to defend it as well. I want you on board in case the mission sends you anywhere else. Joniel and Kyla, I want you to go in and deal with it. Only you two are immune to the infection.

If we are too late and they have been taken over and you can't safely extract Dr Colt's team I want you to wipe them out and retrieve what you can. This could be a trap but I don't have to tell you that. Joniel, I want you to go down ship to planet with your teleport. I'm fairly sure there is an infestation. If not, report and I'll send further orders. If you see any sign of the carapaces developing on the scientists get out of there and we'll have to blow that planet out of existence. So be ready to get out quickly."

Kyla looked up, her brow furrowed. "Is there any chance of saving anyone else? The population on that planet is nearly two million?"

The Prince looked down. "I'm sorry, no. Once they have changed, they have changed. As we aren't getting full life readings they are most likely already too far gone. Even if they aren't we wouldn't be able to find a cure in time. I would assume that the Followers are also sending a team in to capture Dr Colt and his team. I want you to get there first. The next best thing would be to catch them on the planet and take some of them out when we destroy the planet. We'll take that decision when it comes to it."

They walked in silence to the equipment room. They kitted up, ran to the hopper and leapt on board. Rennon did the pre-flight checks in triple time as he'd written a sub routine that meant he just had to flick one switch.

They sat in silence as Rennon took them out of orbit and initiated the Eion Drive and they leapt into the dimensional corridor and sped to the planet. Half an hour later they jumped out of the dimensional corridor and hovered above the blue and green ball floating in space. It had a moon in orbit around it and seven other planets in orbit around a double sun. They went into orbit around the planet on the far side of the moon.

Rennon activated the sensors and began his scan. He furrowed his brow. "I'm getting semi life signs on the planet, lots of them. Not human life signs. I've compared the signatures with what I would have expected from the locals and there has definitely been a change. I'm afraid you are dealing with converts. So it is an extraction and destruction for the base, just as we had feared it might be. It looks like there are many groups but they are nowhere near where the caverns are yet.

That is curious. I'm running an analysis of the atmosphere. We're shielded so they can't detect us. I'm waiting for the results back but it won't take long. Saying that, here they are. The atmosphere is thick with something that shouldn't be there. I can't detect exactly what it is without a sample so I'd appreciate it if you could get me one. With extreme caution of course, that is what has probably made them change.

Don't worry, we're on a closed atmosphere here, nothing out there will mix with the air.

If the air is the catalyst or cause then those people on the planet didn't stand a chance. I'm guessing that whatever is down there is something that the Followers have created. Probably all part of their super soldier research. The life signs are strong, too strong for a human. Take this scanner." He handed Joniel a wrist strap. "I've been working on it and it seems to work perfectly. You can activate it without someone knowing you are scanning them. It could be useful if they are infected and you don't want to let them know that you know. Are you ready? I'll hold this orbit. Don't trust anyone. As far as I can see everyone is infected on the surface but the base may have a closed atmosphere. It depends if they have activated that or if they were on normal air harvesting."

Kel was pacing. Joniel took the offered wristband and put it on. Kyla put a hand on his arm. "There are going to be places you can go, this isn't one of them. You have to understand. In a combat situation a hazmat suit could be breached."

He looked down at her and smiled. "I feel useless."

Kyla smiled. "Well get those hazmat packs out for me. I need four, let's be optimistic."

He got the packs out and helped Kyla and Joniel on with theirs and put the other four into the backpacks. Kyla put her hand on Kel's chest. "Thank you, now we'll see you later."

She stepped over to Joniel. He put his arm around her, keyed in the location and pressed his wrist transporter and they disappeared.

They appeared on the planet's surface almost instantaneously and a few hundred yards from the mountain where the cave was. They immediately crouched down into the long grass and began running at superhuman speed. They ran then stopped, ran then stopped, listening and watching for any sign of other movement. Joniel caught Kyla's arm and pointed out a group of locals who were milling about. It didn't look as though they had been noticed as the locals seemed to be walking and milling, walking and milling and making their way slowly. Joniel pulled out a small stick camera and took a few shots of the people milling about. He also pulled out a scanner and took a reading. He pressed the hazardous sample button and the reader took a sample of the air.

The creatures were obviously what had once been the locals. They were still wearing their everyday clothes or the clothes they had been transformed in. Many were in their nightwear and at least two were wearing nothing at all. One of these was wandering aimlessly holding a bath brush and what looked like a bar of soap. They were grey skinned and staggering around in an incoherent group between where Kyla and Joniel were and where they wanted to go. Joniel indicated that they should go around the group so they ran, silently and crouched in the long grass. Joniel left no footprints, Kyla although fast was struggling to keep up with him.

They got to the trees. Kyla realised first and touched Joniel's arm. He turned and she pointed out the band of locals who were shambling in their direction. They looked strange, different from the others, but from that distance they couldn't tell specifically what made them different. They weren't moving like the others had done, these were fast and they were covering the ground between them at an alarming rate. Joniel and Kyla turned and ran and took a path that was in a different direction from the one they wanted to go but it did take them up onto the mountain.

They both found some undergrowth, hid and froze. Staying still until they were absolutely sure that they had not been spotted. The locals who had been following them seemed confused. They were now milling about and looking blankly all around them. Then following Joniel's lead the couple made their way to the right and circled the group, keeping to the undergrowth where their outline couldn't be fully seen. This seemed to work, the locals didn't seem to be able to spot them. Though they couldn't work out how Rennon had missed them with his scan.

They moved slowly at first, cautious and trying to avoid any sound or too swift a movement that would get them noticed. Once away from the imminent danger and out of sight of the group they sped up until they were able to run and they then managed to get to the base of the mountain where they had originally wanted to be.

The mountain towered above them. Seemingly impossibly high but at the same time an amazing challenge which incorporated rock, vegetation and all the ingredients to instil sheer blind terror even in an experienced mountain climber.

Kyla took a deep breath and fear gripped her. She had thought about the climb but not in such minute detail as to imagine what it would actually be like. Now that the sheer rock face towered above her it was real and she had to face it. She looked at Joniel who was evaluating the climb as well. She knew his mind would already have sorted out the handholds, footholds and any possible hazards. She just didn't have that knowledge and deeply wished that he would just say they could use his wrist device. But, she knew better than that, without knowing the specific layout of where they were going they could materialise in solid rock and that would make for a slow death and a very short mission.

Joniel was a lot more confident. He strode up to the rock and seemed to glide gracefully up, his hands moving to holds as if drawn there by some magnetic force. Kyla was not so skilled. She took a deep breath, partly grateful that he was above her and couldn't see what she was doing. She looked and she struggled to find easy holds. It was slow going for her, every handhold seemed unreliable and she was trying one or two before she put her weight onto it. Similarly with her footholds as they seemed unreliable.

She was concentrating and didn't notice Joniel watching her from his vantage point at their destination. He smiled and climbed back down beside her and put a gentle hand on her back. She looked up at him, the concentration and fear was now obvious to him. He reached into his pack and pulled out a rope. "I forget sometimes my love. You haven't done this before have you?"

She shook her head and clung to the rock.

He looped the rope around her. "There is no shame in telling me. I don't expect you to have done the things I have done. We'll do this together."

He shadowed her, climbing beside her and telling her where to put her hands and feet. When there wasn't a good handhold he supported one for her even though he seemed to be able to climb where there was virtually nothing holding him up.

Then Kyla grabbed a rock which came out in her hand. She slipped and began to slide down the slope towards what was by then a hundred foot drop. Joniel deftly caught her by the back of her suit and pulled her up to put her hand on solid ground. Once she had her footing again they moved on and crossed an almost horizontal rock face.

They climbed over the ledge outside the cave entrance they had been looking for. Kyla sat for a moment, catching her breath as she looked back down the near sheer mountainside she had just climbed up. She also allowed herself a moment to look out at the breath taking countryside. The towering snow covered mountains sinisterly pointed to the sky, the rolling hills below such a contrast of what would have been peace if there hadn't been people wandering around aimlessly. Their plight soon brought Kyla back to the moment and she looked around the ledge.

It was swept clean of any debris or fallen rocks and had been worn smooth by many boots over the years. The cavern itself was remarkably small, hardly big enough for one or two people. It opened out into a tunnel which went off into the blackness. Joniel sniffed the air and listened. He pushed Kyla behind him as a creature leapt out of the darkness. It was man sized and in the moments she had to evaluate the situation it was obvious that it was a man, but covered from head to foot in a carapace. The transformed man was impossibly fast and strong. He caught Joniel in the chest and pushed him back. He rolled with the push and ended up back on his feet just as Kyla drew her sword and just before he went over the edge. With a single smooth stroke she took the creature's head off and the head and man fell to the ground. Joniel circled her took up a position on her right hand side as they entered the cave entrance. Joniel stepped ahead and went first, Kyla turned and followed him, back to back. She could feel his solid muscular back against hers and focused on his movements to be able to keep contact with him. She matched how he walked as she could feel what he was doing so she didn't need to see where she was going. They synchronised their movements and moved swiftly.

As they progressed Kyla heard the advancing creature before she saw him. His feet made a dull flapping sound as the bare flesh and carapace ran over stone. Joniel felt her tense as the creature came up behind them. He didn't turn, he kept watching the cave opened up into a cavern ahead, watching now with the ability to see shapes in the darkness, a talent that he knew that they now both had.

Kyla could see the creature attacking her as a silhouette against the sunlit background of the cave entrance. The creature crouched and got ready to spring. Kyla braced herself as it sprang towards her but rather than leaping directly it bounced off of the wall which caught her by surprise. Its clawed hand bore down on her but she moved with lightning speed and cut the hand off. She stepped aside and cut its leg off with the back swing. It crumbled to the ground and began to crawl towards her. Its razor sharp fangs were snapping with impossible speed. She balanced herself, watching it for any sign that it still could spring then stepped forwards to get the right angle and cut its head off. As the head rolled away it lay still. Without a word she backed to where Joniel was waiting, watching for any shapes that may be moving towards them in the darkness.

One creature bounded down the tunnel out of the blackness towards Joniel. As it leapt to attack, Joniel tensed and Kyla turned as he bent down and crouched under her swing. They both lunged and caught the creature off guard. Its prey was now moved and it met with Kyla's sword which sliced across its chest and Joniel's which cut its leg off. Joniel took up his position watching Kyla's back as she stepped forwards and impaled the beast and then decapitated it. It fell to the ground, its black blood running into the dust of the cavern, its white carapace almost shimmering in the vaguely lit darkness.

Kyla spun around and Joniel rotated with her so that he led the way and she followed up, watching their back. The tunnel was almost silent. The silence was broken by a slight buzz from their communicator which was on semi-silent. Kyla grabbed her communicator from her belt and Rennon's voice came over the crackling line. "They are moving in on you. Something is attracting them."

Kyla swore. "We are about to have more company."

Joniel moved faster down the corridor until they came to a metal door at the end. He punched in the code. The door opened. Kyla already had her backpack off and threw it to him. She smiled. "I'll stay here and fend them off."

He closed his eyes momentarily and took a deep breath. "Be careful."

She smiled. "I always am."

Joniel grabbed both of the backpacks and jumped into the lift and entered his code. The door shut and the intercom crackled into life. "We recognise your code as friendly. Help us, please help us. There are only three of us left. We are having severe malfunctions here." The lift sped down the shaft and the door opened. Joniel threw the backpacks through the door as it opened and the three scientists stood looking at him. He ran his scanner over them. The scanner indicated slight changes but Joniel didn't react.

The scientist who stood in front had a box in his hand. "I've got the pod. We need to get this off base. I've also got my work on here." He held up a memory stick. "I've been scanning the planet there is no life out there now that isn't infected. You need to get us out of here as soon as possible. There is some sort of other new creatures out there though. They are scanning strangely. I can get no data on them."

Joniel levelled a cold stare at him. "Get the suits on and follow me."

The scientist spluttered but took one look at Joniel's mean and moody look and undid the pack. Joniel caught a movement out of the corner of his eye. Instinctively he ducked as two throwing knives flew over his head. He leapt forwards, put his foot on the back of the scientist who was bending down and leapt over him, twisting in mid air to land facing the room. The knife thrower was momentarily disorientated, that was all it took. Joniel leapt across the room, knives appeared from what seemed like thin air and the knife thrower hit the ground, his red blood splattering the immaculately clean white floor. The scientist with the box laughed and opened it. He grabbed the pod that was in a protective padded area inside and thrust it at the other scientist but it never made contact. Joniel's dagger flew through the air and the hand and pod hit the floor as Joniel followed it up. His long knife moved like a blur and the scientist fell to the ground. He pushed the two remaining scientists back and knocked the pod back into the box and snapped the lid shut.

He felt the air moving as one of the two scientists took a swing at him with a scalpel he had pulled from his pocket. It cut empty air as Joniel ducked. With a swift upwards movement he brought his knife around and slit the scientist's throat. Once on his feet he ducked instinctively as the second scientist lunged at him with little skill. He cut the hand off that held the kitchen knife as he spun and then cut across the scientist's throat.

The room was silent. The bodies lay on what had been a clean white floor. He heard a click and instinctively grabbed a backpack, the memory stick and dived back into the lift and hit up. As the lift sped off it was rocked by an explosion below. The lift jolted violently and Joniel was thrown off of his feet. The lift kept rising as he pushed the box into the backpack and slung it onto his back.

The lift doors opened. He could see Kyla fighting the creatures that packed the tunnel in front of her. He reached into his pocket and pulled out a metal ball and threw it. As it fell he slipped his arm around Kyla's waist and hit his wrist. As they disappeared the tunnel erupted in flames incinerating anything in the blast radius.

They appeared back on board the Hopper and the auto sanitiser hosed both of them down with a blue and slightly cold blast of chemically enriched air.. Rennon screamed. "Hold onto something we've got incoming." Out of the front window they could see a ship which had just appeared and was spewing out smaller, close combat, fighter craft. They were needle like planes which headed towards their ship at an alarming rate. Rennon pushed buttons. "Kel, I need you on guns. See if you can cut us a path to get into the corridor."

Kel leapt into the seat, grabbed the gun console controls and began firing. He cut a swathe through the oncoming planes as Rennon made the calculations and switched switches and pushed buttons. The Hopper jolted violently as it took a direct hit which took out the shields. Rennon keyed in the home channel and clearly announced. "Mission X567, Planet Compromised. Initiating Clean Sweep." He took out a silver device that looked like a scanner, flipped up the lid and pressed the blue button. Their hopper was rocked by the wave of energy that came from the planet as it exploded. He pushed a series of buttons and switches and the Hopper lurched forwards. It was knocked sideways by a volley from one of the fighters but it managed to keep enough momentum to get into the corridor that had opened up and the gap closed behind it.

Rennon hit the red button and put the ship onto auto-return. He revolved his seat to face the others. "Well, what happened?"

Joniel levelled him with a cold stare that made him visibly shudder. "The base has been compromised but I have the pod. I wouldn't trust this memory stick though. The scientist said it had his work on it but that was just before he tried to kill me."

Rennon took his scanner out and ran it over the memory stick. All expression fell from his face. He calmly turned to Joniel and stated clearly. "Put that by the back door, quickly."

Joniel did what he was told and as soon as he had stepped back Rennon brought down the blast doors. He then opened the back door just as the device exploded. The explosion forced the Hopper forwards a little but the blast doors held fast and damage was minimal as the explosion vented out of the open back door. When it was spent he shut the doors, checked the pressure and raised the blast doors. The back door was blackened and charred a little on the edges but the outer hull hadn't been breached and they had not lost any structural integrity.

Joniel swallowed hard. "Well I guess there wasn't any information on there that we needed. Ok, well at least I know the pod is in the box. I've no idea why the scientist was trying to infect his colleague when his colleague was already infected."

Renon was scanning everything. "Probably because he assumed he was the only one infected. Well, that is assuming that he actually knew he was infected at all. He'd just be acting in a way that he thought was right. We've no way of knowing what instructions any of them had been given. We don't even know how the pods work. It could be a hive mind, where they all know the same information. It could be a control and they receive messages subliminally. It could be that they receive direct orders. I just don't know."

Even though the scanners said they were alright and they had been initially sanitised they still stripped off their overalls and threw them into the hazardous materials bin to be incinerated in the ship's afterburners, just in case. They made use of the black flight suits on board which fitted them, although Kel was a little broad shouldered for his. Rennon scanned everyone and took blood samples to make sure that they were not infected. By the time they arrived they were silently sitting waiting to land.

On arrival Joniel grabbed the box which Rennon had also scanned and took it to the Secure Items Unit. Rennon put it in a concrete box, put the lid on and keyed in his code so that it became sealed in a force field. He looked up at Joniel. "Well you can't be too careful. Guess we'd better report back. Looks like that one was a trap."

The Prince was waiting for them when they got back. They went directly to his meeting room. Aliniel was sitting with him and they broke off their conversation as the crew knocked and entered. Aliniel smiled, bowed slightly to her father and left the room. Joniel noticed the smile on her face as she passed him and caught her arm. She looked up at him, blushing slightly. She hesitated, the smile falling from her face as she looked up at him nervously. Seeing his eyes looked kind and he was smiling she relaxed. He nodded slightly, let her go and she relaxed and left the room.

The Prince turned to face them. Joniel stepped forwards. He spoke slowly and quietly. "The base had been compromised as we feared. The scientists had been turned and attacked me. The memory stick I got off of them was an explosive device but the pod doesn't scan as being any more of a threat than it already is. It is in a safe box awaiting investigation. It looked like it was a trap."

The Prince turned to Rennon. Rennon stepped forwards. "Our scans showed very little. There is a new creature that they seem to have developed. It is not indigenous to the planet, it does work by transforming ordinary living people and seems to be created using the carapace created by the pod."

The Prince shook his head. "So many dead. I'm assuming you cleaned the planet."

Rennon nodded. "With extreme prejudice."

The Prince nodded. "Very good, at least we put them out of their misery."

Kel stood at the back of the group, arms folded, looking moody.

An emergency claxon went off. It cut through the silence and its repetitive sound was loud enough to be felt on their chests. The Prince stared around their faces. "We are under attack. Now that can't be a coincidence."

Rennon grabbed his scanner. "There's no way there could have been a tracker on board. I scanned the hopper, we used your devices and I scanned everything that came back onto the hopper."

The Prince grabbed the scanner off of Rennon and pulled the battery case off of it. He swore as what looked like a sheet of blue plastic fell out. "Damn it, we have a spy on base. You can't trust any of your readings now."

Rennon bent to pick up the sheet but the Prince grabbed his wrist. "Don't, I've been getting reports of all manner of new inventions and devices being used and they are almost all either explosive or trapped in some way." Rennon looked down at the plastic which had begun to bubble. The prince grabbed his sword from the table behind him where he'd left it and flipped the plastic into a metal wastepaper bin where it ignited the paper inside and the sprinkler system went off locally to put the fire out.

The Joniel unit in the corner stepped forward and began to speak. "Poisonous gas detected, suspicious electronic activity, evacuate the room."

They dived out of the door. Kyla was last out and jumped through as they shut the door. She rolled and regained her feet and they ran down the corridor followed by the Joniel unit.

The Prince was looking at his scanner. As he ran he opened the back, it was empty. The scanner showed that they had an incursion on the planet. Troops were being dropped from ships and they were focusing on their base. He skidded to a halt beside a green glowing panel on the wall. After flipping it open he keyed in his personal code and put his palm against the scanner. Once done the glow turned to blue. He cleared his throat and pressed the big red button. "This is Prince Anathorn. Code Black, I repeat, Code Black. We are under attack. All personnel to attack positions."

They headed for the armoury and joined the stream of people collecting weapons.

Kel grabbed a semi-pulse rifle. "Shall I encode it?

Anathorn was grabbing ammunition for his favoured weapon and shouting orders to the men and women who were picking up weaponry and loading ammunition. He turned to Kel. "No point, this planet has atmosphere and I have a feeling that we're going to be moving on after this anyway."

Once they had as much weaponry as they could carry they left the armoury at a run. They took up a strategic position in the main corridor and waited, aiming at the entrance. All over the base other members of his team did likewise. They didn't have to wait long before the door blasted in and after the dust had cleared they could see foot soldiers flooding through the gap. Their black carapace armour almost a signature that told them they were dealing with Followers, not drug crazed converts.

The first wave was taken down and died in a hail of blaster and gunfire, then the next and the next. They blasted and blasted until their weapons ran out of power and ammunition. One by one they threw the weapon aside and then the foot soldiers pushed their advantage forwards. They stepped over their dead without a look down. More and more flooded from the breached door.

The Prince's entorage were forced back by sheer weight of numbers even though Kyla and Joniel were almost accounting for one per sword stroke. As they retreated past a side corridor Kyla leapt to the side, flipped her sword, cutting the soldier's arm off along with the rifle in it. She stepped forwards over it and kicked the rifle back to Kel while pushing the slight advantage.

Joniel climbed up the smooth wall where there seemed to be no handholds and disappeared into a observation panel which lifted up above, leaving Anathorn to hold the invaders back by almost constant laser fire. When this was out of power he held back the advance with his sword while Kel fired over his shoulder and around him. Moments later there was a scream as Joniel opened the panel above the intruders and dropped a portable blanket force generator down on them. The loop opened wide and fell down over them electrocuting anyone who was caught within its environs. Joniel followed it down, knowing exactly when the force field was spent. He landed gracefully and didn't spare a moment before his daggers flashed at an impossible speed in the circle the net had left amongst the soldiers. They were too tightly pressed to use their rifles and too surprised to react after their comrades had fallen so quickly.

Kyla screamed to Kel, "I need a hand up." She took a run at him and as she jumped Kel caught her and threw her up so that she could catch onto the roof beam. She pushed up the soft tile which made the decorative ceiling and used the supporting strut to propel herself forwards so that she flew over the heads of the shocked soldiers and landed beside Joniel, kicking a few of the soldiers in the head on her way through.

Joniel and Kyla fought back to back and then worked their way out, cutting down the line of soldiers. Kyla grabbed an armful of weapons and leapt up into the roof space. She was thrown slightly off balance as one of the gouts of flame from a flamethrower one of the Followers was using enveloped her. With lightning speed she rolled up into the roof space and fell onto the unprotected sharp metal edge of the support in the space above. She bit her tongue, rolled and kept climbing along the supports carrying the weapons under one arm.

The soldiers fired upwards but she leapt down next to Kel and the Prince and handed them rifles. Kel had a few more shots in the rifle she had given him before that ran out and he was able to grab one of the new ones.

Joniel got caught in the chest by a pulse rifle which a soldier had swung like a club when it had run out of ammunition. He reeled sideways and fell. Kyla saw him fall and screamed which stunned the soldiers enough that they didn't react when she leapt and swung along the underneath of the roof struts and landed next to Joniel. He managed to catch his footing as she began firing with her pistol, taking out the front few as Kel and the Prince cut through the rest. The last soldiers fell and they were able to get to the entrance where the infiltrators had got in. Rennon re-activated the force field on the door and locked it as the Prince activated his communication device which linked him to the main computer. He looked at the readings and swore. He then pressed a combination of buttons and the readings came up on the screen. He stepped to the communicator on the wall and when it was blue he spoke calmly and clearly. "This is Prince Anathorn. The base has been overrun. Code Purple, I repeat, Code Purple. Evacuate the base immediately. Take only essential equipment with you. I repeat Code Purple."

Joniel looked over to Kyla and they both headed off down the corridor in the opposite direction. "Well meet you back at your hopper or the ship. Get back there as fast as you can. We're going to get the girls. We'll use the transport to get up to you."

Kel turned and ran with them. "I'll help you."

They ran down the corridor. Gunfire and blasting was heard all over. There was a loud explosion and the infrastructure shook. Masonry started falling around them and the walls started to crumble. Kel grabbed Kyla as a wall collapsed next to her. She was knocked sideways by the rubble. He lifted her up and over it and they kept running.

They rounded a corner and came up behind Arla and Aliniel who were holding a corridor by themselves. They were fighting what looked like ordinary people, dressed in black. There were none of the armoured Followers with them. Although they had some blasters they mostly fought with rifles and a varied selection of bladed weapons including wood axes and machetes. Arla blocked the corridor with the flashing blade of her sword, pushing her advantage and pushing the soldiers back on the rank behind so that those with rifles had no room to fire. Aliniel was throwing her home made firebombs over the top. They exploded with different colours, illuminating the corridor with a myriad of sparkling lights.

Kel stopped in amazement. He couldn't help watching Arla as she expertly wielded a broadsword as if it weighed nothing. He came up behind them. Aliniel backed off and let him in when she noticed he had a blaster. Kel then began blasting around Arla. She cast a quick look over her shoulder, realised it was Kel and kept fighting.

They worked their way down the corridor until the enemy they were facing backed off into a hall. That gave them an advantage as more of them had the opportunity to fire at once. Kel then threw his spare blaster to Arla and they walked together down the corridor blasting at anything that moved. They kept the men pinned down in the outer room until they got to the security lock. While Arla kept firing Kel put in his security code and the heavy metal security door came down locking the soldiers out.

Arla turned to face Kel. That was when he saw the patch of red that was blossoming on her side. She collapsed and he caught her. The blaster hole in her jump suit was obvious by the black charring on the fabric. He grabbed one of the bandages he kept in his pocket and bound it so that it kept pressure on the wound. He then held it to help stop the bleeding. He screamed at Joniel. "She's been shot, can you give her some blood or something."

Joniel took a transport device from his pocket and put it on Kyla's wrist. She grabbed Kel who was carrying Arla and pressed the buttons, they disappeared. He then grabbed Aliniel and pressed his key pad and they too disappeared from the base.

They appeared on the shuttle where Rennon and the Prince were running the gauntlet of the fighter ships that had been deployed by the ship that had followed them from the planet. He was just about managing to cope with the controls and the automatic firing mechanism that kept the ships at bay.

Kel laid Arla down on the padded bench. Joniel came over and took a look at the wound. He took the medical box down and got bandages out. Kel caught his arm. "You are quick enough to give Kyla blood when she needs it, why not your own daughter?"

Joniel glared at him. "I do not do it because it would not help her at all." He continued to bandage her. "This will hold until we can get her medical help."

Kel frowned. "I don't understand. Surely she is your daughter, she's like you."

Joniel shook his head. "Kel, I mentioned this before but I don't think I explained it well enough. She is but we all start our lives as something like human. It is when we come of age that we choose to either accept or reject our father's blood. It is the gene that we carry that allows us to turn that infection into something that gives life and strength that makes us different. When she is of age it will be her choice but she hasn't chosen yet. I will not choose for her, particularly over a wound like this. It is clean, just a blaster wound and it will heal. I didn't give Kyla a choice because I would have lost her if I hadn't done it. It was made with a fair bit of prior knowledge. I'd already had her blood tested so I knew she could accept my blood. I made the decision for her but she had asked me before and I had denied it to her. I got it right, I could have been wrong and it isn't something you can go back on."

They fought their way through wave upon wave of fighter planes but found their escape route cut off by the main ship.

Joniel put his hand on Rennon's shoulder. "Do you mind if I try something?"

Rennon jumped up and out of the seat. "Be my guest."

Joniel started pressing buttons. "I'm going to try that manoeuvre we pulled off on Keraximus Seven. "

The Prince looked horrified. "We got lucky then."

Joniel smiled. "Well let us hope we get lucky again." He took the controls and typed furiously, keeping them just out of the way of the ever increasing amount of firepower that was being directed at them. As ships erupted into cascades of stars their path got more difficult as more of the fighters turned their attention to the little craft. Joniel looped and moved until he had a trail of fighters following him. Then he flew directly at the gas output on the main ship. It was the port where the overload of heat was vented from the Eion Drive on the star ship. He flipped the controls just as he flew into it and the ship flipped upwards and rolled over and over passing just above the port. The following ships were not so lucky. They couldn't stop and they either ended up in the blast or ran into each other.

Joniel didn't look at the rear camera screen, he flipped the levers as the Prince made the calculations and took them into the corridor.

Intendi stuck his head out of the cargo hold. "Can I come out now? I did what you told me to do my master, I have stayed in here for days."

The Prince glared at him wide eyed. "I've been looking for you for days as well. Why have you been here?"

Intendi looked at him mystified. "You said go to the shuttle."

The Prince laughed. "I said go on scuttle, I meant hurry up and go off somewhere and do something Intendi like."

Intendi looked confused. "I still have some problems with your phrases, is there a manual I can download?"

Joniel looked up. "Rennon, can you take over now please." Rennon took the controls. Joniel got up and went over to Kyla who was leaning on the wall of the shuttle. He turned his back on Kel who was cradling Arla's head on his lap. "Are you ok? Did you get hurt at all?" He put his arms around her and his hand felt damp on her back. He turned her around and saw where her back had been sliced open.

She smiled. "I guess I wasn't so careful." She swayed slightly and Joniel caught her as her legs gave out.

Kel looked away. "I guess we know what happens next."

The Prince smiled. "They do fight well as a pair, don't they?"

Kel glared coldly at the Prince. "They probably do everything well as a pair. I'm not watching this. They should keep that sort of thing in private." He watched the Eion particles floating past the window making rainbow patterns on the glass. The Prince on the other hand was fascinated and watched with curious interest as Joniel offered Kyla his neck. She smiled, licked it and bit down, her fangs piercing deep into Joniel's vein and his lifeblood flowed into her, healing her. Joniel felt the euphoric release from the pain as she released the anaesthetic and felt the blood pumping into her mouth.

Joniel looked up at Anathorn, his eyes blood red and his teeth beginning to extend. "If you don't mind."

The Prince looked away. "Sorry, it's just different, couldn't help looking."

Joniel cradled Kyla in his arms, taking care not to put any pressure on her back. "I thought we'd got away with that too lightly."

Kyla choked slightly as he pulled away from her. She licked his wound so that it sealed up quickly. He looked at her back, it was beginning to heal although the wound was deep. He smiled at her. "Well that is going to need medical treatment as well. It is starting to heal but it was deep." Then he took a quick look around the shuttle and saw that Kel wasn't watching so he kissed her. "It is time to go back to my home darling. We have a fabulous party to attend. Although with that wound I'd rather take you anywhere else in the Universes than back there."

3

The Hopper landed in Joniel's Flagship's bay. The Prince had been on the radio for the entire journey sorting out what had happened in each of the departments, finding out where everyone was and organising stations for them to go to. They had dropped out of the corridor early so that he could get a connection. The death toll had been high, nearly three hundred had died in the onslaught and the base had been lost. Thankfully the protocols for clearing the base had been adhered to so no sensitive information had been left behind.

The Prince looked tired and drawn by the time they got to the ship. Joniel was piloting and he transmitted his security code. Jaz's voice crackled over the intercom. "Welcome home father, just to warn you grandmother is on the warpath. You haven't introduced her to your daughters."

Joniel opened the comms. "Thank you my son. I need a med unit ready for Arla, she's been shot. Kyla has had her back cut open."

Jaz crackled his answer. "I've arranged it. The Infirmary asked have they taken the blood."

Joniel replied. "High priority Arla, no, she is not yet of age and hasn't chosen yet. Kyla has."

Jaz crackled his response. "Priority logged you are docked and good to go. Bring my little sisters in. I haven't met them yet either."

Joniel gave the Prince a room in his private chambers where he could set up an office and communicate with his bases across the galaxies. He settled Rennon into a comfortable room just outside his private quarters and once he had checked on Arla in the Infirmary and left her being looked after by Kel he found a room for Kel next to Rennon. Kyla had been bandaged but she was still with him. They had just got back to his private rooms when there was a knock on the door.

He opened the door and stepped back. A beautiful raven haired woman stepped through the door. Her presence was all commanding. Kyla couldn't help looking at her. Her skin was milky white, her lipstick deep burgundy red, her face elegantly beautiful. She looked like a walking porcelain doll. She wore a low cut black velvet dress which showed off her ample chest and slim waist. She held her hand out and Joniel took it and went down on one knee. "Mother, it is a wonderful surprise to see you."

She looked over at Kyla and seemed to be looking into her very soul. Her deep blue eyes were piercing, intelligent and taking everything in. "My dear, you have been hurt?"

Kyla didn't know how to react. She smiled and looked nervous.

The woman smiled. "My dear, you don't need to fear me. He does of course." She looked over at a very sheepish Joniel. "But that is because he is always in trouble. This time I am pleased to say he is not. I find you very pleasing. You will do well as my daughter in law. If you have any questions or need any help with the very complicated etiquette around here, come and see me. I doubt my son will be much help. He spends most of his time breaking the rules, not following them. You may stand son."

Joniel stood up and his mother put her arms around him. "Welcome back son." She then turned to Kyla. "I will not embrace you as I have heard of your injury. He has given you blood?"

Kyla smiled. "He has, thank you."

The mother smiled. "Good, at least he has remembered his manners. The elders have decided that as you and Arla are injured the Ball will be postponed until you can enjoy it all the better. It will give Joniel more time here to attend to any matters that need dealing with as well." Her look was intense and Joniel read it immediately. "I have put a gown out for you Kyla but I will send you another if your wound has not healed by the time of the Ball. Unfortunately it had a low back. As you do not know our ways I will warn you of one thing. Be careful of Berenel, Joniel's elder brother. He may try to claim you by right of being the elder brother and that his wife died last year. Do not under any circumstances take his hand if he offers it to you after making the claim. That would bind you to him. You are not yet married to Joniel, he could have the right and he could also have the right to claim it by combat. I have no doubt that Joniel would fight him to keep you. I do not want to lose either of my sons."

Joniel looked down. "Mother, I have not told grandmother as she would not understand as it has not gone to the Council of Elders. Kyla and I were married by the Lord Osiris and Queen Isis twenty years ago before our daughters were born. They therefore claim my right of inheritance as they were legitimately born. I was not in a position to ask for permission. Nor was the Council in the position to grant it as we were on a planet that was out of this dimension so had no communication."

His mother smiled. Her face lit up and her eyes sparkled. "I now know something my mother does not. I am pleased for you but I do suggest that I speak to mother on your behalf over this. If this is true then it must be allowed to be known to save bloodshed."

Jonel looked nervous. "Do you know something you aren't telling me?"

His mother looked sad. "Your brother has for some time been trying to gain more power within the enclave. This was to be expected and quite understandable. Your status, which was earned, has upset him and that this flagship is yours and your fleet is greater than his is a constant thorn in his side. This is again perfectly understandable and as you know you have dealt with any political moves on his part extremely well. That you can take such a bride as Kyla with her blood inheritance has added fuel to the fire. I would expect an assassination attempt very soon. In my mind this is unacceptable but he is very much a follower of the old traditions and under those circumstances it would be a natural course of events. Be careful my son. He is a supreme political player and not above any manner of underhanded dealings to attain what he wants.

Be swift to get your daughters claimed or he will use them as political pawns in his game. He is my eldest son so has the right to arrange marriages for them as your father is no longer with us. I wouldn't put it past him to have done so already and made some deal in exchange for one or other or both of them. He would however agree with your grandmother's choice of trying to ensure that the Prince marries into the family, it is the other daughter who is in danger. Then again, if she is a child of yours probably whoever she is married off to wouldn't last long but can we avoid that situation please? I have lost three sons this year, I do not wish to lose any more." She looked as though she was thinking.

Joniel looked down. "Losing my brothers was a tragic blow for the family. We have all paid heavily for allowing the Followers to get such a foothold unopposed. Our trade deals with them were beneficial and our assistance to some of their more politically minded members has proven to be devastating. We have a lot to answer for that we, even with all our history of political manoeuvring, didn't see this coming. If I might make so bold as to ask? Is there something else troubling you mother? I sense that there is something you are not telling me."

His mother smiled. "You are as always astute in your grasp of situations. I have long been at odds with Nekasari, my brother's wife over land and ownership disputes. I am sorry Kyla, you may find out family networks complex. As you can imagine over the centuries we have a number of siblings who marry between families to keep our blood pure. Your father has been dead now for nearly three years and there is pressure for me to take another husband. I have managed to avoid this but I will not be permitted to stay without a husband for much longer. Nekasari has guessed that I do not wish to take a husband and has already challenged me about it. She is pushing the Council to speak to me on the subject. You know what that means. I have worked long and hard to get my position here. Your father was a true and loving man, not a political player I grant but an exceptional man. If I must take another to my bed I would wish to have the choice of who that is."

Joniel sighed. "After this ball is over the dignitaries and grandmother will leave, as will my brothers and yours, taking their wives with them. You are welcome to stay here under my protection."

His mother smiled. "I hoped that was what you would say. I will of course bring my flagship and fleet to join with yours. That is if I survive telling my mother that you two are already married. I did suspect something so I called an emergency meeting of the Council this afternoon. The decision was unanimous that you may marry. By our laws you have now done nothing wrong."

Joniel smiled. "Thank you mother. I will spend this time trying to undo some of the damage caused by being away so much. I will also reaffirm Jaz as my second in command. I understand there has been some political manoeuvring there as well to try to undermine his position. Although my four other sons are adept they do not show the aptitude that Jaz does for being in command."

His mother looked worried. "What do you intend to do?" Her eyes involuntarily drifted to where she knew he kept his daggers. She snapped her eyes back to meet his, angry with herself for showing any sign of her thoughts or worry.

Joniel looked down. "I commandeered a number of ships from the Follower fleet a while back. They are following on with the main fleet with a skeleton crew. I intend to elevate them to full crew status and give my sons command of one each and plenty to keep them occupied. No doubt with a little gentle persuasion they can swap Follower kills for political milestones."

His mother smiled. "You are as wise as you are handsome my son."

She bowed her head to Kyla and turned back to Joniel. "My son, I will see you later. The arrangements are all made for the Ball when it happens. It will be the usual format. Everyone will be seated then you will enter with Kyla and your two daughters and present them to my mother. That will be the point that your brother may challenge. It is also the point that any other man may ask for their hand. If they do it will get difficult. I would suggest that you speak with your Prince and if he would lay claim to one or the other I would suggest he does it then. Please warn your other friends not to speak at all at this part of the evening. The Prince will be tolerated, anyone else would not. Kyla my dear, do not say anything other than no if challenged by Joniel's brother. It is safer that way until you know our ways. You will however have a few days in which to get yourself into such a position. I understand that the Prince has only just met your daughter. We can hope for love at first sight but should this not be the case I trust that you will do all in your power to ensure that the Prince makes a wise decision over his matrimonial partner. I suggest that you instate your sons as soon as you can as they are no doubt plotting something and patricide is, as you know, not uncommon." She looked sad, remembering the day that her second youngest son had killed her husband out of a wish to elevate his position within the family. She also remembered, stifling the tears, the moment she had taken his life to prevent further bloodshed and to avenge her husband.

Joniel bowed his head. "Thank you mother."

She went to reach out to touch him but pulled her hand back, turned and walked regally out of the room.

Joniel breathed a sigh of relief. He turned to Kyla. "Would you like to rest a while and try to heal your back?"

Kyla looked relieved. She was very pale and was swaying a bit as she stood beside him. He turned to her and offered her his wrist. She pushed it away. "You need all the strength you have. I don't know your ways but I have a feeling there could be more than just sleeping going on tonight."

Joniel smiled. "You learn fast. You will do well." Joniel took a wrist device out of his pocket and programmed it. He slipped it onto her wrist. "Go to the bedroom and lock the door. If anyone gets in or tries anything, don't fight them, press this little red button and it will bring you straight to me." He kissed her and waited while she went into the bedroom and locked the door.

He locked the outer door of his private rooms from the inside and went to Prince Anathorn's room and knocked on the door. He heard an "enter" from inside so he went in.

The Prince was sitting at the desk Joniel had arranged to be put in there for him with a pile of paperwork in front of him. He had three communicators with people speaking to him and he was deep in conversation.

Joniel sat on a chair by the door and waited for him to finish. When he came to a natural stop in the conversations, Anathorn turned the communicators off. "Good to see you Joniel. I trust that Kyla is on the mend."

Joniel smiled. "She's tired but I hope she is healing. This must have been a bad wound as it seems to be taking longer than I expected. I need to speak to you on a delicate matter."

The Prince looked worried. "Speak, we have been friends for many years. There is no delicate matter that we cannot speak about."

Joniel looked down. "It is going to be a busy night. Not least that I am introducing my two daughters at court when the Ball happens. It has been postponed which is even more dangerous as I had hoped to introduce them and get out of here quickly. But, I also have other matters to attend to. I would suggest that you keep to these quarters as there are various political matters I must attend to and it is a very delicate time. I'm proud of my daughters of course and nobody can deny they are rare beauties. That in itself is a problem. I have no doubt that there will be suitors waiting to claim them either because they are rare flowers or for political position."

Anathorn rested back in his chair and thought. "Can anyone claim?"

Joniel nodded.

Anathorn was running a pencil through his fingers. "I had hoped to have had time to get to know her and to know how she felt about me but it seems that as usual life overtakes reason. I cannot stop thinking about Aliniel. She would make a good wife. May I claim her?"

Joniel smiled. "By your right as Prince you may. Do you wish to?"

Anathorn nodded. "I am not asking by my right as Prince. I'm asking a father if I may ask for his daughter's hand. I would like to claim her. I want to claim her if that is the protocol. Do I have to speak with Kyla?"

Joniel looked down. "Kyla has not yet been presented at court so she has no voice here as she has no status until she is recognised. I would happily give you my blessing and I have no doubt she would give hers as well."

Anathorn smiled. "What do I have to do? This is presuming that she actually wants me to."

Joniel raised an eyebrow then smiled. "Now that I am glad to hear. When she has been presented, if there is a challenge, as you have already spoken to me I will announce that you have asked and that I have accepted. There is a possibility that someone will challenge. That is the time for a true lover to speak up and he'd have to prove some sort of prior claim, which nobody here can. You of course now can and if you would be so good as to run off one of those pieces of paper we can sign an agreement now which will seal your prior claim. It will then be up to you to convince Aliniel that you are a worthy suitor." Joniel's eyes twinkled as he baited his old friend. "On the day you will have to step up and I will put her hand into yours. Whatever you do, do not let go, whatever happens until the Council have given or refused their permission. The Council will then be asked for permission. They will each have a vote and it goes with the majority. I will speak with each of them individually prior to the Ball so I am sure that the response will be favourable. Once done, she will be under your protection and more's the pity for you, she will be your responsibility. I don't know who will protect you from her though. She can be a real wildcat.

I have already spoken to Arla while we were on the island. She is intending to claim the path of the warrior. I don't think it is any great secret that Kel would claim her but sadly he has no voice here and his claim would not be accepted. You are lucky that you are the Prince. They would not deny you and you do realise that it will open the gate to all manner of political moves on the part of certain individuals. Then, you are pretty clued up on that sort of thing so I don't have to really point it out to you do I?

If Arla claims the way of the warrior she cannot be claimed in the same way. She is free to choose her own love one day. By our law only one of my children may do this. Thankfully none of my seventeen have done that already and I've married them all off.

There wouldn't be many fathers who say this but if you are both agreeable take Aliniel to your bed as soon after the claim as possible. That seals your bond and should we have to leave her here for any reason then she cannot be claimed by anyone else. There is an ancient law that allows a woman who has not been taken in marriage to be claimed if she speaks the words if the bond has not been sealed. I don't want her to be put in a position of being pushed into it. My aunt was and it was disastrous. If you have physically claimed her and she has willingly consented then she will be safe. Our marriages are convoluted state affairs that take some planning. You will also be in danger but even if they kill you they can't claim her without her permission once she is yours. If it is reassuring it is unlikely that there would be many in this family who would want to turn down the True Prince being a family member. The status and political clout you would bring to the family amongst the hierarchy of our kind cannot be underestimated.

There is one saving grace that keeps you safe from Aliniel, if she kills you then she'd be put up for what literally amounts to a public auction and there is no way she'd want that. So you can sleep soundly in your bed."

Anathorn looked worried until he saw the smirk on Joniel's face and realised that he was winding him up.

As Anathorn relaxed Joniel smiled. "Good, I'm glad you realised that I was pulling your leg.

Introducing daughters is dangerous. Mostly for me as any challenges have to be taken up and it has been known to be a good excuse to eliminate someone. I've already been warned to expect an assassination attempt set up by my brother. It may be him, it may be someone who he has either paid or someone who wants to gain his favour. As you may have realised our state Balls are also state political events and can be deadly."

Anathorn looked at Joniel earnestly. "You know I'll look after her. And if I can help you at all I will."

Joniel smiled. "You will help me most by claiming her and cutting off any possible challenge. And truly, I know you will, I have no fear of that. She will look after you too. She's a fierce fighter and has mastered most of my assassination techniques and even created some of her own. Her agility matches mine and she will one day be my equal when she has trained a little more. That is if she can master the mental discipline which she is sadly lacking. She can look after herself. But, in many ways she is still a child. Our isolation on the island didn't give her the opportunity to observe others and to integrate herself into a civilised society. She and her sister had our undivided attention and they didn't have to understand sharing. You can expect tantrums, sulks, abuse and probably a fair amount of disrespect. She will grow out of it. I've raised seventeen, I have been through it all before. Never polarised by the island but she'll come around."

Anathorn contemplated his hand. "So I'm to share my bed with someone who could kill me as soon as look at me?"

Joniel smiled. "But hands that know how to bring pain can also bring the most exquisite pleasure. I have taught her all I know. I have to speak to Kel and Rennon so that they know what not to do. If we are staying her longer I need to make sure that they are aware of the dangers here. If you would excuse me I must go."

There was a sound of wood splintering and a loud explosion. Joniel dashed out of the Prince's room to find a black robed man who lay on the floor on his back. His chest was on fire and Joniel threw a drape over him and put the fire out. "Damn it, I overdid the powder again. That was no doubt the first assassination attempt of the evening. It may have been aimed at Kyla but I doubt it. Damn fool, that was very careless of him and I've now scorched the carpet and ruined one of my favourite drapes. Bloody fool."

There was a knock on the door and Arla walked in. She was taller than her sister and almost as tall as Joniel. She bowed slightly to the Prince but winced in pain. "Father I need to speak to you before the ball tonight. I have just been speaking with grandmother." Then she saw the body on the floor. "Oh, that's a mess, did you know him?"

Joniel shook his head. "Well not personally, I knew of him. I am pleased to see that you are feeling better. So she got there first did she? Alright, let us sit and talk and I'll find out in what way she has set me up this time. Would you excuse me please my Prince, I have a daughter to speak to, then I'll speak to Aliniel?"

Anathorn smiled. "If it doesn't breach any of your codes and etiquette, can I speak to her about the matter we discussed?"

Joniel smiled. "Please do, I would like to know what she thinks about the situation. She is in her room, if you would like to go to see her. Remember to knock and wait. I forgot once and the bruises were quiet spectacular. She has a habit of launching things at the door as it opens if she doesn't know who it is."

The Prince left Arla to talk to her father. Joniel sat down and offered her a chair. She took it and sat down beside him. "Grandmother has explained that one of us could get claimed in marriage. I am worried about my sister."

Joniel smiled. "Don't be. Prince Anathorn has gone to speak with her. He intends to ask for her."

Arla smiled. "He is a very good looking man, she is lucky."

Joniel raised an eyebrow. "And what about you? Are you still determined to claim the rite of the warrior? Or do you have something else in mind?"

Arla looked down at the floor. "I don't know. Do you think that no man would ask for me? If so I will claim the rite."

Joniel smiled. "That wasn't what the discussion was about. It was long before we came here. There are plenty here who would. I think there is one who would happily claim you who isn't from here. Don't play stupid you know exactly who I mean. For now you are safer claiming the rite. You can break it if you meet a man who can beat you in combat. You are good but you aren't good enough to beat Kel. You could always let him win, that solves the problem." Arla blushed. Joniel smiled. "I thought as much. Go, speak to him and make sure he doesn't go and do something stupid when you are presented. The Ball is postponed so we will have a few days here. I will put you under his protection at the Ball."

Arla took a deep breath and was about to speak.

Joniel put his hand up to stop her. "Before you say anything I am putting you under his protection as that is the only way you can physically touch him after you have taken the rite. The rite binds you from contact with any man other than in combat or training. It is also to protect him. You will be accepted here but he is not. Anyone can freely kill him and may well try to if they think you are remotely interested in someone not of the blood. So, do as I tell you or you are both going to be in trouble. Keep any interaction between yourselves within my private rooms here and allow nobody to see any sign of affection when you are able to be seen."

Prince Anathorn walked down the corridor and knocked on Aliniel's door. A gentle female voice called out. "Enter." He walked in.

She was standing by her full length mirror brushing her long dark curls. Her dress was gossamer thin and clung to her, reflecting the light from the vaulted window. Beyond the window a woodland scene hologram was playing. The sun shone down on a glade outside the window. A wild rabbit hopped into the glade and nibbled a few tasty blades of grass, a unicorn stepped gracefully from between the trees and looked about before taking a drink at the tiny pond. Aliniel turned to face him, her skin pale and to his eyes flawless. She smiled at him and he felt a strange warm feeling rising in him. Suddenly he didn't know what to say. She took a step forwards. She spoke first, seeing his discomfort and stifling a smile. "This is a great honour my lord for you to visit me in my chamber." Her smile was gentle, her words soft and they did nothing to help his concentration. She held out her hand. He took it and kissed it. Suddenly he felt confident and took a step forwards.

He smiled at her. "I trust that you are looking forward to seeing something of your father's home."

Aliniel looked down at the floor and looked worried. "May I be frank with you?"

The Prince nodded. "Of course you may be."

Aliniel looked up at him, her deep blue eyes looked worried and had lost their sparkle. "I have spoken with grandmother and she has warned me that someone may ask for me at the Ball."

The Prince took a step back. "Does that worry you?"

Aliniel looked up at him. "It does if it means that my father has to challenge someone. I have been warned that my uncle may try to claim me for someone where it may benefit his position. This will end in a fight and he wants to kill father. That must not happen." She looked at him, almost pleading.

Anathorn still held her hand and he kissed it again. "May I be frank with you too?"

Alieniel smiled. Her look was gentle, her eyes that of a doe, soft and innocent but he couldn't help running Joniel's words about her being a skilled assassin through his head. "You may say anything my lord."

Anathorn looked down at her and tried to keep his line of sight off of her cleavage and on her eyes. "If I asked for you would this please you?" He took a deep breath and felt strangely nervous.

Aliniel pulled him closer to her. "If anyone is to claim me I would that it was you. Why are you asking? You can ask for me at the Ball, I have no say in the matter. No doubt my father would not object to our union."

Anathorn looked down at her and tried to cast off the fragile, vulnerable image that she was presenting. "I'm asking as I want a wife who is an equal. I can claim you in words and then you choose your own lover later or you can share my bed and we'll be united. It is your choice. Either way you will be under my protection. You don't have to win me with your wiles. I would ask anyway."

Aliniel smiled and she relaxed. She went from fragile waif to confident woman in a moment. She pulled him closer to her and reached up and put her arms around his neck, pulled his head down and kissed him. "In this family it sounds as though if you don't take what you want someone else will make that choice for you. I have made my choice."

The Prince was breathless and a little shocked. He bent down and kissed her again and she responded. "Well at least I've given you the choice. Well, we will have some time to get to know each other before the Ball." He bowed and left her as he didn't actually trust himself to leave if he'd waited any longer.

Arla left Joniel with the mess in his room and a slightly shaken Kyla who he had woken up when he went into the room to check on her. She had slept through the explosion as the room was bombproof and sealed but was now awake and looking as though she hadn't slept for years. He put his arms around her but he forgot her back was injured until she howled in pain. He turned her around and pulled the bandages off. He looked in horror at the burn marks where there had only been a cut before. "Who bandaged you?"

Kyla swayed slightly and fell into his arms. "I don't know, someone down in the Infirmary." Then she passed out.

Joniel howled and ran to his desk and dialled a number on the intercom. There was a moment's wait and then the soft voice of his mother came over the speaker. "Joniel?"

Joniel was out of breath and in a panic as he felt Kyla's life slipping away from her. "Mother, Kyla has been poisoned."

The link was cut and moments later a slightly out of breath woman darted into the room. Joniel held Kyla and showed his mother her back. His mother then grabbed the bandages and sniffed them. "You are right. You fool Joniel, why didn't you watch her more carefully. You could lose her here because of your stupidity."

They carried Kyla back into the bedroom and Joniel's mother bore down on Kyla's neck and drained her of all blood, spitting it out onto the bedding and floor. Blood ran down her face, neck and dress and over Kyla but she didn't stop, she didn't care. She wasn't in a frenzy, she was in a panic. Kyla became very pale, her skin started to go translucent but Joniel's mother did not stop. She looked up, her eyes blood red her fangs extended. "Be ready she is going to need your blood. I'm not giving her mine." She gasped for air.

"Your bond is important and this will seal a bond between you forever. I am replacing all her blood with yours." She bit down on her again and the body started to spasm. She then broke free with a long gasp. "Give me your wrist." She snatched his hand and bit viciously into it without using any anaesthetic. He howled in pain. She smiled momentarily when she looked up. "Serves you right you idiot."

She held his wrist over Kyla's mouth and began to work on her throat so that she swallowed. She carried on until Joniel passed out and fell onto the bed. When she had finished she laid Kyla gently on her front on the bed and went over to her son. He was barely conscious. "I'm sorry my son." She stroked his hair and bit her own wrist and poured the blood into his mouth. She shook her head. "You are my most precious boy but sometimes you can be a complete idiot."

Joniel came around and when he was able to stand up his mother washed the blood off of his mouth with a wet towel. She grabbed another towel from the washbasin, tore what was left of Kyla's clothes off of her back and began to wash the wound. Her long fragile hands were surprisingly gentle as she washed the venom off and gently dabbed the burns. "She has a good bone structure, much muscle, I like that in a woman. She has given you fine daughters, you should be very proud. There should be more."

Joniel looked down. "I am very proud. I do not deserve her. Prince Anathorn is going to ask for Aliniel, Arla is going to take the Rite of the Warrior. Prince Anathorn has gone to speak with Aliniel to ask her views."

His mother smiled. "Well you got something right then. I admire the Prince's courage for doing that and if she agrees I admire his wisdom more. They will be a good match. Well if any of us survive this I will be very surprised but if we don't I'd be very disappointed. I must now go to change and wash, I appear to have spilled something on my dress. I am sure you will make her more comfortable. Her wound will be healed by tonight. Take more care of her next time. You have lived here long enough to know that nowhere is safe."

Joniel looked worried. "Arla was treated in the infirmary. Do you think she will be alright?"

His mother laughed. "Yes, and you have a dead doctor to prove it. As she was in the infirmary I had one of my nurses there keeping an eye on her. It seems that one of the doctors was a little too enthusiastic with one of his doses and to show him the error of his ways she permitted him to experience it himself. Didn't you wonder why it took Kyla such a long time to heal such a minor wound? I had assumed she was in your care so I didn't have to worry about such matters. Really my son, sometimes you can be so dim. But thankfully most of the time I am immensely proud of you."

Joniel looked at his feet. "No, well yes. I've been too distracted by other matters. I thought she was alright."

His mother was washing the blood of her face and neck but she stopped and glared at him, walked over to him and slapped him across the face. "Never abandon your duties to your wife and your family. They must come first. You nearly lost your love tonight because of your own foolishness. Don't let it happen again. Don't expect her to know or be as cautious as you should be, or your daughters either. This is not their world. They need you to protect them, to see these things coming. You are punishing yourself, now you have been punished as no doubt that hurt. So get over it and concentrate. This is no place to be off in the clouds. We all make mistakes, it is how we learn from them that is important, you know that."

Kyla woke up and looked around the room at the blood on the sheets and walls. "What happened?"

Joniel's mother sat on the bed beside her daughter in law. "Don't worry my child. It was only an assassination attempt, nothing out of the ordinary." She stroked Kyla's hair. "Your back will heal up by tonight and we will have a beautiful dress for you to wear." She turned out of Kyla's sight and glared at her son. "I must go now. Joniel will take care of you. Joniel, get someone to change those sheets, they are dirty." She stood up and walked gracefully out of the room.

Anathorn passed her in the corridor and was slightly shocked to see the blood on her dress, face and hands. She curtseyed gracefully as she passed him. He couldn't help admiring her beauty or her cleavage. She noticed him looking and glared at him. As she passed him she smiled to herself though. He entered the private rooms and was about to shut the door when two men in velvet court livery walked up the corridor carrying replacement doors for Joniel and Kyla's bedroom. It took them minutes to repair the damage and they left without a word.

Joniel was sitting in a high backed leather chair. The doors to the room were left open and he was watching Kyla sleeping. The Prince stopped when he saw him. "What's the matter? You look deathly pale. Well more pale than you usually do."

Joniel shook his head. "I was a fool and I nearly lost her."

The Prince looked stunned. "What do you mean?"

Joniel buried his head in his hands. "Her bandages were poisoned. We nearly lost her."

Anathorn stepped back in horror. "But this is your home."

Joniel looked up at him. "This is what we are like. Why do you think I let my daughters grow up away from here? Take my daughter away with you and keep her far from this place. Don't let Aliniel be a part of all this. I'm regretting bringing Kyla back here. I wish we could just leave now."

The Prince looked stunned. "Not in the morning?"

Joniel wiped his face. "Do you seriously want to spend a night in this place when my family and the court are still here? Do you have a death wish? Trouble is that we're stuck here until the Ball. I was going to ask you to set up a reason to go. Perhaps to get us called out of the ball after we have done the presentation of the girls. I had this idea that you could take Aliniel with you, take her as your own and we'd sort out the technicalities afterwards. Oh if you could get the girls out tonight."

Anathorn looked stunned. "You think there is a possibility you might get killed in your own home?"

Joniel raised an eyebrow. "With my family and the court here, very likely."

The sleepless night passed without incident. Joniel was exhausted and he couldn't think straight. He needed to watch Kyla all night just to make sure that she was alright. That and his head being running with the many and convoluted possibilities and possible political goings on that could be happening. He didn't' know where to start, for the first time in his life, he couldn't think of a plan as nobody had shown their hand. If there was anything going on, he didn't know what. All he could think of was that it may well involve his mother and with a mother and two daughters unattached as well as Kyla now publicly claimed by him officially, he was in a very difficult position. Plenty of people wanted his position and his fleet. Plenty were just waiting for him to make that big mistake.

That was it! That was his answer. If he could convince his enemies that they would get what they wanted by doing what he wanted now, that would be the trick. It made sense in a moment. He was going off to fight with the True Prince and to many that would seem like a suicide mission. Eventually someone would kill him and then they would have all that they wanted. If they believed that then they may let him go away in peace. It was his mother who was the problem, she was an issue that he had to address. She wasn't going to like it but he had to arrange for her to be bonded with someone. It had been enough years since his father had died, it was time that she was no longer alone. But, who would he accept as a father. That took even more thought.

Who was a likely candidate? It couldn't be anyone with political motivation as his potential new father would have greater status than himself after the bonding. So it would have to be someone who would sympathise with his views and the way he ran his flagship. Granted, the flagship and fleet would still be his, but it was the other power he wanted to hold onto. The ability to speak directly to the High King, something he would have to do sooner rather than later.

It was a pressing problem and one he couldn't easily solve. His mother was headstrong, beautiful and a prize that many in the enclave would dearly want. That wasn't a son's pride, it was his assessment as a political player. He didn't want to use his mother as a pawn and he wouldn't but he certainly wasn't going to let anyone else do so either.

So he had to think, who would actually love his mother. He almost laughed. A creature like him, a political player trying to think about who would love his mother. The answer then came to him. There was only one person he could think of who had loved his mother truly through all the years, even when she was married to his father. It hadn't been a romantic love but it had been a caring love that had brought them together on many an occasion sorting out the many difficulties that the families had faced.

He slipped out of bed, slipping on his silky satin robe and went to his writing desk. He lit a candle, the flame flickered slightly and then stood tall and true, illuminating a bubble of brilliance as Joniel reached into the wooden drawer. He pulled out a piece of vellum, gold in colour and edged with gold leaf. The spiralling knotwork that framed the sheet shone slightly, reflecting the candle light. He pulled a quill from the pot where they stood. He opened the ink bottle with his immaculately manicured fingers and set the lid down beside the bottle. He took the quill and dipped it thoughtfully into the ink, feeling the slight resistance as the quill pierced the skin of the ink. He felt the resistance of the ink as he swirled it around slightly, picking up the red pigment and he brought it slowly out of the bottle, still thinking. He dragged it slightly on the lip, allowing the excess ink to run back down into the bottle and held it for a moment, that one last thought before he began writing.

The quill nib scratched over the vellum leaving an elegant spider like string of words in its wake. Words that would make or break him but words that he knew he had to write.

When done he rolled the vellum, folded it flat and folded in the edges to meet in the middle so it was impossible to read what was inside without opening it. He then took a stub of wax with a wick down the centre and held it into the candle flame so that the wick burned on its own. He held it so the wax dripped copiously onto the join in the vellum and sealed it with his signet ring. The deed was part done. He flicked open a communicator and pressed a blue button. He placed the message into a bag, sealed that with a mechanical device, set the combination and time before liberally covered the bag with contact poison.

The messenger knocked gently at the door and Joniel handed the message in a bag to him, holding just the string. The messenger took the bag as he knew he must, knowing that it had the poison on it. He then ran as fast as he could to deliver the message before the poison killed him. Joniel sent a message to the recipient with the number for the poison that he had used, knowing that the messenger would be given the antidote when he safely delivered the message within the time frame Joniel had given him and knowing that only the recipient could open the message as the code to disarm the device was also sent with the message.

Joniel still couldn't sleep and it was now made worse as he was worried he'd done the right thing. There were other decisions to make and other political moves he could, would and should make. It was sorting out which were the right ones from the ones that would lead him into difficulties that was difficult. That he wouldn't be here made it doubly hard. He knew that Jaz could run the ship but he didn't want to leave him in a vulnerable position either. Every decision had to be well thought out and there wasn't anyone he could talk it over with. He didn't want to trouble Kyla with it and much as he loved her there was no way she could comprehend many hundreds of years of inbuilt hatred and the way some of the people even in his own family worked. No, this was something he had to work out alone. Or perhaps he didn't have to do it completely alone.

He flicked the intercom and pressed the button programmed to call his mother. If she was sleeping it would be on message, if not he'd get straight through. He got straight through.

"Joniel, why are you not asleep?"

Joniel hesitated for a moment. "I can't sleep. There is too much to think about. Can we speak?"

The line went dead and a few minutes later there was a gentle tap on the door. He opened it and his mother was standing there, dressed in a long black velvet dressing gown with ruffles around the neck as elegant as any ball gown. Her hair was immaculately brushed and her make up perfect. She drifted in and Joniel offered her a chair. He quietly closed the door to the bedroom, rendering it soundproofed so neither Kyla and as the door to his chamber was shut too, the Prince, could hear what they were saying.

His mother took a seat and he offered him some of his Trilurian Brandy. She accepted the offered crystal glass, her long red nails making a slight "tink" noise on the fine glass. "So my son, what would we speak about at this hour?"

Joniel sat down after pouring himself a glass. "I would speak about what I should do."

His mother raised an eyebrow. "So, after all these years you actually want my advice?"

"Mother, these are dangerous times and you know far more about what is going on. You have the least to gain from my removal from the situation. We have a good marriage between myself and Kyla. Honestly, I didn't plan it that way. We have a good marriage well on the way to being a likelihood between the Prince and Aliniel, may the gods help him. Arla, well that may be a union I arrange just to get some peace within those who are fighting for the worlds. Kel is a problem, he was in love with Kyla, if I can get him to fall in love with Arla, that will remove a potential threat I obviously have there. There are my cards on the table.

You have a problem here with the etiquette of having to take a husband. The choice there has to be yours but it is an issue. My brother is a threat and that has already been dealt with by my earlier marriage to Kyla."

"My son, I have informed your grandmother and those who need to know. They are keeping the information to themselves as by our tradition as you know it can only be announced at a public function. We are bringing the Ball forward to tomorrow night, that will allow you time to finalise your moves and get your friends to safety. I suggest you leave either at the Ball or very soon afterwards. If I may remain here I will add my flagship and fleet to yours. That will alleviate any threat from those present as between us we outnumber any fleet they can put against us. I will take a new mate, I just don't know who yet.

Your daughter Tagathian is becoming a player as well. I would watch her if I were you. She is not on board at the moment as she and her husband are visiting. I know where she said she was going, but she certainly didn't go there as I have people there and they have informed me otherwise. She is yet to provide an heir to her lineage and I think that she tires of her husband. I wouldn't be surprised if he has some sort of accident on their travels and she returns without him. She may have another lover in the wings. Those I have watching her have told me that Sessarius, of the Family Heliosath, has been paying her a fair amount of attention. It will do her no good, the Elders will not grant her a marriage to him, I have already assured that. It is a situation you will have to deal with as her husband is very popular. You have a choice, you can let it play out, and it may well have done so already. Or you can deal with her and maintain her husband within the family. I do not have the resources currently to undertake this and as she is your daughter you have the final say on the matter."

Joniel thought for a moment. The image of his fiery and feisty daughter flickered into his mind. He remembered when she was born and how she had been a real torment to her mother as a child. He took a very deep breath and let it out slowly. "She is my daughter and so far other than having an affair we are not certain that she will cause him harm. I would rather avoid the difficulties of his removal under suspicious circumstances and the possible implication of my daughter. She is a vicious player as you may have realised but she is not a rational one. She would not play her aces carefully and you are probably right, she will arrange an accident for him which will be blindingly obvious to all who know. She will count on the family name keeping her from harm and probably she is also relying on my intercession to ensure her second marriage. We have nothing to gain from this and much to lose. I will not have her removed, she has a lot to learn. I will summon her back to the family and I trust that in your capable hands she will have a stunning revelation and a renewed passion for her husband. In short I will call her back to the family and hold back the money that I give her for her support until she has spent some time with you. When you assure me that the situation has been diffused I will reinstate her finances and ensure that they are dependent on the longevity and good health of her husband."

Joniel flipped open his communication device, opened a channel to one of his ships and immediately its engines flared and it departed for his daughter's last known location bearing the message that it was commanded to deliver.

Joniel sat back in his chair. "That is one matter on its way to being dealt with."

Joniel's mother smiled and took a delicate sip of the warming amber liquid. "You have done well. Your restraint is a valuable asset. May I suggest that you address the Commanders in your fleet and the hierarchical problem that seems to have arisen? There is no order of superiority in your fleet and it seems that your Commanders seem intent on creating their own. It is leading to a certain competitiveness in all walks of life and a few of them have started political manoeuvers in order to see other Commanders removed. I know that you like to reward or punish as events happen but in this situation I am speaking from experience. I had a similar problem with my Commanders a while back."

Joniel smiled. It had been something he had thought about. "What did you do to alleviate this situation?"

His mother smiled and looked into the amber liquid. "I created a ranking system between them which they could climb as they achieved points and I made sure that there were many points lost for losing anyone in the fleet. They suddenly became very respectful and protective of their fellow Commanders."

Joniel took a drink from his glass and thought a moment. "That system I like and as it already has a precedent I will establish it. I am also going to give Jaz official command of this flagship while I'm away with full inheritance rights. I could be wrong but I think he is the least likely to remove me to make that situation permanent as he's been doing the job long enough."

His mother looked thoughtful. "Jaz is a political player and if he gets what he wants by your continued wellbeing he is more than likely to be content with that situation. He has made various moves which have given him his own power within the fleet. This has been through many avenues that you may not have considered. He has been loaning finances to some of those who have gambling problems and picking up their debts from others. He owns a small proportion of my fleet that way. I'm doing nothing about it as it is keeping my troops from trouble but I know in a crisis he could call in those debts and I might find myself in difficulties. I would assume that the same situation is true with other families' fleets as well but I have no evidence to back this up. If he is assured of his position here and controls them then you will have a good foothold in other families' fleets as well."

Joniel looked shocked. "Jaz, now that is something I didn't expect. His wife perhaps but not him."

His mother smiled. "His wife has her own interests. She has made some dangerous manoeuvers herself this past year and made a few enemies, her sister in law, your second youngest, being one of them. She found out that your daughter was selling off munitions to the Kilosian Family which was giving them quite a foothold both politically and physically. Politically as they were amassing information about what your daughter was doing ready to present it to you and to discredit you. She arranged for the evidence to be removed and then blackmailed your daughter herself and used those lines to remove those who were amassing the munitions and plotting against you. That was something your daughter did not foresee, Jaz's wife on the other hand not only got the munitions back she got the money off of your daughter. I thought she was going to use it to launch some sort of a situation between you and Jaz, making sure that Jaz was very well funded. She didn't. We had some difficulties a while back when your fleet was attacked by Followers and many of the ships were badly damaged. We didn't have the funds to repair them all but Jaz's wife made sure that we were back on track pretty fast with a secret payment to the spaceport we went to for repairs. I wasn't supposed to know about this but one of my people was in the back office picking up a report and overheard the conversation. So I would say on average you can trust them. They will of course possibly use that at some future date but for now, the fleet is up and running and there is no challenge to you. As you don't seem to have any intention of spending time here any time soon or for any great amount of time then I would evaluate it that Jaz is happy with his position as he pretty much runs the place anyway." She took another drink and finished her glass. "My son, if there is anything else that is worrying you I will happily talk about it. It has been too long. I will accept your offer of remaining with your fleet, our two fleets together as I have already said are formidable." She looked down and it was as if there was something she wanted to say.

Joniel reached out for the decanter to pour his mother another drink but she put her hand out and stopped him. "Mother, is there something else you want to say?"

She looked up and there a strange look in her eyes. "Just about everyone on this ship has their own agenda as always. Nothing changes. It never will."

Joniel smiled and his mother removed her hand. He poured another glass for them both and they carried on talking into the early hours of the morning, if there is such a thing as morning on a space ship floating in the infinite blackness of space.

In the morning Rennon decided to stay in his quarters. He knew what life on Joniel's ship was like and he event spent extra time checking and checking again the breakfast he has asked to be delivered to his room. The thought of going to the main banquet hall where breakfast was served was abhorrent to him, or more likely terrifying in equal measure. He made the excuse of having tests to run and stayed in his room with his books and pondered what would happen at the Ball that night.

Arla had visited Kel that morning and remained there most of the day. Neither of them wanted to spend time around the ship and Joniel had shopped far short of forbidding his daughter to wander around. He didn't need to, she was curious but not stupid. She had laid out her gown for the evening, made her plans, sent her luggage to the ship and was spending her time in the safest place she could think of.

Aliniel had volunteered to help the Prince with some of his paperwork which had degenerated into conversation and enjoying the speciality coffees that he always travelled with. This was of course complimented by his equally impressive array of speciality chocolate which made her stay all the more pleasurable. Some work got done, some messages got answered but thankfully for both of them it was a quiet day on the missive front.

Kyla slept in late, her back healing as she had a chance to catch up on sleep in the far too comfortable bed. Joniel took the opportunity to lock the door and spend his time sorting out the Commanders and instating some other protocols that would ensure the smooth running of his fleet. He also took the opportunity to send off various messages to put other plans into action as he gathered information and evaluated it. He hadn't told his mother everything and he was certain that she hadn't told him a fraction of what she knew. It didn't matter, as he thought to himself. A situation where he knew everyone had their own interests, plots and schemes was easier to handle. He just had to second guess what they were going to do first and either make sure they couldn't or make sure that when they did it caused them a great deal of discomfort.

The ships hovered in orbit around an unoccupied planet which circled a sun with equally unoccupied planets, eight of them. The scanners showed no Follower intervention and as each family member's fleet was positioned out of Eion Cannon range there was time for all of this and to anticipate the forthcoming Ball that evening.

By the evening Joniel was exhausted. He hated playing politics but it was a necessary evil. His suit was waiting for him and he was more than certain that it would be remotely uncomfortable but as he'd chosen it himself he would in exchange probably enjoy wearing it. It was a style he liked and he was very fond of high collared suits with black ruffled shirts, tight pants that ended just below the knee with socks or those which tucked into his long boots. It would have to be long boots this night as they were easier to conceal his vast array of thin throwing knives and other items he felt he may need should the situation become difficult. At this point he envied the women their ability to carry more substantial firepower beneath their floating dresses. The skirt cage had remained in fashion for many years just for this purpose as it was adequate to conceal all manner of weaponry. His jacket was specially made of course with many wires concealed within the elaborate stitching. It looked like it was a type of tapestry with fine metal thread but many of those threads had in the past on other coats been a suitable method of dispatching someone he'd been hired to remove. Now it was a reassuring habit that he was not going to give up. He knew there would be many concealed weapons at the Ball. He had the best of all of course as he had secretly had the ballroom fitted with concealed, voice activated, lasers which were coded to the DNA of his family. He could if he needed to give a single command and anyone in the room not related to him would be removed swiftly. Of course on a night like this when it was his family who were more dangerous he had to state names individually. Not that it was a problem and he hoped he wouldn't have to use it.

It wasn't that he hated violence or the thought of the mass battles that had occasionally broken out at particularly heated times in his family's political history, it was the cleaning up afterwards. He rather liked the hand painted walls and the whole elegance of the ballroom. He had designed it and commissioned it and many of the panels were from his palace before it had been overrun by the Followers. He was rather sentimental about the whole room and he didn't want anyone to put holes in it.

More importantly he wanted some sort of peace between his family before he went off again. He was having doubts himself about the possibility of his return. If this was the last time he was going to be here he didn't want anyone he cared about hurt because of it. A lot was hanging on the True Prince taking up his position. It was risky that he was actually on Joniel's ship and the sooner they were all off of it the better.

Joniel thought of all this as he walked back to his room. Of course he had to have eyes in the back of his head as he was always waiting for that attempt on his life. It didn't happen. It had been remarkably quiet since the attempt on Kyla and as the assassination attempt had revealed a certain group within his ship and they had been swiftly eliminated that had put an end to that.

In the room there was a stillness, that always unnerved him. The carpet was thick but he'd had fibres put through it so that he could still hear footfalls on it. Then he remembered and unlocked the doors to the Prince's room and the room he shared with Kyla. Both of them were making preparations for the evening. The Prince looked most dapper in his black suit. It was a Desarian design with a scalloped lapel. The Prince had favoured a waistcoat which Joniel knew was an elegant flak vest. Even the jacket was plated against small arms. He guessed that under the suit, as he did look a little more bulky than usual, there was body armour. The lapel design was one he'd seen before, designed that if the collar was pulled up it would protect the wearer's head while still allowing him to view what was going on through the holes left by the scallops.

Aliniel left the room once it was unlocked and went to her room to get ready for the ball.

Kyla was already well on her way to getting ready and she looked extremely elegant. He couldn't help but be transfixed by the transformation. It was quite a different from her usual attire but the thought that ran through his mind that the transformation was part of what a Ball was all about. It was the opportunity to dress up and look different.

The orchestra played in the ballroom, the chandeliers glistened as the candles burnt brightly and the room was filled with men and women dressed in their elegant finery. They floated around the dance floor in time to the music using steps that had been danced by their ancestors. Along the end of the room there was a raised platform where high back seats had been placed. These were occupied by the Council Members and the Court. They were armour plated and a force field could be instantly created to protect anyone sitting there should there be trouble in the room. In the middle of them sat Joniel's grandmother and mother as the hosts for the evening. They looked truly stunning. They sat bolt upright, backed by the ornately carved black stone chairs. Both were beautiful women who looked like they were in their early twenties. They had matching dresses made of the finest lace and velvet, crafted with diamonds and precious stones which also hung from the tips of high pointed collars which sat like petals around their heads.

Joniel remained outside the room in an anti-chamber, waiting for Kyla and his daughters. Prince Anatorn was sitting with Kel near the front of the room to the left of the platform. Joniel had seen them and was watching them intently. Kel was looking around the room in wonder, his mouth open as he took in the ornately painted ceiling and walls and the stunning attire of the other guests. Kel had made an attempt to dress well in the clothes that had been laid out for him and he was uncomfortably wearing a suit and tie. His long hair was tied at the nape of his neck and his beard had been neatly trimmed.

The music finished and the dancers returned to their seats leaving the centre of the room empty. It looked a huge and open space of impossible dimensions. All that was running through Joniel's head was what a perfect kill zone it was. He turned and realised that Kyla and his daughters had arrived. He gasped when he saw Kyla, the finished work of art, in the dress his mother had loaned to her. She looked truly stunning. Her hair had been dressed and pulled up. A couple of ringlets hung down and just touched her bare shoulders. The dress was figure hugging, off the shoulder and low backed and fitted her like a glove. He didn't even start to wonder what feat of engineering kept it on her as there appeared to be no visible support. He had to recite "concentrate, concentrate" as a mantra to stop himself losing focus as he looked at her. Aliniel looked beautiful in a traditionally scarlet velvet gown as did her sister. Both were elegant dresses but modest and without any of the frills and lace that was present on the dresses of the older women. Their dresses were plain with a neck line that was acceptably decent. The dresses were cut to show off their figures and both of them looked stunningly beautiful. Joniel suddenly felt excessively protective but at the same time immensely proud as his daughters stood there with their mother showing no fear.

A gentle piece of music began to be played by the orchestra and all eyes were on him as he stood outside the open door. He took Kyla's arm. She looked terrified and he didn't blame her. They walked slowly into the room. They were followed by his two daughters. Kyla stumbled slightly, her legs nearly gave out under her but he steadied her. He smiled at her and she smiled back. The room seemed even bigger now that they had to walk across the open floor. Step by step they got closer to the platform. Finally they made it and he stepped away from Kyla and took her hand.

He bowed to the Council and took a deep breath. "I would like to present Kyla." Then he realised he couldn't use her second name. The head of the Council stood up and smiled kindly at him. "We recognise Kyla as your partner." He then turned and took Aliniel's hand. "I would like to present my daughter Aliniel." The Head of the Council bowed. "We recognise Aliniel as your heir." Prince Anathorn raised his eyebrow. Joniel let Aliniel's hand fall and he took Arla's hand. "I would like to present my daughter Arla who has taken the Rite of the Warrior." There was a gasp around the hall then it fell silent. The head of the Council smiled knowingly at Joniel. "We are proud to recognise Arla as your heir and accept her status as a warrior."

Joniel turned to the assembled guests and he saw at least three men who were edging forwards. He took a deeper breath and let it out slowly. "I have received a request from Prince Anathorn for the hand of my daughter Aliniel. Would anyone challenge this request?" The three looked at each other and Joniel glared at them. His face became dark, mean and moody. The three stood back immediately. He looked about the room. "For this night I give my daughter Arla into the care of Kel Elyn. May I remind you that in honour of her position as a warrior she may not be approached by any man." There was a gasp. Joniel was within whispering distance of his mother and grandmother. His mother bent forwards. "Very good my son!" She sat back again. "Don't forget to ask for permission for the unions, get one for Kel just in case." She smiled knowingly.

Joniel turned to the Council member. "Are these unions and a possible future union between Arla and a partner of her choosing acceptable? I ask for your permission."

Kel raised an eyebrow and Arla looked at him and smiled. The Council looked at each other and then one by one they nodded.

Joniel visibly relaxed. "Do you agree that all that I should say has been said?"

The Head Council member, Silasian, turned to him and cleared his throat. He then smiled kindly. Memories of Joniel's childhood flooded back as he looked at him. This was the man who had always cared for him and played with him when his father and mother were away. He had always been like a father to him although he had not seen him for many years. He still looked young and handsome, his dark hair was cut short and his expression was kind and unspoilt by any age lines which did not reflect his many hundreds of years of life. He smiled at Joniel's mother who smiled back but she looked away quickly. The Council member looked at Joniel. "I invoke a right which has not been performed for many centuries."

The hall fell silent.

Joniel's mother looked up in horror and Joniel tensed. Sheer terror made his blood run even colder than usual. His mind raced imagining all the horrific and deadly rite that could be invoked at that point and hoped that his message had been received in the manner in which it was written. Kyla felt his nervousness and started looking around for a way out.

The Council member smiled as he saw Joniel's expression. "I invoke the Right of Trianthia." There was a gasp from everyone, not least Joniel's mother. He got down from the platform and stood beside Joniel. "For those of you who are new to our ways and those of you who have possibly not encountered this situation I will explain.

On this night and only on this night, as there have been three new heirs presented to your family, where one of the matriarchs is without a life partner I may present myself as her life partner which overrides any previous claim or any claim that may be made tonight.

If it is agreeable with the Council I will have the right to provide any protection that is necessary. If accepted, that has been bound in law, any promise that has been made and any prohibition that would stand in the way of our union is dissolved."

Joniel looked worried and protectively stepped in front of Arla. His old tutor smiled and shook his head. He whispered. "Don't worry, I said right, not rite. It is me who should be afraid." He then looked up at Joniel's mother. "By this ancient right will you accept my love?"

Joniel looked stunned. He was about to correct the man who should have said "offer" but realised that the man had not made any mistake. This he had not foreseen or taken into account. When he had written the note he had asked for a suitable mate to be found for his mother. He had never anticipated that the Head of the Council was in love with her. Thankfully that had been the person to whom he had sent it.

Joniel's mother looked stunned and then smiled kindly. "I will accept."

The Council member then looked to the other members. "Do you accept our Union?"

The Council members all nodded in agreement and the one nearest to them spoke. "It is so decreed that from this moment onwards this woman is under this man's protection."

Joniel looked at his mother who was looking very nervous as her new protector bent forwards and spoke so all at the platform but no further away could hear. "There is going to be trouble, get out Joniel while you still can. Your brother intended to get his man to claim your mother so that you had to challenge him. He cannot now so he will panic and use other means."

He stepped back and turned to the Court, bowed and retook his seat.

Joniel turned to Prince Anathorn. "Step up and claim what is yours." Anatorn stepped up and Joniel put Aliniel's hand into his. He turned to Kel. "Step up and accept your duties for the night." Kel stepped up and Joniel put Arla's hand in his.

There was a gasp as Joniel's brother stepped forwards. Joniel's grandmother stood up as the brother approached and he backed away, bowing. She spoke in a steady commanding voice. "I have to announce that earlier today the Council accepted that Kyla shall be accepted as Joniel's wife. As their union has already been blessed by King Osiris and Queen Isis, whose position in the Pantheon of the Ancients is unquestionable, no man may tear them asunder." She sat down, looking a little relieved as Joniel's brother stepped back, bowed and sat down.

There was a silence in the hall which was broken by three pagers going off simultaneously. Joniel looked down as did the Prince and Kel. Joniel looked up and around at all present. "Although I would have greatly wished to have enjoyed your company for an evening sadly we must all depart. I bid you farewell." He hissed in a whisper at the others. "Move it, now, get out of here and don't look back."

Prince Anathorn still held Aliniel's hand and he didn't let go as he guided her gracefully out of the hall. Kel kept hold of Arla's hand and lead her out and Joniel took Kyla's hand. He looked up at his mother and grandmother. They both smiled but they were looking nervous.

The whole of the Council were looking nervous and as they left the hall the Council stood up as one. He could see chairs being rearranged so that both women had the protection of a Council Member. His mother her husband to be, his grandmother a rather distinguished dark haired man who took her hand and Joniel recognised as her long term mate, Jestrathian.

Once out of the hall Joniel headed for the shuttle. "In a week or two it will be safe to return but I wouldn't like to enter our chambers tonight. I took the liberty of removing your paperwork and our equipment to the shuttle earlier my Prince."

Anatorn cast a sideways glance as they walked as fast as they could to the shuttle. "I would suggest that was a very wise move."

The shuttle bay door was shut but it opened at their approach and they stepped inside as the door shut behind them. Rennon was already at the controls and had done the pre-flight checks. They took off as the Prince used his scanner to destroy all bugs and tracking devices. Small puffs of smoke erupted all over the ship. When he was satisfied their ship was clean they took off.

They got into space and headed for the Princes Palace on Alkar'na'thurion.

4

The night dwindled in endless silence as the dawn rose over the Prince's palace. Its silence brought a million worries to troubled minds but for some that morning, joys like they had not dared to imagine. To the lonely warriors there was not only hope, there was love.

The dawn's golden light crept through the rose garden and kissed the ancient stonework of the fountains and white marble statues. It slunk silently across the sweeping drive and caressed the wind blasted marble of the basilica that had stood unchallenged for many hundreds of years.

The Prince crept silently from his room to take his place back in the world. He smiled as gentle thoughts caressed his warrior mind but out of duty he put them aside as he took his place at his desk. His fingers lingered over the keyboard for a moment, savouring the last of the time he could devote to his gentler emotions before he pressed the keys and opened his electronic communiqués. Report upon report came in at its appointed time and he read them one by one. His joy fading to the despair of one seeing the numbers lost as living breathing souls. His head rested on his hands as he attempted to think of more answers as the questions kept on coming. The more he answered the more arrived.

Kyla stood at the bedroom window, watching the dawn creep across the gardens. She was lost in thoughts of how her children had now grown up and worrying for their future. Joniel joined her. His gentle caress as he ran his fingers down her neck and over her shoulders pulled her away from darker thoughts that crept in unbidden. He gently kissed her neck and whispered. "Live in the moment my love as that is all we truly have."

She turned to face him and he cradled her face in his hands and looked deep into her eyes as he whispered. "Remember this moment of peace and the love we have. Hold onto it when things get dark. Whatever happens I will love you."

A tear rolled down her cheek.

Joniel wiped it away with his thumb. "Why tears my love?"

Kyla's eyes sparkled through her tears. "It is such a perfect moment that I would like to hold onto forever."

Joniel smiled. "Nothing is forever but there will be more moments. I promise you."

Kyla put a finger on his lips. "Don't, just don't. We can't make promises like that. We have there here and now, we can only try our best to have tomorrow or the day after. But, I could not bear it if I had to go on without you."

Joniel looked down at her, his face serious. "My love, you would go on. You are strong. You would be the woman I know you are. You would be strong for everyone else, do what you have to do and then in private you would cry for me. But, let us banish such thoughts. It is a beautiful morning. If we let dark thoughts like that darken our door we'll never be happy and we might as well be dead. So, kiss me my darling. Let us steal a little longer before we join the world."

She kissed him and he swept her up into his arms and laid her on the bed. His look was mischievous. "Ok, so let us steal a lot longer before we join the world. It can last without us for this time I think."

Rennon sat in his new room and looked at the boxes of equipment. His arms suddenly felt very tired from constantly opening the boxes, constantly setting up his laboratory and constantly being alone. Thoughts drifted back to that first time on the ship where he had thought his loneliness was over. Her face haunted his memories. Unbidden the same thoughts drifted to the betrayal and the pain of laying in the room without hope as someone he had come to really like had been the one who had tried to kill him. He renewed his vow never to let anyone that close to him again. A vow he knew deep down he would break in a moment if the right person came along.

Dawn passed into later morning and they all sat together in the dining hall. The Prince was surrounded by papers and deep in thought. Aliniel sat beside him, reading over his arm and occasionally pointing to things. Joniel smiled as the Prince constantly looked surprised as she evaluated situations in a way he had not seen and then gently suggested ideas.

Kel and Arla arrived late, both looked a little unwell. Kyla looked up in concern and Joniel put a hand on her arm. He smiled at Kel. "I trust you both left us something in the drinks cabinet and that you didn't break all the furniture in the Great Hall."

The Prince looked worried.

Arla smiled. "We didn't break a thing though this oaf tried his hardest."

Kel growled and poured himself some coffee from the pot on the table. He poured one for her too and put it in front of her. She looked up and smiled at him.

Rennon sat opposite Kyla and Joniel. His laptop was set on a wooden board so that he didn't damage the ancient wood of the vast dining table with the heat from the base of it. He was deep in thought, his hand reaching out occasionally to grab his mug and bring it to his mouth. Kyla kept the mug refilled for him. He made notes and flicked through screens.

Then he looked up and caught the Prince's attention. "I think I've got it. It's taken a while and I've had to run the data through a few times to check. The origins of the Followers are of course those pods. The worms need the fluid to live in. It is the fluid that causes the carapace growth but also mental instability, paranoia and a susceptibility to suggestion. Once imprinted that suggestion becomes a memory. So breaking the conditioning is not going to be easy. In all aspects it is a real memory and part of the victim's psyche. We're also dealing with various different aspects. I can't identify these yet. We'll have to deal with each part as we can. The waters are very muddied, it's not as clear cut as one thing being the cause."

The Prince looked up. "That can't be good."

Rennon shook his head. "Couldn't be worse I would say. I've analysed the substance over and over again and run tests on animal subjects. It's very good for training animals by the way but I wouldn't recommend it as they grow the carapace as well. The carapace is a reaction to the conversion process. The fluid multiplies in the system and a bi-product is secreted through the skin. When it reacts with oxygen it becomes a hard calcium deposit on the skin as the other part of the compound evaporates. The addition of carbon dioxide drives the deposits deep into the cellular structure where it encounters oxygen in the blood, turning more of the unfortunate soul to carapace and killing off all nerves and blood supply to the calcified skin. The ridges are created by heating and cooling depending on where the victim is exposed to the fluid. By what I can see the mind control is achieved by introducing miniscule amounts of the fluid to the water system. I have figures here from water tested in Follower areas. It is naturally occurring in the water courses so I would suggest that they are seeding it in the rain and then arriving to imprint their message."

Aliniel looked down at the paperwork. "How do we fight that?"

Rennon looked exhausted. "There is something in the royal blood that gives immunity to the effects of the fluid. I have to thank Kyla for her constant supply of blood for research." Joniel glared at Rennon. "With the addition of an antigen and by creating a compound I have been able to project that those as yet unaffected by the fluid can be rendered immune. But that would require a vast quantity of blood that we do not have. I am working on a way of chemically synthesising the compound. Then we too would be able to seed the clouds with it and let it rain down naturally. The people concerned need never know."

The Prince looked up. "It gives us hope but no, I would not sanction such an act. If it is done it will be done with the agreement of the population." Aliniel put her hand on his arm and smiled at him.

Rennon was flicking down screens. "Well then in my opinion the best thing we can do is hit their research and storage facilities. If we introduce the antigen to their vats it will render their contents useless. If we can do this covertly then they will continue their campaign but using totally ineffective fluid which also renders those it touches immune to further exposure."

The Prince smiled. "Are you fairly certain that this would work?"

Rennon flicked up a screen. "According to statistics it should. According to the physical tests I have carried out there is a high percentage chance it will succeed. I can't say any more than that."

The Prince looked thoughtful. "Any hope is better than no hope at all. I will be committing people's lives to this. To raid their bases and storage facilities will be dangerous. He looked at his hand held scanner and called up a page. Our resources are dwindling as more planets fall. If this is a viable option I will have to act fast. Rennon, I'll let you have the location of the facilities that we know about already. Can you draw me up a plan of how we can most effectively deal with them? I can't waste man hours, if this is going to work we will have to get the anti-fluid out there before they realise what we are doing and then I think create a diversion to give them something else to think about. If we merely go for the facilities they are going to know something specifically relates to them. If we hit other things that are important as well we may stand a chance of them not realising what we are doing if we are discovered. The question is if we are going to get that close to the vats, why don't we just destroy them?"

Rennon looked down. "I will run some tests as to what damage would be done for allowing the fluid into the environment in one particular area. It may take some time."

The Prince looked up. "Time is something we do not have a lot of. If an explosion would send this airborne or make the situation worse there is no point trying it.

Daily we lose control of planets and each time that means lives lost. We will be at a point soon that we can no longer put forward a viable resistance to these people."

Kel looked up. "Well can't we just go out and give them something to think about?"

The Prince smiled. "Kel, I know you want to take the fight to them. Believe me when I say it that I really want to as well. The damage we would do to them would be minimal. The loss of life would not be worth the reward. At the moment all I can do is keep those who haven't been infected safe."

Aliniel looked up. "You said infected. What if there was a virus that attacked the infection. You are talking about immunisation but what about a direct attack. What are these bugs that the fluid is protecting? It doesn't seem to harm them."

Rennon looked up, stunned. "You know I was so bogged down in looking at the fluid I never thought of looking at the pupae. I'm wondering what would happen if we hatched one?"

The Prince looked really worried. "It's a bit of a risk isn't it? We don't know what the pupae will develop into."

Rennon raised an eyebrow. "We're running out of time, people and chances here. We'll have to try something. With your permission I would like to ask one of our research establishments on the moon bases to undertake experiments to try to hatch one of these pupae. If something happens at least it will be contained. I can't see any record of one being hatched and experimented on."

The Prince looked troubled. "Do you think this stands any chance of success?"

Rennon looked up, the exhaustion evident on his face. "I don't know. I'm out of options and out of ideas. It's the only avenue I can think of that I haven't gone down so who knows."

The Prince took a deep breath. "I will sanction it. Put together a briefing and I'll get it sent to a remotely located base and carried out. Kel, I know you are keen to be out on a mission but you cannot until we can give you the antidote. What of these two?" He looked at Arla and Aliniel. "Are they immune? Do they carry the blood?"

Rennon looked up. "I have tested both of them. Aliniel has the blood, Arla doesn't. So Arla is not immune." Kyla looked at Joniel.

The Prince looked directly at Joniel. "What would it mean to either of them if you gave them your blood?"

Joniel closed his eyes, took a deep breath and opened them again. "I had hoped that wouldn't be something that would be important. It is their decision to make. Physically it would give them enhanced strength, agility and longevity. But Aliniel is immune already so it wouldn't make her any more immune. Arla on the other hand would gain immunity. Emotionally it means that they would have to watch those they love and care about grow old and die."

The Prince looked at Joniel in earnest. "Is that why your people are so cold and vicious?"

Joniel smiled. "A gentle soul rarely survives the emotional pain. That was why I didn't give Kyla my blood earlier. It is our birthright to be cold and vicious. You have seen what living there is like. Aliniel and Arla will be different. They were raised without that environment. If Aliniel wants to accept my blood, that is her choice. It will give her a better chance of healing but there is dependence and you would find yourself in the same position as we were. You would never again be able to make love as if she lost control at that point of elation, instinct would take over and she would see you as prey. She wouldn't be in control. I doubt that either of you would want to choose that."

The Prince turned to Aliniel. She smiled and kissed him. Her voice was gentle. "I would happily forsake immortality, let us be happy with the life that we have."

Kel grunted at Arla. "Don't you even think about it."

Arla slapped him and nearly knocked him backwards off of his chair. "I wasn't you great Shamshach."

The Prince smiled kindly at Kyla who was looking wistful. He spoke gently. "I can never experience how you must feel as an immortal mother having to listen to your daughter choosing to forsake immortality."

Kyla smiled. "One lifetime of happiness is better than an eternity of shadow. I'd already made my decision and it was a long path to get there." She smiled. "But thankfully, pending any tragedy that is not a worry I have any more. The Order usually have no problem with immortality as they are mystics and wise women for the tribe so people come and go but they remain eternal. They may not take a lover until after they have attained mastery and by that time longevity is something they are more than used to. Perhaps that is the difference between it being heaven or hell."

The Prince laughed. "I would never ask a woman her age but the more you talk, the more I realise how old you might possibly be."

Kyla smiled enigmatically. "And I'm not going to tell you. Part of our training is to go to planets with different time dilations. So I can live out many years there while only a year passes here. It makes for effective training as many mystics can be trained up within one generation of the tribe."

The Prince smiled. "Well that sounds practical. We're a romantic lot but let it be our strength. If we aren't looking for love we can concentrate on what is important. Now we have to find Rennon someone."

Rennon looked up. "Give me a break. If you find me another fanatical Follower convert I'll give up on love entirely. The next one will have to be someone of the blood. It's the only way to be sure. And not one of your psychotic she bitches from the Flagship thank you very much." Rennon rubbed his neck.

Joniel noticed the bite mark and smiled. "It's always the quiet ones. How did you survive?"

Rennon smiled. "I used chemical intervention then sent her packing and locked myself in my room. I'm a scientist. You wouldn't be able to use it as a way around the problem. I knocked her out before she got that far. No, I wasn't popular afterwards, that proved problematic as it was almost as dangerous and as you can imagine knowing what I know now I'm not very impressed with her either for putting me in the possible food situation."

Kel grunted. He looked at Arla. "Just give me the antidote if you have one. I tire of sitting around doing nothing. I want to take the fight to them. Are we fighting them anywhere?"

The Prince took a deep breath and frowned. "We are constantly at war with them and fighting is going on everywhere. The star bases are deployed keeping their eastern forces occupied and they have wiped out at least five Follower planets. I have battleships in active service fighting their forces on our North and Eastern fronts. Fifteen battle stations are fighting in the Endurion Galaxy. They have fleets of back up ships and they have managed to get ground troops down on the Minories Planets. Using hazmat suits they are avoiding contact with the fluid. But of course any penetration of the suit and the individual is lost. The other three galaxies have united forces actively opposing the Followers. Our diplomatic contacts have paid off as most planets who know about the truth of the situation have committed troops to the main force. We have a strong alliance out there. I don't generally bore you with all those details.

We have a network of people spreading information about the origin of the Followers but that falls on deaf ears where the Followers have already converted. Our only hope is to get that message out as soon as people come into contact with the fluid. Then we implant our message first. I have agents contacting anyone who has broadcasting equipment and a video was made before my father went back in time. This has been copied and dispersed through the galaxies. We are but the tip of a very big iceberg."

Aliniel smiled at the Prince. "Which is why he's so tired. He's having to co-ordinate that lot. Having a new High Council helps and now that they are established and co-operating it is making it easier for him to concentrate on other matters. They are deciding on and handling many aspects he used to control."

Kel grunted. "I didn't know you did all that stuff. I just thought you were answering your messages."

The Prince laughed. "I am, it's what is in the message that changes things."

Kel laughed. "That is fair enough. When can I get this serum so that I can get out there to do my job?"

The Prince smiled. "If it is what you all want I will arrange it. I must remain here. Aliniel, will you stay here with me?" Aliniel smiled and nodded. "Arla you are welcome as well but if you would rather leave with the others."

Arla smiled. "I would rather go with the others. No offence sister."

Aliniel smiled.

The Prince looked down. "Very well, why not return to your old ship. It has been active on minor missions in the Celurion Galaxy. The Joniel Unit decommissioned itself but I have my own bodyguard now. It has apparently malfunctioned or there may have been something more sinister going on. It was apparently programmed with a sub routine that couldn't be overwritten. Thankfully it wasn't anywhere near me when it exploded. It would appear it was a bit of a Trojan horse but your programming Rennon meant that although it couldn't override the explosion it could choose where it was when it exploded. It jettisoned itself into space in a minor escape pod."

Kel looked up. "What's one of those horse things?"

The Prince smiled. "It comes from Earth mythology or history. A big horse that fighters hid inside and then it was given as a gift to the enemy."

Kyla smiled. "And they got close to it? Well I suppose we fell for it as well. It's easy to be critical with 20/20 hindsight."

The Prince looked thoughtful as he looked down at his communicator. He flicked through screens. "It seems that current reports indicate that the Followers are actively targeting those who carry the bloodline. Last night there was an offensive to wipe them out. I'm deploying ships to pick up survivors and to bring them to safe havens. I want you to return to your ship and scour the galaxies and bring as many as you can to the safe havens. Kel, I think you are going to find your action now. Rennon, what can we do quickly to get him a vaccination so that he can go out on active service?"

Rennon looked at his screen. "Immediately, nothing. I don't have a viable vaccination."

Kel glared at Joniel. "Give me the blood."

Joniel looked down at the table. "There is no guarantee that the blood would have any effect on you. It doesn't on everyone."

Kel growled and turned to the Prince. "It makes sense. Give it to me and then she can have it too and we'll be able to get on with what we need to do."

Joniel stood up, his eyes flashed red and his pupils elongated to slits. "You will never dictate to my daughter what she will do when it comes to our ways. She has made her decision. You will have to wait for a vaccination to be prepared."

Kel stood up and faced him, his muscles tensing. "How dare you deny me this?"

Joniel glared at him. "It is not some pint of ale to be quaffed at a bawdy house, or a tonic to be taken to make you faster and stronger. It is a commitment and the down sides far outweigh the bonuses. Kel, could you control yourself in a room full of mortals when the hunger took you? Would you be able to cope with feeling love on one hand and a need to feed on the other? You do not have the mental makeup to be able to handle this."

Kel lunged at Joniel. He leapt up onto the table and sprang across it. Joniel nimbly sidestepped him and Kel flew forwards off balance and crashed into the cabinet behind where Joniel had been standing. Joniel reached a hand out casually and caught the vase which was falling onto the floor and put it on the table.

Joniel smiled. "I rest my case. There is a very good reason why our children reach the age of consent before they can be given the blood. Not every child chooses to. Some are not allowed to. Many leave the Enclave and live out their lives as mortals. I will not give you the blood."

The Prince stood up as Kel picked himself up from the floor and glared at Joniel. "Rennon, I want you to focus on the serum. If you are certain you have a solution and you have run every test, give it to Kel. Kel, we want you on the team and we need you on active service. This is not a plot to keep you away from the action. We just don't want to be fighting you on the other side. If you would excuse me I need to work on some paperwork for a while." He gave Aliniel a meaningful look.

Aliniel smiled. "I will help you." She helped him to gather up his papers and they left the room.

Kel and Joniel stood face to face and glared at each other. Joniel's fangs had extended and he glared at Kel, mouth slightly open, his eyes blood red. Kel tensed his muscles and stood, feet apart poised to grab his blaster. Kyla put a hand on Joniel's arm. Arla leapt over the table and landed behind Kel. She put a hand on his arm and turned him away from Joniel.

Kel looked down at Arla who punched him in the stomach. He hit the floor, winded and looked up at her. "Why did you do that?"

She glared down at him, her muscular frame tensed, her blonde curls falling around her shoulders. "I did that because you wanted to control me and I want you to remember that no man does that. That also means you. You can make your decision and take the blood if you want to but I will make my own decision. I agree with father. Until you can control your anger you would be dangerous. Now, get up and come with me."

Kel growled. "I'm not going to be ordered around by you either."

Arla smiled. "It wasn't an order, it was an invitation." She smiled and left the room, Kel followed her.

Rennon looked up from his laptop. "At least I didn't unpack this time. Can we please stay somewhere long enough for me to get on with my research? Going back to our ship would be a wonderful idea, though I don't relish the memories. I suppose you two couldn't just nip back to that planet for another nineteen years and get me one of those could you?"

Kyla looked at Joniel. She smiled. "I would like nothing more than to return to the planet. Though I doubt you would want one of the headstrong minxes we produce."

Rennon smiled while typing on the keyboard. "Probably not but it would be fun finding out."

Joniel laughed. "So what do we do now?"

Kyla thought about it. "I've had enough of facts and worries, let's go to the great hall and kick hell out of each other for an hour or so then one of those showers sounds like a good idea followed by…"

Joniel laughed and put his hand over her mouth. "Rennon, will you be alright here?"

Rennon looked up for a moment. "Well pending any psychotic suicidal she bitch deciding to rip my head off or some drug crazed Follower leaping in through the window I should be fine thank you."

In the grounds there was movement. Three guards lay on the floor and a fourth fell, his throat cut. Black shapes moved through the shadows and made their way towards the house. They moved silently and swiftly, killing anyone who got in their way. They got to the house and moved around it, looking in through windows. Some climbed effortlessly to the second level.

Kyla hesitated as she heard the faintest scrape of metal against stone and looked up at Joniel. She grabbed his arm just as the windows smashed and three individuals dressed in black, their faces covered by a black mask, leapt inside. They landed effortlessly on the floor. Their silent landing lost in the tinkling of falling broken glass from the windows.

Rennon grabbed his laptop and leapt over the table. Kyla and Joniel leapt over the table in the other direction and launched themselves at the uninvited guests.

Joniel landed in front of two, Kyla in front of the other one. They had both pulled daggers as they leapt. Kyla slashed at her opponent, trying to get the momentum to help her and the benefit of surprise. The Follower blocked her with awesome speed and strength. He pushed her backwards with a gauntlet which was knife proof and armed with claws. She allowed the momentum to push her back and rolled

154

to her feet out of range of the claw that narrowly swished past her stomach.

Joniel landed a blow on the first of his attackers but the other smashed the back of his gauntlet across Joniel's jaw sending him reeling sideways.

There was a gunshot from across the room and the second of Joniel's attackers reeled, holding his side as blood flowed out of it. Rennon fired again and the intruder fell to the ground. Joniel rolled to his feet and as part of the movement finished the intruder off with his knife. He then jumped up to face the other one.

Rennon fired again and Kyla's opponent reeled backwards. He was stunned enough for Kyla to slash his throat and he fell to the ground. She then turned on Joniel's opponent and plunged her knife into his back as Joniel slashed from the front. She used all of her strength to use the knife to hold the intruder still while Joniel finished him off.

Rennon shut his laptop and slung it under his arm and they ran to the Prince's quarters.

The Prince was in the shower while Aliniel was sitting by her dressing table brushing her hair. She felt that something was wrong and got up, reaching for her sword which was beside the bed. She drew it and stood with her back to the wall which had the window in it. As the glass broke she was ready and as the first intruder came through the window she slashed him across his stomach. This not only injured him, it threw him off balance and she was able to rotate her sword and plunge it into his back as he fell to the ground. The second intruder crashed through the window the other side of the bed.

Aliniel crouched and the intruder turned on her. She sprang catlike onto the bed and bounced at an angle he was not expecting. His clawed glove cut through empty air as Aliniel rounded on him and as she slashed with her sword she cut his arm bearing the glove off. Blood poured out onto the bed as he howled with pain. She silenced him with a swift backstroke across the neck. He fell to his knees and she took his head off.

The Prince came out of the shower with a towel wrapped around his waist. He reached for his sword but the room was quiet until Joniel and Kyla burst in through the door. There were sounds of glass breaking all over the house. The Prince threw clothes on and grabbed the box he kept all his paperwork in. They dashed out of the room and down the corridor.

Kel and Arla were screaming at each other and were totally surprised when two intruders leapt in through the breaking window. Arla screamed and grabbed her sword as the attacker who faced her slashed her arm with his glove. The second attacker went for Kel who had his back to the window. The attacker plunged his bladed glove into Kel's back. He screamed and fell forwards, rolled and grabbed his sword. He managed to regain his balance as the world began to go very fuzzy. His limbs felt heavy and he fell to his knees. Arla turned on her attacker and slashed just as the room began to spin around her.

The attackers were standing over them when Rennon and the Prince broke through the door. Rennon stepped aside and levelled his gun at the intruders. The Prince stepped to the other side leaving Kyla and Joniel the chance to get into the room. The intruders both put the blades of their gloves to the throats of their captives. The first spoke. "Back off or they die."

Rennon shouted. "Let them go". This drew both of the attacker's attention as Joniel threw a shock net over the two intruders, Kel and Arla. It flashed blue as the electrical charge was discharged and all four fell to the ground. He leapt forwards and cut the throat of the two intruders. He grabbed Kyla's wrist and programmed her wrist band, he programmed his own and they grabbed the others and the net, pressed the button and returned to the shuttle. Rennon jumped into the pilot's chair and did the pre-flight checks. The Prince and Joniel scanned for devices, bugs and transmitters while the Prince communicated with his retinue and commanded them to abandon the building, get to their shuttles and get away. Then they took off and leapt into the corridor.

The Prince scanned everyone. Kyla was busy bandaging Kel and then moved on to Arla. "There has to be something, they are finding us too easily." He hesitated over Kel. "There is a very small reading here. I wouldn't have noticed it if I hadn't been looking for it really hard. Kel has a tracker in him. I don't understand why I haven't seen it before or why the devices didn't neutralise it."

Joniel looked up. "Probably because it was shielded and the shock net shorted the device out. Kyla you could have one on you too."

Kyla looked at him and swallowed. "Go on then."

Joniel looked stunned. "Go on what?"

Kyla shivered slightly. "Use the net, it will take any shielding down and you can scan."

Joniel glared at her. "No, it will hurt."

Kyla glared back at him. "Do it."

Joniel took out a small case and held it in front of Kyla. "Well if you are sure."

Kyla hissed at him. "Stop talking and letting me think about it and just do it."

He pressed the button. Kyla screamed, fell to the ground and passed out as the blue light danced over her. Joniel picked her up gently and lifted her onto the bench. He took Rennon's scanner and ran it over her. "Nothing, she's clean." He then sat with her until she came around.

Kyla rolled off of the bench and stood up and went over to Arla and Kel. "They should have come around by now. Can I borrow that scanner, flick it into med mode for me would you? I want to check for something. It wouldn't have come up before but it may come up now." The Prince entered the code and the scanner switched screens.

Kyla ran the scanner over them both and swore. "Dammit, those blades were poisoned. Worse than that, they have been infected by the fluid." She sat between them, one hand over each and concentrated.

Rennon shouted. "We've got company, a bloody star destroyer is on our tail and a whole battalion of fighters. What do we do now?"

The Prince looked up. "Get us out of here, doesn't matter where, jump into the corridor and we'll see where we end up. We'll have to keep jumping until that device is out of him. Kyla, will they be alright? Joniel, I need you piloting."

Kyla looked up. Her face was streaked with tears. "I can physically hold them here. I can't stop the spread of the fluid though. Joniel, we're going to lose her."

Joniel crouched beside her as the shuttle rocked. They were knocked sideways then the other way. Rennon screamed. "The shields aren't holding. Joniel, I need you piloting, now. I'm not good enough for this."

Joniel leapt to the pilot's seat and flipped the controls. The shuttle shot about at his command in the emptiness of space evading the blasts as the Prince made the calculations and they jumped into the corridor.

Rennon took over the controls and set them to autopilot as Joniel leapt to Kyla's side. "Is it too late?"

Kyla looked up at him, tears flowing unchecked. "I don't know. I don't know how the fluid works."

Joniel crouched beside Kyla. "It is too late to turn her. They will control a creature far stronger if we do."

Kyla looked up at Joniel. She looked broken, somehow fragile. "We can't allow that to happen. Surely if the fluid is suggestion we can suggest to her that she isn't like them."

Joniel shook his head. "If we leave her she will certainly be under their power. The small amount in

160

the water system leaves people open to suggestion. The carapace warriors are something else. Rennon, what do you say, no facts and figures, bottom line, now."

Rennon thought as he got up from the console. "The fluid is in their systems. We can vaccinate, we cannot turn someone back. It fundamentally changes them. I'm sorry, it is too late."

They watched as crystals started forming on Arla's lips. Kyla screamed, it was a pitiful and hopeless scream that echoed around the shuttle. Joniel lifted Arla's head onto his lap and took his knife out and looked around at the faces. Tears rolled down his face. The knife fell from his hand and he bowed his head. His voice was weak, almost a whisper. "I can't do it."

The carapace was forming around Arla's mouth and she moaned slightly. Kyla moved closer to Joniel and sat down beside him. She picked the knife up and put it in Joniel's hand and wrapped her hand around his. "We brought her into this world together. We love her enough to save her from suffering." Kyla pushed Joniel's hand and he carried on with the pressure that cut Arla's throat. They both held her while her life slipped away.

The Prince turned to Kel who lay unconscious on the floor. The crystals were forming on his lips and mouth as well. The Prince pulled out his pistol, pulled Kel up against the bullet proof plating of the outer hull, put it to the unconscious man's head and pulled the trigger. He let Kel fall sideways onto the floor. He then lifted him and laid him onto the bench.

Joniel had his arms around his daughter, Kyla had her arms around both of them as the Eion Particles moved past their window. Prince Anathorn put his arms around Aliniel as she cried.

They sat in silence for moments that felt like hours. Nobody wanted to move, nobody wanted it to be real.

Joniel looked down at his daughter, his mind a mess of confusion and questioning what he had just done. He knew deep down he'd done the right thing. The thought of her a carapace creature with no control over her own mind was beyond any horror he could contemplate. She was free of that now, the crystals were still multiplying but the progression had slowed. He watched as most of her face became covered in the hard shell and it started to spread down her neck.

He looked over at Kel, he too was becoming encased. The chemical reaction was still happening despite both of them being dead.

Rennon ran a scanner over them. "I think we had better do something to restrain them. They are both dead but the reaction is still happening. As the final result is a husk it is possible that the end product carapace warrior may be created anyway. You have saved them the conversion but you haven't saved us the threat yet. We could put them in the airlock."

Kyla looked at Rennon in horror. "I would not deny my child a decent burial. Is there anything we can do to restrain the creature and kill it? Wrong word I suppose as they are already dead. This is even more worrying that the fluid may turn those who are dead into these things. Can we stop them?"

Joniel stood up and watched the progress of the deposits. "I don't know but we could try taking their heads off. It would sever the nervous system."

Rennon looked down at the prone bodies. "Well it can't hurt but as the calcifying kills off nerves it may not do any good. We can try."

Kyla took her sword and with two deft strokes she removed the heads from the corpses. No blood flowed, just a white liquid which formed a solid lump when it came into contact with the air. It was like a lava flow, flowing out onto the floor as blood would have done, solidifying as candle wax does when flowing out of a candle and cooling on a table. It flowed until it flowed no more. The bodies stayed prone, they did not move.

Joniel pulled both of the bodies so that their hands were behind their backs and he tied them with wire. He looked up. "This is just in case they do still move. I think we have stopped them though. We are going to have to destroy the bodies though. We cannot leave even the vaguest of possibilities that they can be used for anything. Again, I doubt that they would be as I think the carapace is an end product of the process but it would be a dignified end for them. Rennon, it is horrific to suggest it but is there anything you can learn from them?"

Rennon looked down on his friends and the thought horrified him. In his head he was seeing them as friends. The scientist in him was hiding under a duvet somewhere just wishing this would go away. "I do not know what I can learn from them but I wish I didn't have to try. I will however run some tests. It may take some time and I believe I should take some samples of the carapace and the liquid that came out of them. I left my lab back at the house but as always I have my scanners here and what was there is stuff I have duplicated all over now. I think I can pretty much rig up a lab from what I have stored in the hold of this shuttle if you will allow me the time."

The Prince checked on the communicator in the cockpit. "I've had reports from most of the other shuttles. We lost quite a few people there, most to the carapaces and sadly in the evacuation many were left behind so they are not only lost, they also now also count among our enemies. We do however have time as most of the ships are also making their way to the meeting point. The risk of infiltration here is high so each ship has a different co-ordinate. We will travel around and pick them up one by one so that they can be appropriately scanned without revealing the location of our main fleet. So, Rennon, you have some time to do what research you wish to do but please keep it succinct. We do not have days, I can give you hours though and I believe you will also wish to take them somewhere that can be their final resting place.

5

The Prince brought the shuttle down to land on an uninhabited planet on the edge of the Dariunus Nebula. The sky swirled with an orange hue and the blues and greens of the lichens gave it a mystical appearance. Lavender flowers grew in clumps all over the place. Yellow lichens trailed like hair from tall stick like growths and fluttered in the gentle breeze.

The Prince completed the engine shut down and lowered the ramp. He stood up slowly and walked into the back of the shuttle. Joniel stood stock still. Kyla was beside him as they looked out onto the colourful planet. Joniel had his arm around her and she was leaning on him heavily. As Anathorn approached them he could see that Kyla was shaking badly. Anathorn put a hand on her shoulder and squeezed it reassuringly. Aliniel put a hand on her arm and Kyla put that arm around her and pulled her daughter close to her. Joniel kissed her on the forehead. "It is time." He lifted Arla from the bench and walked slowly down the ramp followed by Kyla and Aliniel. Kyla nearly fell as she stepped forwards and her legs buckled. Anathorn stepped forwards to support her and helped her down the ramp. Then Aliniel took over and Anathorn went back up to Rennon and followed them carrying Kel on a stretcher.

They walked slowly in silence through the forest of lichens. The gentle breeze fluttered the lichen hair and there was a scent of flowers in the air. The path was indistinct and wild but they managed to pick their way through the tendrils which crossed it at intervals.

At the top of the hill Joniel lay his daughter down on the soft mossy ground. He crouched for a moment and stroked her golden hair. He then pulled the cloth that had been wrapped around her neck up to cover up the cut and the calcified part of her face. Kel was laid beside her. Joniel took Kel's hand and hers and put one in the other. He then backed away to put his arm around Kyla and Aliniel as Anathorn stepped forwards. He laid a cloth over the two bodies, covered it with igniting fuel and stepped back.

Joniel stepped forwards and knelt at the feet of the bodies. There were tears running down his face. Kyla stepped forwards, leaving Aliniel with Anathorn to stand beside her husband. He spoke slowly and with deliberation. "I promise with all that I am that you will be avenged." He stood up and turned around and even Prince Anathorn took a step back. There was a look of pure anger in Joniel's eyes. He seemed taller and there was a dark shadow about him. He looked down at Kyla. "Kyla, I promise you, our daughter will not have died in vain. I will do all in my power to bring these people to justice and I mean my justice." He turned back to the prone bodies. "Kel, we didn't see eye to eye but I still respected you. Goodbye my friend. Arla, you were ever loving, ever beautiful and I hope now that you are at peace. Goodbye my daughter."

Kyla looked at him but her expression was blank. Tears still flowed uncontrollably down her face and she appeared not to be focusing on anything in particular. Aliniel ran to her and clung to her and was visibly shaking as she slid down to the ground to sit at Kyla's feet. Kyla shut her eyes, took a deep breath and opened them again. "You are right. We are not victims or we will die slowly one by one." She took Aliniel's arm from around her and reached for Anathorn's hand. She put Aliniel's hand in his. "Take care of my child. I give her into your keeping." Anathorn helped Aliniel up and supported her back to where Rennon was standing.

Joniel looked down at Kyla and saw so much pain written in her expression. As she stood up he clenched his fists so hard that his nails dug into his palms and drew blood. He took a box out of his robes and held it for a moment. He looked down at the two bodies on the ground in front of him. He flicked the switch and the box burst into flame. He bent down and threw it onto the bodies which ignited with an orange flame. He then stepped back and stood beside Kyla and they watched as silver tendrils spread from the box and covered the bodies then exploded into violet light before combusting with a brilliant white light.

As the flames subsided Kyla bent down and picked up some of the earth and let it fall through her hand. "I take earth, from where life came and will return, I pass it through air which gives us life. As I pledged my life once to the service of the White Lady now I take that power and I release it. Let it break the final binding. Take my pain, use it as you will. I release you by right of blood. I release you by right of anger. I release you from your bond, I release you from your vow taken to keep peace in the Galaxies. My Queen Isis by my blood I demand retribution." The air began to crackle around her and flashes of white light shot from her hands. She reached for the knife on her belt and pulled it from its sheath. Joniel tried to snatch it from her but he was too late. She plunged her hands downwards towards her heart. There was a crack like thunder and Kyla's wrist was caught by an elegant long fingered hand. The blade was stopped by a black haired woman dressed in gossamer white who now stood in front of her. She had stopped the knife just a breath from Kyla's chest.

The woman smiled. "That will be quite enough. No my child, that is not necessary, the texts are far too poetical. You have asked and I have felt your pain. I will not stand by and see innocents suffer, not any more. The vow is broken by the sacrifice that has already been made. I and my husband will stand beside you both as we are now released. We commit our fleet, battleships and facilities to the cause. Your sacrifice was too great but I have heard your call." She smiled at Kyla, her face serene. "Kyla your loyalty has been without question, your love without bounds. You have mastered all the orders of healing. I would not take that from you for one moment of justified anger. I have used that anger to break our ancient binding, we are now free. A healer's true anger and justified hate is power strong enough to do that."

Kyla looked at peace. "I would gladly have given it if it could have saved her. Take whatever you wish from me. Can you give her back to me?"

There were tears in Isis's eyes. "I cannot. I will do what I can now." She smiled at Joniel. "To right the wrongs done by my brother I give you another gift of healing. Once the change has begun it cannot be stopped but if you can heal quickly enough you will be able to neutralise it immediately after the blow is struck." She touched Kyla on the head and she collapsed. Joniel caught her just before she hit the ground.

Isis turned to Rennon. "I think if you analyse the energy that Kyla can now use to heal you will be able to duplicate the frequency to create a device to distribute more widely. I would assume you would prefer a more scientific approach to this? It is the strongest form of healing, it may be able to reverse the effects of the fluid if you research and adapt it."

Rennon looked stunned and nodded.

There was a crack of thunder and a tall thin muscular man appeared, his nose was hooked and his black hair hung to his shoulders. In his eyes they could see the universes as pinpoints of stars on a deep black background. He stepped to stand next to Isis. "We respect your love as only those who know what it is to live lifetimes apart. But this is a time for the practical, not poets. Prince Anathorn, as my wife has indicated we are now able to commit our ships and troops to the war."

Prince Anathorn knelt before Osiris who stepped over and put his hand on Anathorn's head. "Without your skill in handling this war so far there would be nothing now to salvage. I am in your debt. You shall remain as my Prince but would you accept a King's command?"

Anathorn did not hesitate. "Gladly."

Osiris smiled, his elegantly handsome features slightly hawk like. "That is good. I will communicate with you via the usual channels. If I may download my security software first as you seem to have a few more eyes and ears in the system than would be wise." He held his hand out and Anathorn handed him his scanner. Osiris clipped in an organic looking stick. "That should help. Any machine that is in contact with that unit will spread the protection software. Anyone trying to hack it will get a very unpleasant surprise."

Isis reached into the flames and pulled out a small metal device. "This is what has brought them to you. It isn't bio linked so they will not know that Kel is dead. It will help us to lure at least some of them where we want them to go."

Osiris smiled. "Indeed." He took the device and put it in a pocket in his robes. "That will give us the chance to manipulate them for a change. I think a few bio units who look a lot like you but with a little less vulnerability should keep their forces tied up for a while. It may give you a bit of peace which you so rightly deserve or a chance to move about more freely."

Isis stood in front of Kyla who was being held up by Joniel. "I can't take away the pain you have felt as it is part of who you are now. I can tell you that you will have the blessing of another child. I hope that the son you will conceive tonight will be born into a happier and more peaceful world. Let that be something that drives you on, not anger." She smiled and took Kyla's hand. She then took Joniel's hand and held the two hands together. "I am sorry that it took this to release us. If I could have given you the healing before I would have done but it would have been in direct contravention of our agreement and bond."

Osiris stepped over and took his wife's arm. "We must bid you farewell now as we need to organise our troops and deploy our ships." There was a wicked gleam in his eye. "Prince Anathorn, you must take them to your private home tonight, nowhere else. I will contact you with further information. Do not attempt to go anywhere or get involved with anything that you see happening tonight." He touched his wrist device and Osiris and Isis disappeared.

Kyla looked up at Joniel who had managed to raise a smile. He bent down and kissed her on her forehead. "Where are we going to go? He said to your home my Prince, where is that?"

Rennon looked up. "I would say that my vote is to find somewhere where there are a minimum of murdering and psychotic bastards trying to kill us. I would expect that there will be a huge offensive by these new ships for a while so we had better find somewhere as far as possible from Follower territory."

The Prince smiled. "Whitewater. It has a low technological level and is off of the main trade routes. I have a ranch there."

Kyla tried to smile. "Sounds like a good idea."

They got back into the shuttle and as they took off the Prince got a huge document download, swore and sat down to start reading it. Aliniel sat beside him, her head on his shoulder as he read through the pages. She yawned slightly and fell asleep. He smiled as he heard her breathing change.

Rennon was seated on the bench opposite the Prince with his scanner in hand. He was still trying to work out what had been changed. He kept smiling to himself and occasionally he uttered a "Well I never" or an "Oh my god that is amazing".

Joniel and Kyla were sitting in the cockpit but Joniel was flying, Kyla had her head rested on the high back of the chair and was drifting in and out of sleep, tears still rolled down her cheeks and she made no attempt to wipe them away. Joniel looked across at her while she was sleeping, reached over and brushed away a stray hair that was hanging over her face.

They were approaching the ranch and Joniel circled it as he looked for a good place to land. It was a lot like

Whitewater Town but the house was bigger. It was a huge structure that looked like it had many rooms on two levels under a pitched roof. Smoke swirled upwards from the chimneys and people were milling about, going about their business. The solid brick house had been freshly painted white which contrasted well with the grey of the roof.

The compound was mostly covered in grass. There were three paddocks, one of which had a circle worn in it. A young man was exercising a large black stallion who was going through his paces around the circle and proving hard to control.

A couple of dogs were sleeping on the veranda of the house. A small herd of sheep were grazing on what looked like a manicured lawn until they were chased off by an irate middle aged man wearing an apron and brandishing a meat clever. They weren't going to wait around to find out what he had in mind. He then returned to the barn. The door was half open and he could then be seen smashing up and slicing beets with the clever and throwing them into buckets.

Joniel was looking for a safe place to land where he wouldn't land on any of the animals or people and that was proving a little difficult. Finally a gap emerged.

As they flew down to land in the stockade on Whitewater the Prince received another update. He put the scanner in his pocket and they stepped out of the shuttle, cloaked it and walked across the compound towards the ranch house. It was on two storeys, the upper storey built into the pitched roof. There were a large number of windows. A stockade had been built around it which encompassed about a hectare and there were guards patrolling the walls, around a platform which allowed them to walk around the top on the inside and see out. The Prince had already sent his code so they were expecting them and merely glanced over to see what was happening when they had de-cloaked and got out of the shuttle.

A tall, thin, grey haired man with long grey moustaches came out to greet them. A beaming smile on his face showed how glad he was to see Anathorn, he saw the Princes guests and took on a more formal stance. He bowed slightly to the Prince when he approached. Anathorn laughed. "Jake, there is no need for all that, you know that. These are my friends. Good to see you again."

Jake smiled. "You weren't so important when you left. You are Prince now. I feel I should bow or something. Maggie has cooked you a meal that would flaw a full grown bull. I hope you are hungry."

Anathorn laughed. "Ravenous and I expect my friends would enjoy a big meal too. I don't need to ask if you have got rooms ready for us all. How are the animals?"

Jake smiled. "I'd have been mortally offended if you had. You will find things all right and proper sir, just as you asked for. Your mare is doing well, she isn't ready for riding though. She's got a new born at foot. She had a beautiful Palomino by Gustauf. He's doing well too, he's in with the bonded mares who are due to go back to their owners in a month. They have all paid and it looks like Gustauf has done his duty. I'm sorry to have to tell you but we lost Acken last winter I'm afraid, that old dog loved you. He was old and he fell asleep and didn't wake up. Other than that the steers have multiplied well, you have a good heard of nearly three thousand now and you have about two hundred head of sheep that went to the market last week so your accounts are looking very healthy. Your standing stock are doing well, they are out on the wild lands on the east pasture at the moment. We have branched out into goats as you suggested and the dairy and cheese making is doing really well. The rhasvarks you brought back have done well. You have twelve now."

The Prince smiled. "You have done well. It seems peaceful around here."

Jake smiled ironically. "On the surface it is but there are a few underlying problems. I had to drop two of the boys last month. They got into gambling debts and tried to sell off some of your stock to pay them off. Mikard caught them at the sale, recognised your stock and got them arrested. I didn't let them come back here. There are a few other things going on but nothing too dramatic. Can we bring your bags?" He was looking around for the ship.

Anathorn laughed. "The ship is over there, we've cloaked it which I suppose isn't such a bright idea."

As if on cue a huge black dog chased a tabby cat across the yard. The cat was in luck as it was small enough to miss the ship, the dog wasn't so lucky and took part in a dramatic athletic manoeuvre where it bounced backwards, flipped over and rolled in the dirt.

Anathorn looked horrified. "Poor dog or should I say lucky cat? Is that one of Atatha's kittens? She's really grown." He turned to the others. As you can see we have a fully functioning farm here of about two hundred acres. It was where I invested all my ill-gotten gains and I suppose now it is where I will come to get away from the rigors of being a Prince. Or, under these circumstances where I and on this occasion, we, are kept until we are needed.

In case you are worrying the rest of our crew are still on board and are in orbit the other side of the planet. That was what the instructions were. It appears that we have Follower sleepers on board and they are going to be eliminated by certain members of Osiris's crew. How the plan to get on board I am not going to ask.

So, Jake, would you show everyone to their room so that they can relax a bit. We can meet up at dinner. Take time and if you need anything Jake will help you."

Kyla and Joniel were shown to a spacious double room which had a spectacular view across the open countryside to the woodland in the distance. If they had been happier it would have been perfect. Kyla ran a bath while they looked around the room. Clothes had been put for them in the wardrobe and there were washing products in the bathroom for them.

Rennon was more than happy with his room as it had a view of the countryside and wasn't a box on a space ship hurtling through space.

Aliniel was happy to be shown to Anathorn's room even though he said he'd see her later as he had things to do. She walked into the room and looked around at the personal things that were there. There weren't many. He had a collection of horse ornaments that were very fine. He also had a few countryside paintings on the wall. She looked in the drawers as she couldn't help herself. She wanted to know. She was disappointed as the drawers were mostly empty.

There were things like a comb and clothes but nothing really personal.

She put her things down and ran a bath and went to the wardrobe where clothes had been left for her and she assumed his clothes had been there awaiting his return.

Aliniel pulled a dress out of the wardrobe. It was long and had a full skirt which bunched from the waist. She had been reading about Earth history and she placed it firmly in the Victorian era, like everything else. Thankfully the facilities were completely up to date although they were not as computerised as she had seen on the ships.

That evening, after a large and expertly prepared full roast dinner with all the trimmings and a pudding they sat out on the sweeping porch that surrounded the ranch house in the dry heat of the fading sun, unable to move. They were too full. The women wore elegant cotton gowns, the men jeans, shirts and waistcoats. Kyla sat on a long swing seat with Joniel, she had her head on his shoulder and was watching what was going on. He put his arm gently around her. Aliniel was sitting alone beside a table playing a solitary game of cards. Anathorn was kicked back on a rocking chair with his feet on the table while Rennon was fidgety. They had taken his laptop off of him for the evening and he was forced to sit with them. He looked strangely out of place without it. He didn't know what to do with his hands and he constantly looked as though he was getting ready to get up and go somewhere.

The wind was getting up a little, blowing little pieces of straw around the place. The last rays of sun turned the sky a brilliant orange and evening faded into night with a smooth progression. Anathorn sat up and lit a hurricane lamp and set it on the table. Kela was watching her daughter.

Joniel bent down and kissed Kyla on the forehead. "Are you tired?"

She smiled at him. "A little."

He turned to Anathorn. "I think we'll turn in if that is alright with you."

Anathorn looked up lazily. "I hope you sleep well."

Joniel got up and helped Kyla up. They walked back into the house. Aliniel stayed where she was and Rennon looked about, looking a little lost. "I somehow feel a bit of the odd one out here. I think I'll turn in too if that is alright with you all. I'll see you in the morning. I really can't stand sitting here and not knowing what it going on. I feel so useless. I think I'd rather sleep through it. If we get blown up, don't let me know about it. If we get attacked for the record I'm sleeping in my clothes and my bags are still packed."

Aliniel got up and went to sit on the swinging seat. "Well, what do we do now?"

Anathorn smiled sleepily. "We're going to take our reinforcements and kick their sorry asses back to where they came from, or oblivion or anywhere else that we fancy."

Aliniel laughed. "Do you think it will be that easy?"

Anathorn laughed as well. "No but for tonight I want to think it will be." He looked up into the sky and froze. In the sky there were flashes of explosions and then he suddenly realised that planets were missing. "Something is going on up there. Much as we expected." He pulled his communicator from his pocket. He'd turned it off as Osiris had taken full control and had commanded him to stand down to save any confusion and delay with having to inform him of situations. He hastily switched it on again and messages flashed up. Osiris had copied him in on every message but had locked him out of actually responding to anyone. He began opening them. "I don't believe this, there is a full scale war going on up there at the moment. Osiris has deployed his battle cruisers and planet busters. Where they can't take a world they are blowing them out of existence. That man doesn't take any prisoners. I'm getting the statistics in now. The death toll is running into the millions. He's got ground troops on most of the major planets and he's taken out several key installations.

I'm looking at planets up there that don't exist anymore. Their names are listed but their light won't go out for a very long time.

Queen Isis's troops have retaken the Milky Way and are covertly removing all Follower infiltration there. The list of planets that have been cleansed is growing by the minute."

There was a huge flash in the sky. Anathorn looked it up on the scanner. "That was the Follower Command Ship going up."

There was a blue flash from planets in the distance which seemed to jump from planet to planet. "I've just received a communiqué. That was the Followers fighting back. They had self-destruct devices set on various planets in the Anibola Nebula and they have blown those planets up. I'm sad to say that the loss of life is phenomenal." He shook his head. "I know why Osiris is keeping me out of this. He's doing a clean sweep. Should we wake Joniel and Rennon?"

Aliniel smiled wistfully. "No, I have a feeling that Isis said what she did today to make sure that Kyla was kept away from watching this. She is a healer and she has lost too much today. It would rip her apart to watch all that death as just numbers on the screen.

Leave them in peace. Rennon would only want to interfere and if the Followers found out we are here they could do a strike on this planet."

Anathon sighed. "You could be right my love." He looked down. It looks like they are moving in on the Follower strongholds on the core planets. It's going to be bloody. They have most of their firepower concentrated around there. Our troops are being kept very much to the side lines as well. This is totally Osiris' show. Then I would anticipate that Osiris' troops have been waiting for a long time for active service again if they bound themselves not to intervene for so long."

The numbers kept on growing and the communiqués kept on coming in. At about midnight there was a communiqué from Osiris himself to Anathon. He opened it, read it then read it aloud.

"Greetings Prince Anathon, I trust that my message finds you well. If you did try to take off to assist tonight you will by now have found that I have disabled your shuttle. If not and you followed my instructions then I trust that you have watched the situation unfold with interest. Remember that you made this possible. If you and your companions had not survived this long and found out what you did we would not be in such a strong position tonight.

You will have to forgive me for keeping your troops away from the action. They have seen much service over the past years while my men have seen none. They are also trained on the equipment we are using. There will be plenty of time for them to see active service in the clean-up operation which will begin tomorrow. It will be your job to retrieve what you can of the Followers' research and to remove any last vestiges of Follower control.

I have a command ship waiting for you when you are ready to take up your Command tomorrow. For tonight I will let fire and my wrath rain down on my brother's troops. This should have been our war, not yours. Innocent people have been killed to satisfy his lust for power.

The armies of Set have now suffered significant losses such that they will never again be able to get such a stranglehold on the galaxies. It will be your job to make sure that all pockets of resistance are removed and any perpetrators who may seek to reinstate the regime are eliminated.

For tonight you must, I am afraid, watch what is going on from a distance. Tomorrow will be your time. King Osiris, Commander of the Osirian Fleet."

Anathorn sighed. "I suppose we can only sit this one out." He looked down at his scanner and through the night he gave Aliniel an update on the figures. She looked strangely thoughtful.

Anathorn noticed and looked over at her smiling kindly. "What is the matter?"

Aliniel smiled a little. "Oh, nothing. I was just thinking of all the innocent people who got caught up in this. Those are planets exploding, that doesn't differentiate between those who are Followers and those under their thrall."

The morning dawned bright and clear. Anatorn had been out riding just after dawn having not been to bed from the night before. As they came out onto the porch he rode up on his Pintaloosa and dismounted, tying his horse to the rail. "I trust you slept well. I have lots to tell you so please, make your way to breakfast."

Breakfast was spent recounting the battle as they had seen it the night before. Rennon was fascinated. Kyla was visibly shaken. Joniel listened in a moody silence.

After breakfast their shuttle sped off into the crisp morning air. It orbited the planet then jumped into the corridor. They travelled in silence, fears were unspoken. Kyla sat with Aliniel. Joniel piloted while the others looked at the screen, running and rerunning short clips of the battle as they became available as news clips.

For half an hour they flew through the corridor, Joniel wasn't piloting once the ship had taken over but he stayed in the pilot's seat, lost in his own thoughts. The proximity alert went off and he made the calculations and they jumped out of the corridor into a small piece of empty space. He transmitted their code as they left the corridor at the precise coordinates they had been given by Osiris.

There was silence in the cockpit. They all looked in wonder as the colossal ship stretched out in front of them.

The ship was an extremely large battle cruiser that looked as though it was just off the production line. They approached, transmitting the code they had been given and a clamp grabbed the shuttle and lifted it into the hanger. The doors shut behind them and they heard the hiss of pressurisation. The shuttle came to a gentle landing and the clamp retracted. Joniel flicked the switches to shut the shuttle down and the rear door opened.

They were met by a contingent of soldiers in full body armour. The armour was modern, the insignia and decoration was based on hieroglyphs. A middle aged man in plain white robes who stood with them stepped forwards. "I am Neitis and I would like to welcome you to the Horus. My master has bid me show you around your new command Prince

Anathorn. I trust that you have received the specifications of the vessel and the crew breakdown?"

Anathorn smiled and nodded. "I have indeed. She is a very impressive ship and the crew seem very adequately qualified." He had indeed received it, pages of it. He'd skim read it but had omitted to notice the scale on the plan so the actual size of the ship was equally a surprise to him. He also hadn't read the reams of pages about the crew, again he'd skim read it and everyone seemed to be more than qualified for the job they were doing. After reading a few he was happily reassured that although he knew nothing about a ship of this calibre, they did, so they were hopefully safe from imminently crashing into a planet somewhere.

Neitis led the way and showed them around decks upon decks of crew rooms, a galley, command room and all manner of training rooms. Finally he showed them to their private rooms. Each had a suite of rooms set aside for them. When the tour was done Neitis left them in a comfortable sitting room which was to be their private meeting place.

Anathorn looked around the assembled faces. "Well, this is more than I expected. Her firepower is phenomenal, like nothing I've ever seen. She is the flagship of a fleet of twenty battle cruisers. They are all under my command. It is beginning to sink in now that we might just stand a chance here of turning things around."

A voice behind him made him jump. "I certainly hope so." He turned to face Osiris who was standing folded armed behind him. "Don't worry, I do that a lot. I can't tolerate all that walking down endless corridors. I don't usually arrive without an introduction but as there is haste needed here I thought you would be happy to forego the usual etiquette."

Anathorn bowed his head. "Of course my lord."

Osiris raised an eyebrow. "Well, you have your orders, other than that general directive you have a free hand to go and do what you wish. All I ask is that you report in occasionally and tell me any important information. Is that agreeable?"

Anatorn nodded. "I will do your bidding my lord."

Osiris smiled. "I would hope so. Joniel, I hope that I may call on you for certain special tasks that I need undertaken."

Joniel bowed his head once then met Osiris's glare. "We will do all we can to ensure the destruction of the Followers."

Osiris's smile faded. "Your anger is great."

Joniel nodded. "I had to kill my own child. I will never forgive them for that."

Osiris looked down. "That is a heavy burden to bear. Do you want me to take the memory away?"

Joniel took a deep breath. "Not yet. One day perhaps. I will have my revenge first."

Osiris nodded slowly. "Anger that is held too long becomes self-destructive to the bearer though. I carried my anger towards my brother for many years, but now it feels so good to be finally having an opportunity to vent how I truly feel."

Joniel looked confused.

Osiris smiled. "Many years ago when we were young in the world my brother tricked me. He trapped me in a coffin and cut my body into many pieces and spread them around the old world. Isis found me and put me back together. She breathed life back into me but I have never forgiven my brother for my death and that hatred festered. For many years I have forsaken any of the worlds out of anger. I even left my wife to live out her life alone. I would not help, she would not join me in my indifference. So I know exactly how you feel. One day you will ask me to take away the memory that is no longer necessary. For now, you need to make it right in our own mind. I can understand that. In our final victory perhaps we will all have what we all need. You have learnt your lessons well and you have served me well. Now I must bid you all farewell." With a smile he disappeared.

They looked at each other in silence. Outside the black emptiness of space, pin pricked by tiny points of light stretched to eternity. The moment wasn't lost on any of them. They had all lost so many people because of the views of others inflicted on them because of some else's beliefs. Now they had been given their personal power back. Even Kyla, a healer, was silenced by what had happened in the worlds. The Followers were a cancer, they were the cure. Those who lived in denial in Follower worlds, mindlessly believing in the rules they were given, were living in a false hope and according to reports they were finding out the reality of the regime they had so happily welcomed.

Prince Anathorn stood outside the Command Room of the Horus. He then keyed in his personal code and the door opened for him. He was met by a scene of bustling activity. There were people everywhere. Some carried small hand held scanners and were looking at the readings and typing in more figures as they walked around the room accepting information from the terminals. Some were seated at terminals watching monitors and screens where reams of figures seemed to flick up and down. He took a deep breath and strode in. Everyone looked up. He smiled as they stood and saluted him.

Anathorn stood for a moment, surveying the scene. He had read the main chapters of the manual the night before so he knew to stand still and accept the salute in silence. He then took a step forwards and everyone relaxed. He cleared his throat and spoke. "As you may already know I am Prince Anathorn. You will have been briefed that I have a lack of technical knowledge so I am going to have to rely on each and every one of you to do your job. You have my permission to explain a circumstance to me when I am making a decision. It is therefore also your responsibility to suggest what, in your opinion, is the best possible manoeuvre in a given situation knowing the capabilities of this ship.

I hope that you will find me approachable. We are going to be a team and I hope that this becomes more than just a title. I hope that later I will get an opportunity to meet you all personally but for now, shall we go and see what this ship can do? Mr Sanderson you have a "go" take us out of here. Log in co-ordinates for Milea Ventura and inform the fleet, when they are ready we'll make the jump to the corridor. Please take it as read that when I give an order to move, unless I say otherwise I mean for you to contact the rest of the fleet first and move us as a unit."

Mr Sanderson, a short blonde haired youth looked up momentarily. "Aye Captain, I mean Prince." He looked at Anathorn pleadingly.

Anathorn smiled. "Well, Captain will do."

Sanderson smiled. "Thank you Captain." He then keyed in various codes on screen and data started flooding back from each of the other ships in the fleet. The view from the huge windows shifted from the black and pinpoint lights of stars to the swirling colours of the Eion Particles in the corridor.

There were welcoming faces all around him, and slightly relieved ones that he didn't give a long speech. It had said in the manual that the length of speech was the choice of the speaker. It had also given various hints on content. He'd decided to keep it short and speak to people later. He went to his chair and sat down. There were switches and screens in front of him. He looked at them and tried to recall what they were but it had all become a bit of a blur and then Aliniel had distracted him.

They jumped out of the corridor over a small group of planets on the rim of the Ionis Galaxy. As soon as they arrived six fighter class battle cruisers moved into orbit with them and sent a challenging hail. Anathorn gave the order to power weapons and raised the shields. He gave the order to fire just before the enemy fleet. They got at least one salvo in first, disabling the enemies' main guns and ability to jump into the corridor.

The ships in the fleet co-ordinated their firing and within minutes the enemy fleet was destroyed. The cruisers burnt with plumes of orange and red light, bright against the dark backdrop of space and its myriad of stars. Suddenly Anathorn felt very small faced with the black infinity of that panoramic view. The ship felt so large, it was almost the size of a planet, the rest of the ships under his command were not much smaller. Each had a full crew and supporting staff together with a force of ground troops and engineers. The gravity of the power he had been given to wield sunk in. The gravity of the situation did also. There had been many people on those ships and they were all now dead. That had been his command, his responsibility. Knowing that the Followers brainwashed many of their believers it was a difficult moment. Capture had not been an option, not with the firepower they had. Firepower that was now no longer in the hands of his enemies. Democracy and right of choice had to be restored, they were fighting for the freedom of speech and to be able to live out a life in the way someone chose. That was a fight worth taking up. He had to put aside the horrors of what he had just done and the lives that had been lost. He wouldn't sleep well over it, but for now he could let himself and his crew enjoy a victory.

Rennon was in his new laboratory. He had his boxes with him. They were beginning to show their age and the amount of times they had been rescued from near abandonment on evacuating an area was beginning to show. He took the contents out like old friends and found them homes on shelves and in cupboards. He marvelled at the inertial dampeners and gravity modifiers which he knew would keep glasses and tubes on shelves whatever angle the cupboard ended up at.

Outside the internal window to his laboratory he could see his research crew. To him the laboratory area seemed vast. Within it thirty people were all busy and seemed to know what they were doing. He sat down and pulled out his laptop and connected it to the system. He pulled up their resumes and began going through them. He wanted to know who they were, a bit about them and most importantly what they could do. He was reading when there was a knock at his door.

He got up and opened it. He was met by a fragile woman, dressed in a lab coat with light brown hair tied back in a ponytail. She smiled. "Sir, I have been instructed by Prince Anathorn to tell you that I am not a psychotic murdering she bitch. My name is Neris Stevens. I am reporting for duty as your assistant." She looked a little bemused.

Rennon laughed. "Don't worry, it is a private joke. My last lab assistant was a Follower spy and managed to blow my lab up, steal the contents of my laptop and left me for dead."

Neris smiled sweetly. "Oh, I am sorry to hear that. If you check my resume you will see that I am totally unqualified for such extra-curricular activities. I have only trained in lab work so sadly I will have to forego the blowing up of the lab and trying to murder you duties. Can we settle for me bringing you tea or coffee occasionally? I find that much more suitable to my talents."

Rennon laughed. "Yes, I think that would be much more appropriate. Mine is white with no sugar."

Neris smiled. "Very good sir."

Rennon smiled back. "You can call me Rennon." She left and he went back to unpacking his boxes. He couldn't help smiling and he wasn't quite sure why. His laptop had begun downloading specifications from the ship and he busied himself looking through them.

Among his new documents was a message from Dr Samson. "Greetings from the Argo. We are all fine here and enjoying the delightful cooking and care that we get from Ma who is now the commander of this vessel. We were are a part of the post firestorm clean up mission like you and hopefully one day we'll be in the same area and can meet up."

6

Anathorn had just logged off from a communiqué with Maran. He rubbed his eyes and took a mouthful of strong black coffee, sighed and leant back in his high backed leather chair. He looked older. The strain was beginning to show on his face as was the lack of sleep. He looked down and realised he was still in the clothes from yesterday, he was yet to go to bed. Aliniel came in and stepped behind him and began to massage his shoulders. "You are very tense. Try to relax. You are doing a fantastic job. It has only been two weeks. Don't expect to know everything immediately."

He smiled. "I'm fine, it's a lot easier now." She ran her finger down his spine.

He laughed. "That does nothing for my concentration." He turned and grabbed her arm and pulled her down to sit on his lap. She put her arms around him. "So, how do you like your new mate? Will I do?"

She kissed him. "Despite not being in my bed last night you are doing just fine. Was that Maran?"

Anathorn raised an eyebrow. "She's doing well. She has settled in to heading the group that is uniting the tribes across the galaxies. She is having a little difficulty with the technology though and her spelling is driving me mad. She writes as things sound but she has a strong accent."

Aliniel smiled. "She was my mother's tutor as you know. She has started training me."

Anathorn looked worried. "You didn't mention you were training for the Order."

Aliniel kissed him. "Don't worry. I'm training for the basic healing only. I've already made my choices haven't I? There is no way I'm taking the path of celibacy. Not now." She smiled. "My mother took it before she had known a man. I know what I'd be missing."

Anathorn smiled. "I'm glad to hear it." Then Anathorn hesitated and looked thoughtful. "You mean?" He looked sheepish as he realised what he was saying to Aliniel about her mother.

Aliniel laughed. "Yes, she was."

Anathorn blushed as a message flashed up on screen and Aliniel jumped off of his lap and stepped aside as she saw it was a visual connection. Anathorn accepted the message, opened the channel and Osiris' face appeared in the communication box.

He looked a little tired but he smiled as he saw Anathorn. "We have some trouble in the Destiny Sector. It seems there was a small research laboratory there which passed undetected on our first sweep. Intelligence has come our way that there is a Follower ship on its way to extract the scientists and retrieve their research. I thought your people might enjoy an opportunity to go off ship and get there first. I have transmitted co-ordinates. I trust all is to your liking there?"

Anathorn smiled. "I am indeed very pleased with my new command. Thank you sir."

Osiris tilted his head slightly. "It was a pleasure. Until we speak again I wish you every success." The communiqué was cut off as the co-ordinates arrived.

Anathorn relayed the co-ordinates on to the Command Room with instructions for them to be keyed in but kept on hold. He then typed a message into his private pager which had the others on speed dial. "Report to Prince Anathorn. You have a mission."

Fifteen minutes later they sat around the large dark wood meeting table in the Operations Area of the ship. Anathorn had downloaded the information into private reading pads and had laid them out on the table so that everyone had a chance to look at them.

Anathorn stood up. "As you will see it's a small border planet, inhabited by miners mostly. It has already been swept by Osiris' shock troops so the Follower garrison that was stationed there has been removed. There are suspicions that there are still Follower spies amongst the inhabitants but if there are they are obviously keeping a low profile. I'm still not sanctioning Intendi for off ship missions so you won't be able to use his scanning skills. Anyone who you bring back will have to face him though, just in case.

Initial scans of the planet didn't reveal any hidden base so we can assume it is underground or shielded. I'll supply you with hand held scanners that may be able to tell you more once you are on the planet's surface. The magnetic field around that planet is strong so that may be interfering with our readings. Probably explains why we missed it before.

The best guess is that it is in this area." He pointed to a spot on a map which was projected onto the wall.

"It is an uninhabited and relatively undisturbed area of gullies and mountains. I would suggest that you land around there and take a look around.

Speed is of the essence but I don't want you to go in as unprepared as we were last time we undertook an extraction."

Aliniel pouted. Anathorn caught the expression and its meaning. "I need you with me here. Although the likelihood of assassination is minimal I would rather not take the risk, or the risk of losing you." He smiled at her, one of his velvet don't you dare contradict me smiles and she sat down and looked away.

Anathorn turned to Rennon. "I want you to go as well. You will know which machines to take and we may need you to break into any built in hard drive. I'm sending you in as a small force as that will stand the best chance of going in undetected. The population needs to be left alone to rebuild and to be reassured that we aren't going to be dropping by and shooting the place up every five minutes. This is a covert extraction as I understand that Osiris is hoping to set an ambush for the Follower rescue party. We are to leave as much as possible undisturbed on the perimeter of the facility if and when we find it."

The hopper set down on the eastern side of the planet. The greens and browns of the foliage were a stark contrast to the violet sky, made that way by the dust particles from the ore which floated in the air due to the extraction method. The soil was violet, green grass springing from it and exotic flowers clung to tree trunks. As they walked between them they gave off a heady aroma.

Kyla took point with Rennon just behind her with his head down looking at his scanner. Joniel was taking a look ahead and he had disappeared into the undergrowth when they first set off.

Their route took them along a little used path and headed up into the mountains and through a narrow ravine. Rennon kept turning around, trying to get a reading. He was having little success. "This damn planet's EMF is disturbing the equipment."

Kyla thought for a moment and held her hand out, palm down. "Will you let me try something? There is part of my training that helps me to locate objects or people. It is supposed to be used to find those lost and injured but I'm wondering if I can adapt it."

Rennon smiled. "I'm not going to say a word. Go for it."

Kyla took a deep breath and focused her mind and concentrated. She turned and checked direction after direction. "I think I've got something. I can feel something in that direction." Her legs gave out from under her and she slumped to the ground. She was dizzy and staggering but pointed towards the mountains.

Joniel had been watching them and changed his direction to match theirs. As the trees ran out he came back to join them. He fell in beside Kyla who had her hand out and was concentrating. Again and again she tripped over branches and rocks. He put his arm around her. "Is that alright, does that help?"

She gave him a weak smile. There were dark circles under her eyes and she seemed to be having difficulty keeping awake. "That helps. I will see the way better if I can close my eyes, they are so heavy, can you help me? I haven't done this for a long time and never out of the safety of the Training House." Joniel supported and guided her so that she could walk with her eyes shut which made it easier for her to find the energy signature she was looking for.

Kyla stopped. "I can feel something else." Then she gave out a shocked whimper. "Trouble."

A shot rang out and Kyla reeled backwards, blood flowing from her shoulder. Joniel picked her up and lifted her behind a rock where there was enough cover to hide her. He slapped a trauma patch over the wound and pulled out his blaster. Rennon was already blowing holes in the hillside randomly as he had no idea where the shot had come from.

Joniel disappeared into the undergrowth moved from rock to rock with lightning speed as he crossed the ravine and disappeared up the mountain side on the same side as the shot had come from. He managed to use the smallest amount of cover. Rennon saw him go and stopped firing. He made his way silently along the ravine and found himself a secure position behind the lone gunman who was safely hidden behind a thick stone wall, or so he thought. He shinned down the rock face and dropped silently behind the man, stepped forwards and put a knife to his throat. The gunman shifted his weight slightly and Joniel just caught a glimpse of him pushing a button on his belt. He didn't hesitate, he leapt and rolled out of the fox hole as an explosive charge went off, blowing the gunman to pieces. He muttered under his breath. "I guess I won't be interrogating that one."

He rolled and ran down the goat tracks that led down to the gulley they had been walking along. He passed Rennon. "I would suggest you scan here. That was a guard post." He carried on to Kyla who was sitting with her back to the boulder. She looked pale and the patch was soaked in blood. Joniel put a hand on her other shoulder. "Would you mind giving up being shot, I can't stand the worry."

She smiled as he grabbed the patch and tore it off. He then looked at the wound. "The bullet has lodged in there. Plenty of damage and that has got to hurt. So, shall we immobilise it or heal it and we can take the bullet out later?"

Kyla smiled. "I'll take the healing please. We don't know what we are going to meet."

Joniel nodded. "Good call. He handed her his wrist." She licked it first and anaesthetised the skin before biting and drawing off the blood that she needed to close the wound up." She lay back and looked up at him. He licked a stray drop of blood off of her lips and smiled at her. "Come on then, let's get on with the mission lazy bones."

Rennon held his hand out. "I've got it, three clicks south of here. Let's move out but we'll watch out for more of those outposts. I've got three on my scanner now that I have their signature. Joniel, if you would do the honours."

Joniel smiled and took a look at the scanner over Rennon's shoulder. "I'll clear them and come back, it's easier that way." He smiled and scampered up the goat track and along impossibly narrow ledges until he leapt over the ridge line. He ran along the ridge, keeping down and mostly out of sight using bushes and other small pieces of cover.

The first guard post was further along the gulley. He lay down on the ridgeline above and pulled himself out over the edge slightly so that he had a clear view down onto the guard who was diligently watching the valley around him. Joniel took out a small elegant gun with a long barrel. He carefully aimed and fired. A long slim dart flew down and embedded in the guard's shoulder. The guard grabbed at it in disbelief before he fell to his knees and then the floor. Joniel ran along the top of the ridge to the next one and did the same. As he fell Joniel was moving off to find the third. The third guard was on the other side of the valley. Joniel took out his silenced pistol and made himself comfortable behind a bush where he could watch what was going on. He waited and was soon rewarded when the guard stood up to take a look down the valley. Joniel's shot was instantaneous and the man fell to the ground. A single clean shot had pierced his temple.

Joniel ran along the top of the ridge, keeping low, back down to the group. "All clear." He grinned.

They moved down the gulley, Rennon holding the scanner out in front of him and following the proximity arrow that had now appeared. "Not far now. I'd say just about here."

There was nothing visible but with the scanner Rennon was able to find a portion of the wall and Joniel's keen eyesight picked out the crack of the door. Altering the frequency on the scanner tripped the lock and the door swung open. From the moment they could see inside Kyla started firing catching three very surprised guards unawares. She blew two away before they could move, then she got the other one. They stepped quickly inside and shut the door behind them.

The cavern was empty except for a plain metal camping table and four chairs. Joniel slipped into the room and down the tunnel which was the only exit at the back. Once outside the light from the guard room he used his sight to pick his way along the dark stone tunnel. He could hear something in front of him as he moved silently along the right wall. Candlelight flooded from one side. He crouched down and looked around the corner. A lone man was using the urinal. Joniel couldn't help smiling. He waited a moment and then stepped into the doorway. The man had turned and was just doing his flies up without looking up when Joniel launched two thin throwing daggers at him. The man looked down at his pierced chest in disbelief and his hands involuntarily reached up to hold them as he fell to his knees and collapsed onto the floor. In one fluid movement Joniel kept moving into the room and slit the man's throat with his dagger, retrieved his daggers, washed them in the sink, dried them and moved the man around the corner out of sight from the tunnel.

He stopped and listened. All he could hear was the dripping of water somewhere in the distance. He retraced his steps and re-joined the others. He arrived smiling slightly. Joniel shook his head. "I just find it totally wrong to hit a guy at the urinal. I was laughing at my twisted morals. I'll happily kill anyone, just not there."

Rennon laughed. "So that is the safest place when you are around then?"

Joniel smiled enigmatically. "No, you have to leave the room one day."

The smile fell from Rennon's face.

Joniel disappeared into the darkness of the tunnel, the others followed on with torchlight. The tunnel dipped down underground for about half a mile and opened up into a single cavern which was lit with electric light. Joniel slipped into the shadows and hugged the wall, moving slowly so that he didn't attract the attention of the four scientists dressed in lab coats who were going about their business of packing the last of their equipment into boxes. He reached into his pocket and pulled out a similar gun to the first, this one had a red ring painted in Kyla's nail varnish around the end. He took aim and fired four shots in quick succession. The scientists grabbed their necks as the venom paralysed them immediately and they fell to the ground unable to move or cry out.

Joniel waited for the others to catch up with him. He then moved off into the rooms beyond the cavern until he heard voices and came back. "We have people ahead."

Rennon was busy packing the last of the useful and portable things into boxes. He had cable tied and gagged the scientists. Joniel looked down at them. "They will be out of action for about half an hour."

Joniel moved silently, Kyla at his side. She kicked in the first door. The door flung back on its hinges to reveal what looked like a bunk room. Six guards were playing cards. Four fell in quick succession as Kyla fired again and again with her silenced pistol. Joniel blasted the other two before the room fell silent. Joniel launched a thin dagger at a guard who was just getting out of bed and another at one who had grabbed his pistol and was reaching over from the top bunk to the right. They leapt into the room, back to back. The room was clear. There was nobody left alive.

Joniel slipped out of the room and moved down to a junction and listened. He couldn't hear anything so he returned. The two followed him and moved to the junction and turned right. This led to a line of cells. Each cell held a carapace creature which lay dead on the floor. Each was holding its throat. Each had a tray of half eaten food which had fallen on the floor.

At the end of the cells there was a room with a table with restraining bands on it. Rennon looked around the room but all equipment had been removed.

The corridor to the left of the main corridor was the kitchen and dining room. It too had been packed up and was empty.

A corridor went off deep into the mountain. Joniel set off down it, slowly, carefully and silently. It went on for about half a mile, gradually sloping down. The smell of damp stone became tinged with sulphur. The air seemed unnaturally cold. The sulphur became choking. Joniel pulled out a breathing device. He returned back to the others. He coughed before emerging from the shadows in front of them. "It's clear up ahead but it is going down a long way. There's sulphur in the air so you'll need breathing devices. I'm going back. Follow me up at a steady pace." They then followed him up far enough back that their light didn't disturb his vision.

The tunnel went down into the mountain and the carved walls became a natural tunnel. The floor became damp, then wet. Trickles of water ran down the walls. The floor was becoming increasingly slippery as green dark dwelling wet algae covered the floor. Joniel was finding it hard to keep his footing. He was more skating than walking by the time he felt a cavern open out in front of him. He hugged the left wall and looked inside.

The walls pulsated. He could see movement but whatever was in there was almost as cold as the walls. He held onto the wall as his foot slipped out from under him. Something snapped onto his ankle, blades cut into his leg. He bit his tongue trying not to cry out. He felt panic running through him as he tried to pull his foot free and was pulled off of the wall as a chain started being reeled in pulling him across the floor by his ankle. As he was being dragged he reached down and tried to grab the device. Pain shot up his leg as he slid across the floor. He had no purchase. He ignored being dragged and concentrated on the device. He tensed his muscles to pull himself into a ball and grabbed the man trap with both hands and pulled it open. He was free and tried to stand up. The floor was completely covered in slippery moss. He managed it but as soon as he took a step his foot slipped out from under him, partly from the slipperiness but mostly because the bone was broken. His injured leg was beginning to go numb and he was feeling light headed from blood loss as he crashed to the ground. Pain seared every nerve and the fear of remembering the time he'd been paralysed made him feel physically sick.

He reached down into his pocket and pulled out a box which contained phials of white liquid. He poured some onto the moss in front of him, waited and put his hand down there. The acid burnt him a little but most of it was spent. He managed to pull himself up to his feet, balancing on the tiny patch of moss free stone. He poured another and another and made his way back to the tunnel he had come from. He was nearly there when a shock net fell over him. He screamed in agony and fell to the ground convulsing as a voice was heard laughing above him and he passed out.

A light appeared at the cavern entrance as the others arrived. Before they could react a metal door slid down behind them. The cavern was filled with light as a bank of light bulbs above was switched on which momentarily blinded them all. A voice spoke from above. "So, aren't I the lucky one, I get to meet you all at last. Welcome but I'm afraid you will find my hospitality far from warm."

Standing on a ledge high up on the far wall of a roughhewn cavern with an obvious shimmering force field protecting him was a creature. It looked like it had the shape of the man but it was similar to the carapace warriors. "Don't worry, I'm not going to bore you with my evil plan. I know I can't hold you there either as sooner or later Joniel is going to get to you and you will teleport out. I'm assuming you have already killed my guards and any of the scientists that you have found. I'm pretty certain you are going to take what you can from this facility. The question is, how fast can you run? You want my research. So you are going to have to work for it. Or it will go up with this mountain. Sorry, cliché I know but the old ones are good ones. I've set the facility to self-destruct. I'm going to teleport out now and by talking to you I have wasted precious last moments of your lives or the possibility of you getting hold of my research. So, off you go then, get yourselves out of this one." He pressed his wrist and disappeared with a maniacal laugh.

Joniel was unconscious and his leg was pouring blood out onto the wet algae.

Rennon was working on the security lock on the door. He had pads attached to the wall and was feverishly tapping keys on his scanner.

Kyla lay down flat on the slippery stone and reached forwards, securing her foot on a rough part of the tunnel entrance. She managed to get to reach out far enough to grab Joniel and pull him back. When he was back in the tunnel Kyla concentrated hard. She held out her hand and white light encompassed Joniel just before she collapsed. Her skin looked grey. Joniel came around, saw her and rolled to her side. He was about to bite his wrist to give her blood but then realised what she had done. He waited while Rennon managed to get the door open which was about the same time as Kyla came around.

They moved as fast as they could down the corridor with Joniel limping in agony. They got back to the laboratory. As they got there a low rumbling began deep within the cave system. Joniel thought for a moment and moved to stand beside the pile of boxes and took out his last energy net. "Kyla, take Rennon. I'm going to try something." Kyla nodded as Joniel set the coordinates on her wrist strap, grabbed Rennon who was too busy with his hand held scanner to notice what was going on and they disappeared.

Joniel set the co-ordinates on his wrist strap, gritted his teeth in anticipation of the pain and as he activated the net he pressed the button. The energy net created a circuit around the boxes which bound them to him and the whole lot arrived back in the shuttle just as the others were walking up the ramp. Joniel collapsed as Rennon leapt into the pilot's chair and did a swift pre-flight check, pulled up the ramp, detonated any bugs and tracking devices and took off.

Kyla sat on the floor with Joniel. His muscles were in spasm and it was all she could do to stop him flailing about. She just about had him pinned down when he woke up. She leapt off of him and he sprang to his feet and fell sideways as his injured leg would not hold his weight.

Joniel winced as he flexed his muscles. "Remind me never to do that one again." Then he saw Kyla and they sat down on the bench. "What happened? Why did you pass out?"

Kyla smiled. "I used too much of my inner strength there. Basically I had overdone it a bit but not to the point of it being lethal."

He smiled at her. "Have you attended to your shoulder?" She shook her head. "Don't forget I healed it with the bullet in it. The sooner we get that bullet out the better." He pulled down the medical box from its locker and took out a bottle of disinfectant. He then took his knife and disinfected it. Kyla looked away as he reached over and made sure he was balanced. As he couldn't manage that standing up he sat down beside her and made sure he had a steady hand before anaesthetising and then cutting into her shoulder and removing the bullet.

Rennon was watching him intently.

Joniel tried to stand up afterwards but he was in agony and he could hardly stand. He could feel that his leg was swelling up and the pain was almost unbearable. He sat beside Kyla and she put her hand gently on his leg and concentrated. Her face was expressionless as she slipped into unconsciousness and fell against him.

Once they were back on the Horus Joniel's leg was dressed and immobilised and he was able to sit with her as she lay on a bed in the Infirmary. There were no pipes attached to her, no monitoring devices. They were doing nothing to help her and in his mind this started conjuring up all manner of nightmarish possibilities. He kept checking she was alright until he fell asleep with his head on her bed.

Anathorn sat in his office and looked over the paperwork. There were reams of it. Message after message came in. Facts, figures, reports and more reports and he had to read them all. They all related to his fleet, nothing was coming back about what they had found on the planet. He flicked the intercom to Rennon's laboratory. Rennon answered almost immediately. "Yes Anathorn, can I help?"

Anathorn smiled. "Any news about what we found?"

Rennon hesitated. "I'm working on something now. King Osiris has shipped back all the information and has left us with the research material. You need to come down here when you can."

Anathorn thought. "Did you all get back alright?

Rennon looked down. "Sort of, Kyla is in the Infirmary with Joniel, he got his foot caught in a man trap and she's overloaded her healing. They will be alright in time."

Anathorn signed off of his computer and ran down to the Infirmary. He was rushing in but saw Joniel asleep. He then entered very quietly and kept out of range of Joniel's dagger arc. Kyla looked grey skinned and he really didn't like the look of her. He picked up her wrist and felt for a pulse, he couldn't find one. He felt her neck, no pulse. He rushed to the alert button and pressed it.

Sirens went off and Joniel awoke with a start. He saw the Prince bending over Kyla and realised that a medical crash team was in the room. He backed away as they started to try to resuscitate Kyla. Anathorn walked over and stood beside him. "I found her just now. I didn't like the look of her so I checked her pulse. Does she have a pulse?"

Joniel glared at him. "She does, a weak one but still a pulse."

The team had begun their work. They shocked her again and again. They worked on her and then finally as they were about to give up there was a feint blip on the monitor they had now attached to her. Then there was a pulse.

The doctor came over and got a chair for Joniel. "She's a very sick woman. As well as her injuries this time we have to take into consideration all the past injuries she has sustained. Her bones are still knitting from some past missions and her heart is very weak. It has had so much strain, as has she. We'll do all we can for her but a body just wasn't made to take that kind of punishment. I have read that report of those initial injuries that happened when she was captured by the Followers. The damage then was phenomenal.

I was surprised her body survived it then. Since then there have been countless other occasions. I understand that she was also recently poisoned. He body was still weak from that. I advised her not to go on that last mission with you but she would hear nothing of it. Now she is going to have to listen to me and you are going to have to make her listen. That is if she survives this. The next twenty four hours are critical. In truth I had left her without the equipment to let her slip away in peace."

Joniel turned and grabbed the doctor by the collar and pinned him up against the wall. Anathorn grabbed his wrist and stopped him from doing any serious damage to the doctor. Joniel glared at the doctor. "She needs blood, I must give her blood."

The doctor glared at him. "We will not have any of those practices around here. I have already given her a full and regular blood transfusion and that is all that she needs."

Joniel's eyes turned red and Anathorn let Joniel's wrist go and grabbed the doctor instead. Anathorn screamed at the doctor. "Why are you doing that? Giving her human blood in that fashion is exactly what is causing her to be in the state she is in. Joniel, look after your wife. I will take this fool out and explain to him a few things about the care and preservation of my off ship team."

The doctor was literally shaking as he watched Joniel drain Kyla's blood and give her his. Joniel wasn't bothered where the blood went as he spat it out. The room looked like there had been a blood bath by the time he had finished. He sat on the bed, both of them covered in blood, cradling her in his arms and rocking her. She moaned and woke up and smiled until she looked down. Joniel just about managed to catch her and hold her down as she went into a feeding frenzy. He was much stronger than her and soon enough she calmed down and he was able to release her. He grabbed a fresh gown from the table and tore the blood stained one from her, bundled up the blood stained sheets and bundled them out of the door.

The doctor stared in horror. "Her notes didn't mention any of this. They said she had a blood thinning disease and needed regular transfusions. I have been giving her them since you arrived on board."

Anathorn grabbed the blood stained set of written notes. He showed them to Joniel who looked over them carefully.

Joniel looked up, his expression serious. "That report at the top has been added to. Look, the ink is a very slightly different colour. It seems you have a very cowardly assassin on board who wants someone else to do his work for him. If you don't mind I'm going to take my wife into my own care. I think you have done enough damage."

Anathorn lifted Kyla off of the bed and carried her back to the room she shared with Joniel. He then left them alone.

By the time he had sat beside her she was beginning to gain a bit more colour to her cheeks. She smiled at him then a serious look came over her face. "That is twice I've been nearly assassinated while in an Infirmary. Did you find out who poisoned me when I was on your ship?"

Joniel stared at her moodily. "No, I didn't. You were unconscious when you were treated. There was no record on the notes and the security footage had been wiped out. You think they are linked? If so then it has to be someone who is travelling with us. The only person who has been with us on both occasions is Rennon."

Kyla opened her mouth then shut it again. She thought about it and then spoke quietly. "It can't be, well not voluntarily anyway. Anathorn has been with us as well but I can't see what he'd have to gain. I can't see why Rennon would do anything either. So what do we do?"

Joniel looked thoughtful. "I'd like to say nothing but this is your life on the line here. Next time we might not be so lucky."

There was a knock on the door and Joniel impaled the door with one of his throwing knives. He looked very sheepish as the door opened and Prince Anathorn walked back in. He coughed. "Well I'm glad I didn't just walk in." He was looking at the spike sticking out of the back of the metal door. "You are a bit jumpy."

Joniel stepped forwards, looked outside the door and shut it. He then pulled his knife out of the back of the door and covered the hole with some tape. "Anathorn, we have a problem."

Anathorn looked concerned. "I know that we do. Ker, one of the off ship team members has accused you of trying to murder your wife. He has done it in accordance with the Ancient Laws so I have no alternative but to take you into custody."

Joniel looked horrified. "But I didn't do anything. I wouldn't harm her, ever."

7

Joniel sat in his prison cell. It was a box of a room with smooth impenetrable walls. The light was embedded in the ceiling and there was no window. The door fitted flush to the wall and there was a solitary window in it and a hatch for passing food through. The room was sparsely furnished. A toilet was fixed to the wall and there was a pallet bed which was fixed to the floor. His leg hurt but he had been denied pain killers as all drugs were forbidden while in the brig.

Thoughts rampaged through his mind. He thought of Kyla, unprotected. He questioned why he would be suspected.

He heard the metallic scraping sound of a door opening down the corridor and he froze. Looking for cover there was none in the room. He got up and went over to it and tried to look down the corridor but he couldn't see far from the small square. He didn't see anything until a face he recognised appeared at the window. The face belonged to Ker, he knew the name but he couldn't think what the man actually did on the ship. He trawled his memory to see if he could place him. The man was laughing.

Ker was barely past being a teenager and still unable to grow more than a token beard which he looked like he tended with great pride. He was a wisp of a man, wiry but extremely fit as he probably spent most of his time in the training rooms. That bit was easy for him to evaluate, what Ker's position was in all this he didn't know.

Ker turned on the speaker outside the room. He laughed and then spoke clearly and slowly, his mouth close to the microphone. "So you don't feel so high and mighty now, do you? What is it with you and ruining my life? I thought you were alright about me being with Kyla? Or was that one of your cunning plans as well? Make us think that you were supporting us then get her paranoid enough that she can't trust me? You have drugged her, haven't you? I hope you are happy with what you have done, you have succeeded. She has told me exactly what she thinks of me. She even seemed surprised that I thought we had a relationship. You have really worked your poison on her. Well any time to gloat is going to be short lived."

Joniel watched Ker very carefully through the glass. He was looking for some sign of why Ker was not himself. He saw it, there was a feint blue glow around his eyes. He could see it in the shadow as Ker had his back to the light. He got closer to the door, keeping out of the way of the food chute. "Ker, you are not yourself. Try to calm down and listen to me. There is nothing between you and Kyla. There never was. This is the effect of a drug that has been working on you and a suggestion that someone has made to you." He desperately trawled his memory, looking for something he could use. Then he remembered something. "You have a wife and a child, why would you want to be with Kyla?"

Ker laughed. "Listen to you? Do you think I'm going to listen to you so you can infect me with your verbal poison, I don't think so. This isn't something you just say sorry for and I can't see why you are making up those lies. I don't have a wife or a child other than Kyla and our unborn child. Kyla is my wife and now I've lost her because of the lies you have told her and the drugs you have used on her. So now you are going to lose something you love. You are going to lose her as well. Think on that. You can't call anyone. I've drugged the guards. You are going to have to sit here and think about it until someone comes and tells you that your wife is dead. You may have had all those years waiting for her, now you can have the rest of your life without her." He turned and strode off down the corridor.

Joniel screamed and despite the pain tried to claw his way out of the cell. He threw himself at the door but it held firm.

It made no sense to him. Ker's thoughts and memories were completely tangled and he obviously had no idea what he was even thinking. There was obviously nobody around so that part of what Ker had said was true. So there was no reason for the rest of his threat to be untrue either.

Ker strode out of the corridor and to the office. He opened up the custody box which hadn't been put away and took out Joniel's dagger in his gloved hand. He held it up to the light and grinned. "And with your own knife as well." He slipped it into its sheath and strapped it around his waist under his jacket. He caught his reflection in a window and smoothed down his hair. The security camera he had disconnected earlier was hanging from its wire broken and useless.

He left the room and carefully closed and locked the door behind him. He then walked down the corridor as if nothing was wrong and went to Kyla and Joniel's room. Kyla was sitting by her dressing table with her back to the door when he barged into the room. She turned and faced him, standing up as she turned and backed away from him. He pulled out the dagger. "No pretty speeches, no kind words about how I feel." He lunged forwards and grabbed her by her hair and drove the knife deep into her stomach. "Joniel can kiss his long awaited love goodbye. He has destroyed our life and our love. He is deluded but I can't let you be a part of that delusion. I must save you. I must purify your soul so that you may live at peace in the spirit world. I must break that bond between you and that evil creature." He pulled the knife out and let the blood flow onto the floor. He pushed her down onto all fours. "Look at your life blood draining away. These are the last minutes you will spend and your poor love is broken and screaming in a prison cell. You could have had me, we would have been happy. Look on the bright side. At least he will be released in the morning as he is at least innocent of one murder, yours." He pulled her head back and slit her throat.

The door burst open and a security detail grabbed Ker, stopping him from turning the knife on himself. Anathorn stepped in behind them and took the knife off of him. "Take him away and release Joniel from the cells. Take Joniel to the Infirmary. He is bound to need his leg redressed by now and I'm sure he will want to see his wife. Yes Ker, that is one of King Osiris' body doubles that he had made for us. Very handy that he had it on board his ship and was able to send it over when I realised something was wrong.

Take him away and get him ready for psyche evaluation."

The Prince's communicator was flashing. He opened up his messages. They were coming in thick and fast from all over. He opened one, then the next. Immediately he sent a message to the Guard. "Code 546R". He shut the device and ran to his office. Instantly he paged Rennon and the others. They arrived shortly afterwards. Joniel was in a remote control wheelchair, his ankle strapped and bandaged.

The Prince indicated seats for them and poured them each a cup of hot coffee. "We have had a disastrous night tonight. All around the fleet sleepers have been awakened. They have been sparked off by the slightest upset and the seriousness of their actions depends on what set them off. Many key operatives have been murdered. I am sorry to tell you that Ker was one of those sleepers, either voluntarily or involuntarily. It is more than likely that Kel would have been one too."

Rennon was paying attention, his computer was shut down. "I thought we got him out of that secure facility a bit easily. It has always been on my mind. What about Kyla here, she was there too."

Anathorn looked down. "I have executed Code 546R and anyone who has ever been in Follower hands who is not of the blood and immune has been taken to the cells. Kyla we have already deduced that you are immune. I would suspect that your training would have protected you, although I cannot be totally certain of that one. I don't want to take any chances." The laptop made the noise that heralded messages arriving over and over again. "If you would excuse me I need to keep up with these messages. I wanted us all together for this, we are all prime targets."

There was a knocking sound from the Prince's tall cupboard. He opened it and found Intendi's arm knocking. There was a single running from it to the mess that had once been the Prince's android. He got the pieces out and gave them to Rennon who laid them out on the meeting table and began reassembling them. Rennon managed to activate the computer unit. Intendi screamed. "Get out of the room."

They dived out of the room just as there was a loud explosion. Joniel was blown out of his chair on the way out. Kyla shielded him from the worst of it and was blown over the top of the chair and flew across the hallway and hit the wall opposite and slid down it. Anathorn had dived to the right with Aliniel. Rennon, laptop and Intendi under his arm was picking himself up off the floor. Kyla got up and leapt to the door and shut it as gouts of flame burst out into the corridor. They heard the swish of the sprinkler system, set off by the flames.

Kyla slid down to the floor head in hands. "How much more of this can we take?"

Anathon walked over to her and offered her his hand. "As much as we have to and I know you will." He took a quick look over at Joniel who was climbing back into his chair and put his arms around her. He stroked her hair as she started to shake uncontrollably. "We'll survive or we won't. It is that we try. It isn't as if we have any choice either. I am under no delusion that any of us are heroes. We just know what will happen if we don't succeed. We dealt them a blow, we didn't expect to get away with it without any retribution. I had suspected something like this but hopefully it has revealed the sleepers."

Kyla took a deep breath as she stood up. "What are you going to do with Ker?"

Anathon went silent for a while and put his arms around Kyla. Joniel raised an eyebrow.

Aliniel was looking at him strangely. She stepped over and put a hand on her mother's shoulder. "What is the matter? Is she hurt?"

Anathon kissed Kyla on the forehead. "Probably more than any of us will ever understand. She is not just a member she is one of the High Priestesses of the Order of the White Lady. Have you any idea what all this feels like to her? I made a point of studying them and she feels something of every death. She is being brave but inside I would imagine she is being ripped apart. We are all too quick to think that it is Kyla, she'll be ok but look at her, she is tired."

Aliniel pouted. "Don't treat me like a child! Go on then hug my mother. I suppose now I and my sister have even more in common. Or would have had if she had lived." Kyla pushed away from Anathorn. He could see the pain on her face. Joniel looked up at her from his chair as she walked past him to her daughter. Her daughter looked at her and scowled. "What, fed up of grabbing every man on this base?"

Joniel saw the torn dress and the purple welts that were blossoming on her back as she walked past him and tried to get up from his chair, forgot his injured leg and fell back down again in agony. She caught her daughter's wrist and held it tight. "You are young. You have a lot of life ahead of you if you are lucky. Some of us have seen more pain than I hope you will ever have to endure. You will learn that when you go through some of the most unpleasant times in your life you can have men around you who are friends. You are lucky to have Anathorn's love. If your love is true then don't throw it away as jealousy will do that. It will eat into you. I love your father and only your father. But I have friends that I love as deeply as any person can love another. You will understand one day but as you don't understand yet it is best to watch, learn and ask questions if you don't understand before jumping to misinformed conclusions." She turned away and walked a few steps before her legs gave out under her.

Aliniel looked on in horror as her mother nearly collapsed. Her voice was weak, like a frightened animal. "Mother, I didn't realise that you were injured."

Anathorn caught her and steadied her. Her voice was weak and she managed a smile. "I'm alright but I'm getting really tired of people trying to shoot me, stab me and blown me up."

Anathorn laughed. "May I suggest I issue you with a flack vest or even better full protective body armour?"

Joniel managed a smile. "It might help. Will everyone please stop damaging my wife, it seriously hampers my love life."

Aliniel giggled and blushed. The others turned to her and simultaneously stated. "Grow up!"

Joniel held his wrist out.

Kyla picked it up, looked up at the others and kissed it. "Blunt trauma, no use at all but I appreciate the thought." She bent down and kissed him passionately. "But that definitely helps." She managed a smile.

Anathorn glared at Aliniel and she looked away. "That is better. Have some respect." Anathorn ran his fingers through his hair. "What the hell do I do now? I don't know who to trust."

Rennon coughed. "Well I'd better get to work fixing Intendi then hadn't I? May I suggest that when fixed you keep him with you and keep him on active evaluation mode at all times."

Anathorn looked puzzled. "I did just that. Then he disappeared. I sent a detail to look for him but then more messages came in and I got distracted."

A siren went off and Anathorn turned to his communicator. "Damn it, hull breach in Sector 9. We're venting atmosphere. I had better not lose this sparkly new battle cruiser." He hit the live link. "Get that breach blocked up immediately. Security I want a full search and scan of the ship. If anyone in your group acts suspiciously, arrest them." He shut his eyes. "Probably not the best thing to say as I'll have half the security squad in the cells by morning, if we get to morning." He checked the communiqués. "Same on every other ship. Infiltrators, bombs and total distrust and chaos. How can I tell these infiltrators without Intendi?"

Kyla looked up. "You can't. The drug makes them susceptible to suggestion but after that it's their own mind and their own beliefs. You can't detect that. Not without Intendi." She was looking at the twisted remains of what had been Intendi.

Anatorn looked down. "So, what do I do."

Kyla smiled kindly. "Exactly what you are doing, the best you can."

Anathorn glared at Aliniel who looked away. He held his hand out to Kyla who walked carefully over to him. "It's me who needs this hug. Thank you for being my strength and for the record I am in love with your daughter. Is that alright with you?"

Kyla smiled. "As long as you look after her and make an honest woman out of her."

Anathon spluttered. "That would make you the mother in law."

Kyla grinned. "Skip the jokes, I'll break the mould."

Joniel coughed. "Hands off my woman if you don't mind."

Anathorn smiled as he saw that Joniel was smiling. "So what do I do?"

Joniel thought and Rennon clicked on his keyboard. "You order sweeps and searches. This ship is vast but they aren't going to go for something irrelevant. I'm guessing they haven't got an infinite supply of people."

Kyla smiled gently. "I will call the White Lady."

Anathorn glared at her and Joniel tried to get out of the chair. Anathorn spoke quietly. "You are not strong enough."

Kyla smiled. "We know that, this is a flawed system."

Anathorn frowned. "What do you mean?"

Kyla laughed. "Most of the time I end up on the floor. Please hold me up this time. I really can't handle any more bruises."

She took a deep breath and concentrated. White light began to coalesce around her. She held her hands out, palm facing palm. Energy shot off up and through the ceiling and Anathorn caught her as she fell. She looked up at Anathorn who was trying to get her back onto her feet. "Well, let us hope."

A message came up on Anathorn's communicator. "Tied up with insurgents on ship, will contact you soonest. Isis."

Anathorn raised an eyebrow. "Why couldn't you just use a communicator like she did? It looks like infiltrators have got everywhere but how? Isis' ship has been out of our dimension for millennia. That is a frightening thought. That means they may also have infiltrated Nai's realm. I thought I hadn't heard from him for a while."

Anathorn put his arm around Kyla and she relaxed onto his chest. She spoke quietly. "I didn't think, she's in our realm now so I suppose I could have just called. How can they have corrupted Nai's people, they are immune?"

Anathorn laughed. "Among Nai's people there are some of the most evil creatures ever created. They wouldn't have been controlled. They would have dealt with the Followers for personal gain and probably quite willingly. This could be worse than we thought."

Joniel looked up at Anathorn, he couldn't help casting a glance at Kyla who looked so comfortable in the Prince's arms. "That means that anyone at any point in our past could have come across a Follower, not known who they were and been indoctrinated."

Anathorn kissed Kyla's head without thinking then looked nervously at Joniel. "That is quite a worry."

Aliniel coughed. "Shouldn't I be the one who is giving you support?"

Anathorn smiled at her. "I love you and you do support me but the healing that she is giving me is really helping the shrapnel from that blast that is stuck in my back. But if she doesn't stop soon." He emphasised the "soon". "Then she is going to pass out, isn't she?"

Kyla looked up. "I don't know but I hope someone will catch me."

Anathorn looked over at Joniel. "Well if your husband is agreeable it is always a pleasure. But please excuse me. I really have to deal with these communiqués. So Aliniel if you would like to come and support me we will go to my office which I hope is still in one piece and not liable to explode imminently. I think a detour via the Infirmary might be a good idea. If you would be so kind as to make sure that the doctor doesn't try to murder me while he is removing this shrapnel from my back."

Anathorn helped Kyla across to Joniel. Joniel glared at her moodily. "Don't ever forget that you are mine."

Kyla smiled. "Eternally." She leaned heavily on his chair. "Rennon, I think we had better go to our chambers. Hopefully you can repair Intendi."

Joniel took her arm. "I think we should move that arrangement to the Prince's rooms. Let's go and make sure he gets through the night. Rennon can you gather the equipment you need to fix Intendi?"

Rennon nodded.

Kyla smiled. "I wouldn't have suggested it but I agree."

Anathorn was working his way through the communiqués as they arrived. He looked up and smiled as the others came in. "Is everything alright?"

Kyla smiled and winced slightly. "No, but we'll make the best of it and if you think you are going to go undefended tonight you have another thing coming."

Aliniel smiled. "He isn't undefended. She put a hand on his shoulder and he looked up at her."

Joniel took a look around. "So, is it uneasy the head that bears the crown or is it alright if we all pitch in?"

Anathorn looked around them. "We've got problems springing up all over. The initial assassinations seem to have abated. Now we have explosions going off all over the fleet. We can't have eyes everywhere. Nothing has crashed yet but I have some serious venting going on in ships 17 and 19."

Kyla looked at the paperwork. "Didn't Intendi find anyone?"

Anathorn looked thoughtful. "We caught quite a few but for some reason he kept going missing. He kept misunderstanding my orders and ending up in some really strange places. I began to feel he was malfunctioning."

Rennon looked up. "I doubt that. They were probably jamming him when they found out what he was. That would have confused his systems. Why didn't you mention it?"

Anathorn was reading a communiqué. "I didn't have a chance to think. The fuel tanks have gone up on 15. If this goes on I could lose the fleet. I've got security patrols out but they aren't finding anything."

Joniel looked up. "Are they loyal?"

Anathorn frowned. "I don't know. They should be."

Joniel put a hand on Kyla's arm. "Is there anything you can do?"

Kyla smiled. "I have been thinking there is one thing I can try." She sat on the floor and shut her eyes. All pain and anger went from her face and they felt a gentle peace come over them. It was like a touch of a feather to start with and then a slight feeling of euphoria.

Anathorn was looking intently at the screen, his brow furrowed. "It seems to have gone quiet. What did you do?"

Kyla opened her eyes and looked very serene. The worry had gone from her face and she smiled at Anathorn. "I put your fleet in a state of peace. The actions are triggered by anger and fear, so I took the anger and fear away by surrounding them in peaceful white light."

Rennon had been tapping away on his laptop and he looked up. He had been putting Intendi back together but had put him down for a short while and picked up his laptop. "I think I've managed to prove what the Followers have been doing. The ship has a log of who is on board at any time. It can't log who they are but the system knows how many people are there. I have run a sub routine for each ship both in real space and in the corridors. We can rule out real space. If the Followers interfered with time there then there would have been intervention by the Talisinians who step in to stop any time related anomaly. I was proven right. The figures show that there have been hiccups in crew manifests all over the fleet. This ship didn't have any but as most of the hiccups were over the past fifty years this ship is too new. The crew on this ship however have been posted all over the fleet and by cross referencing I have managed to pull together a list of where and when these visitations occurred. This may be something that would interest Nailindris. If it is his people who have been working with the Followers then he will also have the technology to take us back. Then we can take out these visitors before they can influence our people."

Anathorn was already typing and he hit send. They waited for a response.

There was a flash of blue light and Nailindris appeared in the room. His face was blackened with soot and there was fresh blood on his ornate armour. He removed his helmet as soon as he arrived. He staggered slightly. He turned and bowed politely to them. "I received your communiqué and I have put my people onto it. The traitors who dealt with the Followers will be found. That is an aside to having a huge problem to solve ourselves of course.

My caverns have suffered the same attacks as your ships. I have lost countless of my people and equipment that is irreplaceable has been damaged beyond repair. This has left us without the ability to keep the gates shut and our world is being overrun. So I must be brief. If we can go back in time and stop these Followers on a ship by ship basis then we can stop all this. Well make it not have happened which is even better. I have contacted the Talisinians and explained the situation and what we intend to do. They have issued me with guidelines that we must follow to the letter. They cannot intervene here as it is outside their jurisdiction." He looked down at Joniel and his eyes were drawn to his leg. "That is not a good state of affairs. We need you Joniel, and your daughter, your particular skills will be very useful tonight. Looking at the figures, once they have visited a ship they never return. So in all we have 56 incursions."

Rennon looked up. "I have surveillance material which can pinpoint each of these people just after they arrived on ship and before they had contact with any crew member."

Nai nodded. "Then all we need to do is to take you back to that point and you then eliminate the Follower."

Kyla looked up. "That wouldn't work."

Nai frowned. "Why not?"

Kyla smiled. "Because the Followers would then know and try something else. Do we know who they influenced?"

Rennon called up more figures. "We know who acted against us. I can cross reference this with the crew manifests on the ships that the Followers visited. Where are we going with this?"

Kyla smiled. "If we can make the Followers believe that they succeeded then they wouldn't know until now that they hadn't. Killing isn't always the answer. Joniel we need to get you back on your feet."

Joniel glared at her, his demeanour dark. "I can't take any more of your blood."

Anathorn smiled and walked over to Joniel and offered his wrist.

Joniel pushed it away. "You need to concentrate, the last thing you need when tired is to have to make up the blood as well."

Aliniel walked over to her father. He shook his head and she looked disappointed.

Rennon looked up. "If I offered you'd have human blood in your veins and that can get infected." He went back to typing. "Not that I wouldn't offer of course so you can take this as my offer."

Kyla turned to face him. "You wouldn't take me if I was in the same state. This isn't an assassination mission, it's a persuasive one. You'll have to sit this one out my love, literally."

Anathorn frowned. "What do you mean?"

Kyla smiled. "I'm going to follow the Followers, find out who they indoctrinated and when they leave, turn that indoctrination against them. I am guessing that they are going to administer the fluid in its weakened form. How much time do I have before the suggestion phase is over?"

Rennon checked his notes. "Experiments have proven that you would have up to two hours."

Kyla looked at Arla. "That should be more than enough time. If I step in when they have left I can countermand what they were told. Nai, can you make this happen?"

Nai looked tired but he smiled. "I think I just about can. I won't go through the risks and the stress it will put on your body though, I know you are going anyway." He thought for a moment and took his scanner out and typed into it. He then waited and there was a tiny bell as a message came back. "Good, the Talisinians have agreed that I may cause a time flux. They have granted me permission to alter time slightly, but only tonight, and only in the way that I have agreed. This is very specific and I must not put a foot wrong here.

Yes you can go back and countermand their indoctrination and you will be in your own real time on these missions but it will happen in just a fraction of a second here. That is the only way I can think of saving you from your body shutting down Kyla. I'll add my voice to all the others who will doubt be telling you, your body can't take much more. Queen Isis has intervened as well on this. You copied the original communiqué to her and her husband and she has assured the Talisinians that you will be good to your word. You can only go there, speak with those who have been interfered with and come back. I will give you this device." He held out a silver ball that seemed to have just appeared in his hand. "It will make them forget that you were there. No doubt the Follower is using a similar device."

Joniel looked up. "Can you take us back to the planet afterwards? She needs to heal."

Nai looked at him sympathetically. "I wish I could but that is no longer possible, you knew that when you left. The planet came back into phase as soon as the last person left. If you want to help her, give her blood."

Kyla stood beside Nai who was just finishing reading another communiqué. "The Talisinians have agreed that what the Followers have done is a violation of the time agreement. They have therefore suspended time throughout the galaxies. If you would give each of those you speak to the command word they will then utter that when they are activated. That in turn will allow time to continue. If we get this right the only thing that will happen is the various people will say a word at the same time. This room has been held out of time so we are now acting independently. So no more communiqués until we sort this one out." Anathorn put his communicator down. "All you will see here is a flash but in that time Kyla will hopefully have visited all of the locations we have worked out. Then we will wait and see which of the assassinations and explosions didn't happen. Are you ready?"

Kyla nodded. There was a bright blue flash. Kyla staggered slightly and Aliniel supported her.

Rennon ran a system scan. "It looks like it worked. As far as I can see all ships and personnel are back where they were just before they were activated."

Aliniel was supporting her mother who was swaying and had begun to shake. Anathorn took his jacket off and put it around Kyla's shoulders and led her to a chair which Aliniel moved next to Joniel. They sat her down and Joniel put his arm around her.

Anathorn smiled. "So now we are looking at a resounding success and having kicked those Followers' sorry butts. Shall we at least try and feel some sort of pride and happiness? Then thinking about it, it didn't happen so there is nothing to celebrate." He looked around the others. They were tired, some were injured and everyone looked like they needed a good night's sleep.

Nai looked around too then looked at Anathorn. "I don't think that partying is what these people need anyway. I must go now and see how the situation panned out for my people. I also have some creatures to punish for their treason or whatever other title I can come up with for their betrayal. Not that they will have done anything so there will probably be nothing to punish." There was a flash of blue light and he disappeared.

Anathorn stood up. "I won't be long, Rennon, would you like to come with me. I think we ought to go and find Intendi." The others then realised that Intendi had disappeared off of the table. "As all the damage didn't happen what happened to him didn't happen either. Kyla, I won't suggest that you go back to the Infirmary, I would imagine you don't feel altogether comfortable in there now. Aliniel, could you monitor my communiqués for me until I get back. If there is something that requires immediate attention, page me. Rennon, you did a great job working that one out. All of you, you have really helped to turn this around. I'm truly glad that Kyla didn't go back and alter time. For all the bad, I am grateful that it has brought me good friends like you."

Joniel laughed. "That will do nothing for your image Thorn."

Anathorn smiled. "I haven't gone by that name in a long time."

Joniel smiled wickedly. "Good job, no doubt the missus would not be too pleased if you did."

Aliniel stepped over to her father. "Oh, what was this?"

Anathorn glared at Joniel. Joniel winked at him. "I'm only winding him up. I could tell you all manner of sorry tales about this old pirate but then I could be making them up just to cause trouble. Love him for who he is now."

Rennon was tapping on the keyboard and messages were coming back. "If you would excuse me, I am needed in my laboratory."

Anathorn looked up. "Is there a problem?"

Rennon looked up and smiled. "You mean was my assistant taken over by the indoctrination and hatched some devious plan to blow my lab up? Actually no, she has done a fantastic job of helping me to collate the figures and even came up with a few hints along the way. I'm just going to go and congratulate her on a job well done. If you need me, knock first." He smiled wickedly and left the room.

8

Kyla sat bolt upright and turned on the light. It was barely six o'clock and Joniel was fast asleep beside her. He woke him and he too sat up. She still looked tired. "I've got it."

Joniel sighed. "Why do you keep doing that? You are here to sleep, not think. You need a rest. Although I totally respect your great ideas and I appreciate you need to find answers, we both do, but I worry about your health. You must rest. Was it another attack? Is there something in the room?"

Kyla smiled. "No, not this time. Whatever I say now is going to sound patronising. The truth is that I've been thinking about Anathorn and you aren't going to be best pleased that I'm thinking about him while we are together in our bed."

Joniel glared at her. There was real venom in his eyes.

Kyla jumped slightly. "Right, you are going to tell me about the Prince and him being Thorn, right now!"

Joniel kissed her. "No I'm not. Some things are better not told and I think you can guess anyway."

Kyla glared at him. "You are going to tell me."

Joniel laughed. "I don't think much of your interrogation techniques." She glared. "Alright, I'll tell. Thorn was a gutter pirate. He spent his life in every low life place in the galaxies picking up freight, smuggling, anything really and most of his money went in the whore houses by the waterfront. He liked waterfronts for some reason. I met him when he was thrown out of a bar drunk one night. I was on my way back from a job and he knocked me over. He was out of it and I looked after him. We became friends and have been ever since."

Kyla looked horrified. "And you think that will be an appropriate partner for our daughter?"

Joniel smiled. "Well at least she'll be satisfied and he is a Prince now, always seemed to be actually. He had a commanding way about him even then, but as he was drunk most of the time nobody noticed. Go to sleep woman, you need to rest."

Kyla smiled. "I'm not tired."

Joniel kissed her. "You soon will be." He reached over and turned out the light.

Later that day they stood in Anathorn's office.

Anathorn looked at Kyla kindly. She stood in front of his desk, one hand on the edge of it. Her eyes were dark, there were bags under them. Her whole demeanour was that of someone totally and completely exhausted. "You need to rest."

Kyla smiled back. "You don't understand, I need to keep the white light shielding around the fleet. Someone is trying to interfere with it so I have to keep putting it back. I can feel the energy and it is being directed at me. You didn't think I was the only one in the galaxies who has trained in this way did you?"

Anathorn looked worried. "I hadn't thought of it that way. We've removed the threat now though haven't we by stopping the original indoctrination?"

Kyla shook her head. "I don't know, I can't think straight but what I can do is maintain the shielding and make sure that nobody else gets set off. And what of all those other innocents who would die if just one person gets activated?"

Joniel stepped to put a hand on Kyla's shoulder.

Anathorn looked concerned. "I didn't know, why didn't you tell me?"

Kyla smiled and put her forehead against his chest. "I lived in my own little world where Maran and similar people to her accepted that sort of thing as everyday. I forget that you and the others here don't know about such things. It didn't seem important to tell you as I assumed you already knew. I don't know if I need to do it or if I don't but I don't want to take the risk. It is one thing I can do so I'm doing it."

Anathorn looked up from his laptop. "I informed Osiris about our success. It seems that looking at the results it has been pretty successful across the board. There have been one or two people who have managed to do things but we have no idea if they were indoctrinated or truly believe." The Prince sat up and stared at Kyla, his face changed, he looked serious, commanding. "No amount of shielding is going to stop that. Kyla, stand down, that is an order."

Kyla opened her mouth as if to speak but Joniel gave her a warning glance. "You can't go on much longer."

Kyla smiled. "Joniel, these attacks are on me as well. I'm using every defensive tactic I have but I'm getting worn down. It's getting so that I can't sleep or they will get through. Not just night horrors, real thought forms that can do real damage to me."

Joniel looked up at Anathorn. "She has been waking screaming when she does sleep and I was sure on one occasion there was someone in the room. There was nobody there when I turned the light on."

Anathorn looked worried. "I'll contact Maran." He started typing. Moments later a message arrived and he turned the screen on and rotated it so that everyone could see her.

Maran looked exhausted. Her face was covered in scratches. "My Prince, your communiqué is most welcome. How may I be of assistance?"

Anathorn looked worried. "Are you experiencing psychic attacks?"

Maran gave him a reluctant smile. "I can assume that by your contact and your question that Kyla is experiencing a similar offensive."

Kyla smiled. "Greetings to you Maran, seeing you again is most welcome. I am indeed. It started with a feeling of contact and night horrors, waking in a hot flush and feeling something was there and now it is a full on offensive. My shields are being broken through as I get more tired and reflecting the attacks back isn't working. I've dealt with most of the basic forms of attack but they are getting much stronger."

Maran smiled reassuringly. "My little one, I am as well. Even with my mastery I can't hope to keep them off for much longer. I fear what will happen when they do break through. Those who are less well trained have already either fallen into a coma or they have been taken over.

It is coming in the form of tendrils that get through your shielding. Reach inside, take a look and pull them off for as long as you can. The healing that Isis gave you to give has worked wonders around the galaxies. The offensive would not have been so successful if we hadn't had the hope of those infected being turned back. Hold on for as long as you can my child." She shuddered slightly and a shadow seemed to come over her face, she grimaced and it was gone. "Anathorn, if she falls then hope is lost. Do not let her sleep. She will get taken over eventually but they cannot ever take over one of the white light permanently. Keep the body inviolate. Don't allow it to be damaged, whatever she does. She has one of the strongest minds that I have ever trained and a willpower that I know will survive whatever they do to her. If anyone is going to fight this she will. I just hope that you haven't exhausted her in other ways so that she hasn't got the energy to fight back."

Kyla looked thoughtful. "We need to track this back."

Maran looked confused. "What do you mean my child?" The dark shadow seemed to flow across Maran's face.

Kyla smiled and her eyes were bright if only for a moment. "We need to stop being victims and being forced to keep to defensive disciplines. I just sent energy back the other way and it hit home. We have a warrior nature as well as a healing one."

Maran looked horrified. "No, what was the first lesson I taught you? If you are taking a step down that road it is a dangerous one. Healing must never be used to harm."

Kyla swayed slightly and Joniel stepped closer so she could lean back against him. "I have not forgotten my training and healing should never be used to harm, even if it could be. I trained with Marisinkata, on Mount Eramon on Sanik. I have training in both healing and the mystic arts."

Maran's look of horror intensified. "That teaching is forbidden to a healer. You must be a healer pure and unsullied by the psychic arts. You were touched with darkness when you healed Joniel, wasn't that enough of a tarnish on your soul?"

Kyla raised an eyebrow. "Apparently a necessary one as I need those arts now."

Tears ran down Maran's face. "My sweet child, you mustn't walk down that road. Abandon it now, cast out those powers and put them out of your mind."

Kyla looked confused. "Why not? I have attained mastery with no failing in my healing ability or any objection from the White Lady."

Maran glared at her. "That magic will taint you forever. Wasn't it bad enough that you kept that evil creature alive? I have heard that you have taken him as your lover. Has he tainted you that badly that you have not only blemished your soul but you let him violate your body too? Joniel I cannot tolerate seeing you with your evil hands on a creature of light. To this day I do not know why you were not damned forever by the White Lady for your actions. To have trained with Marisinkata, the despised and cursed one who was cast from our Order millennia ago, it is beyond me. How can you stand there and profess to be a healer when you have done that? I do not know you." Maran cut off the communiqué.

Kyla collapsed. Joniel held her up as she became like a rag doll in his arms.

Joniel turned to Anathorn. "That is not like Maran. Whoever is controlling her doesn't know that we spent nearly a thousand years as friends and she knew who and what I was. Kyla, come round. Whatever you can do, do it now, you have just told your enemies what you plan to do." He shook Kyla, she gradually came around. He screamed at her. "Kyla, strike back at them with whatever you have."

Kyla looked up at him. Her hazel eyes turned to burnished gold and her pupils transformed to slits. "I call upon the ancient energy of the earth and the planets. Joniel, I'm going to walk the veils, I'm going to try and do something to fight back." Aliniel sat down on the floor beside her mother as her mother's expression went blank.

The spirit of Kyla was standing on a barren planet. All around her was black and amber. Smoke arose from holes in the crust. The air was hot and sparkled with a myriad of dust particles which reflected the golden light of the sun which scorched the land. The earth was cracked and through the cracks seeped molten magma. It burnt her feet and her body. Searing heat forced her back but she pushed forwards, step by step. Skeletons and burnt corpses lay around her, all facing in the direction she was going. She concentrated and put up a shield. A barrier of water blossomed around her and the heat abated. She called up energy and held it as a ball of light in her hand. She carried on walking but each step brought intense pain.

She concentrated and called up an image in her mind. A beautiful black horse appeared beside her, his head noble, his feathered legs strong. She shielded him with water and leapt onto his back. "Take me to where I need to go, make haste."

He reared up and lunged forwards. She had trouble staying on his back but soon she felt like she was flying as he covered the miles as if they were nothing. The terrain was the same wherever she looked so she followed the bodies and her instinct. She could feel where to go. The steady rhythm of the hooves steadied her thoughts and helped her to concentrate.

As they rode, volleys of burning arrows started raining down on them. She smiled and called on a physical shield above the pair of them. Then she concentrated and the arrows turned and flew back. The scream of pain as they hit home echoed across the landscape.

In the distance she saw a black pyramid. Flame erupted from the ground around it and beams of light shot out and blasted the ground at intervals. Terror grabbed her and her shield began to falter and the horse stumbled. Then she thought of Joniel and the euphoria that ran through her steadied her and banished her fear. Her shield re-established itself and the horse galloped ever faster.

Kyla reached deep into her soul and called up every bit of pain she had ever felt, every upset, every hurt both physical and mental and for every one she had survived her strength grew. She pulled the energy together and the ball of light in her hand grew. She smiled as she saw a pair of eyes forming over the pyramid. She laughed. "You have thrown all this at me all my life to break me, now it is my strength, I do not need it anymore. I transmute this pain to a weapon to use in truth and light against you." The light flew from her hand and burst over the pyramid. The pyramid and the planet she was standing on exploded in a ball of white light and Kyla was back in her body in the room with her friends and lover.

Joniel felt the energy, it was like a force coming out of her. He struggled to keep a hold of her as he felt himself pushed away. Then she relaxed. He lifted her and carried her to a chair and set her down. "Well we can hope that worked. I certainly felt something and I don't think I'd want to be on the receiving end of whatever she just sent."

A communiqué arrived and Anathorn opened it. "It is from Maran's helper. Maran has apparently collapsed but she is still alive. I'm getting communiqués from all over. What happened there? Please explain to my simple mundane mind."

Joniel smiled as he reached down to Kyla and stroked her face. "I'm not totally sure but I think she went into the spirit realm and has just hopefully won a psychic battle with whoever was doing this. She's explained it to me a few times. Energy is seen as things she can understand, she visualises it that way and then uses the images she has created. So it could be that she's met whoever it is there in a sword fight or some other fashion. The energy would be the same whatever she saw it as. It is just manipulated in a way that she can understand. It arrives in the same way, hence the night terrors. She is seeing those creatures arriving and having to deal with them as if they are physical. They are how her attacker has visualised the energy attacking her. If the will is strong enough the energy actually appears as those creatures."

Kyla came around. She put her arms around him. "I'm alright my love, I think I just gave whoever was at the other end of that attack something to think about."

Anathorn smiled. "Too right you did. I've got more messages on here than I've had through the battle. It seems that there are people collapsing all over the place who have been under some sort of control. I'm now wondering if the fluid makes the mind easier to control by this Psychic."

***Kyla smiled. "That would be one answer. It is probably why those doing the analysing are having a problem isolating the fluid in the system. Once the attack has got through it sort of latches on and the person can become a puppet if the control is strong enough. It is manipulation of energy. We are electrical creatures after all and our brain sends out electrical impulses. What they are doing is a bit like putting someone on a leash and making them do what they want. Most of the time the victim is just normal but when they pull the leash then the control is back again."

Anathorn sighed deeply. "So it isn't devices?"

Kyla thought for a moment. "They are researching so it is unlikely that they are going to stick with one thing and not develop others."

Joniel frowned. "What we really need to be doing is trying to find the head of all this. What about that assistant back in the cavern. If he was the origin then surely if we track him down and get rid of him it will give us a chance. I'm also wondering what those grubs grow into."

Anathorn smiled. "We hatched one, it didn't grow into anything much, just a tiny moth like creature. We ran some tests and analysed it but it didn't live more than a couple of days."

Kyla raised an eyebrow. "The pod and the fluid are probably a bi-product and a defence mechanism. The moth is probably an innocent in all this. It was just likely pure chance that the assistant got infected and it was his own natural paranoia and wish for advancement that the pod enhanced. He is now projecting that onto what he is doing. If he is insecure, which I would estimate is likely it's obvious that he's going to want power and to feel in control. Do we have any information on this assistant?"

Rennon was tapping away. "We do. He was a research student from the Kerinnial College of Future Technology. He was quite an outstanding student until he got into a disastrous relationship with another student who was selfish and destroyed his career through wanting all his time, manipulative. His grades plummeted and he missed his finals that year and had to retake. Your father took him on mostly out of respect for his father who was an old family friend. The boy then disappeared off of all record. I'm assuming that was because he was travelling and working with your father on the project. The rest we know."

Kyla thought about it. "So there were definite emotional problems there. It had to start with a disastrous relationship didn't it?" She shook her head. "Even the most brilliant of minds are not immune to that crazy drug. So there you may well have our answer. He's lost what he thinks is the greatest love of his life. He is not emotionally mature enough to handle the situation so he's also lost his career and hope in life, as he sees it. So we have a lovelorn student who has experienced being manipulated, so what does he do when given the chance? He goes out and manipulates others fuelled by anger and frustration."

Joniel looked down at her. "So do we pity him or shoot him?"

Kyla smiled. "He was patient zero, that carapace will never dissolve and we'd have to keep him incarcerated. Sadly I'd have to say have pity enough to shoot him. If we could turn him back he has all those deaths on his conscience. Add guilt to his already immense pile of reasons to commit genocide and he'd be a bomb waiting to go off. We can certainly try but at the moment just removing him in any way possible would be an answer. Wherever he is, if that was him sending the psychic attack, he's going to have a headache and probably be feeling intensely insecure so we can expect some sort of reaction soon. He's insecure so I wouldn't expect him to stop and think about a plan." Kyla fell to the floor and began screaming.

Joniel grabbed her and restrained her, grabbing her flailing limbs.

The Prince received a communiqué from Maran. He opened up the channel. Maran looked panic stricken. "Prince Anathorn, I didn't know what I'd done. It happened while I was under their control. I am so, so sorry. Is she still alive?"

Anathorn glared at Maran. "What have you done?"

Maran stared wide eyed at the screen. "They had me under their control and I was convinced that she had become evil and that Joniel had darkened her soul. I wasn't thinking rationally. There is a link between a

Master and Apprentice, however high they raise in the ranks after that. I was convinced she was evil so I evoked the Ancient Rite of Damnation. It is irrevocable. I have taken her gifts from her but as she has already lived beyond natural years that will also kill her."

Joniel looked up. "No it won't she's had the blood as well."

Maran shook her head. "That will save her from physically ageing before she dies but the Rite is strong. Healers have to stay inviolate, that is how they heal, through their purity. A defiled healer is tantamount to an evil creature in the eyes of our Mistress. I am so sorry Joniel, believe me I love you like a son and I'd never think of you as an evil creature."

Joniel screamed. "Call Isis, she is the Mistress. Maran for the record, if you define an evil creature I probably pretty much fit the technical description. I've brought this down on her haven't I?"

Anathorn's fingers flashed over the keys. "No time for that Joniel, you were what you were but who was the one who sat up with you past dawn when we drank our way through your guilt complexes."

Moments later there was a flash of white light and Isis stood in the room. She ignored the rest of them and went directly to Kyla. She stood over her and put her hands on her head. "I can't believe how my words are misinterpreted by those who follow me sometimes. I sent them a directive that was supposed to give them a firm path to follow not so that it could be corrupted to use as a weapon."

Joniel looked up at her. "Can you save her?"

Isis looked down at him. Tears were running down her face. "I can save her life. The Rites that were so worthily earned are gone. Maran has every right to take them by the laws as she took them in good faith and honestly believing in what she was doing. That Maran was controlled wasn't something I thought about when I created that Rite." She took her hands away. "She will sleep now. It is the best gift I can give her. Make her comfortable."

Anathorn had had an anteroom set up with a bed so that he could catch some sleep while waiting for messages. Joniel lifted Kyla gently and limped in there and laid her on the bed. He left her and shut the door.

Isis was dressed in muddy and blood splattered armour. Her long black hair was matted with blood and there was soot and blood on her face. "We can only face what Set and his cohort throws at us as it happens." She walked over to Joniel and laid her hands on his ankle. "I think we had better get you back on your feet young man."

Anathorn bowed to her. "We have been discussing that it might be worth targeting the assistant who was first infected."

Isis thought a while. "I would suggest that would be a high priority. I must go now. I have done what I can. I will give some thought as to how Kyla can perform the Rite of Atonement which is the only way to take back what was taken from her. The trouble is that according to the conditions of the Rite which relates to why she was damned she has no crimes to atone for. Her love for you is pure."

Joniel looked down. "But I'm not. Can she atone for keeping me alive?"

Isis smiled at him kindly. "Sadly she cannot. How can she atone for keeping you alive when you are not evil? You are not to blame for being born with a cold heart and learning regret which is unknown to your people then developing it into a way you can fight for the greater good. I'm sorry Joniel, you can't help her either. Perhaps we don't have to though. She will wake up and she will be strong again. She has the Rite I gave her, Maran had no right to take that. She will learn to live without her healing and the self sacrifice that it brings with it. She will still be able to manipulate white light and she has the other disciplines. She can heal you Joniel with her blood. In time it may be a blessing, especially coming into the final days of this war. The gentle act of healing and the benefit it gives to long term recovery isn't going to help us in these days. She is still a trained medic. Perhaps it is time for her to let that gift go as it was destroying her. Look at her, she was exhausted. Even a great act of evil can sometimes have beneficial outcomes if you look for them. I must now bid you farewell and wish you luck." With a flash of white light she disappeared.

Rennon looked up from his screen. "I've run projections and I've put the figures through again and again but I can't come up with any clear idea of where the assistant may be."

Joniel lifted an eyebrow. "But we know where he was. Can we go back to there and then and deal with him?"

Anathorn looked up from his laptop. "No, we wouldn't be able to as it would alter time. He has done too much since then that has had other repercussions."

Joniel smiled. "Actually I wasn't suggesting that we killed him. I was thinking that we put a marker on him that would mean we could find him now."

Anathorn thought for a moment. "So how do we do that?"

Joniel shook his head. "What I'm thinking could cause far reaching problems we'd have to make sure it was a one off. What I had in mind was for Nai to move a tracer from one dimension to another, the another being this one and the location being within the assistant."

Anathorn raised an eyebrow. "Is that even possible? I'll ask Nai."

Joniel shouted. "Stop, don't type it, just in case. It would have frightening repercussions. Nobody would be safe. Can you call Nai?"

Anathorn clicked the keys and there was a flash of blue light. Nai frowned. "Well if you could have been any more mysterious then I would have been surprised. You have my attention. So, how can I help?"

Joniel turned to face him. "I've got an idea. Is it possible to move a tracer from one dimension to another and put it inside someone?"

Nai looked down. "Technically yes. But they would detect it if they were scanned."

Joniel smiled. "Is it possible to go back in time and do it?"

Nai looked around the room, he looked puzzled. "Yes, but it couldn't effect the time line between it being done and the current time."

Joniel took a deep breath. "So if you went back to when the assistant threatened me in the cavern you would be able to put a tracer in him? Do you have anything undetectable?"

Nai raised an eyebrow. "That has to have a really bad flaw in it as it seems such a simple solution. It complies with the laws as far as I can see. Well, shall I find out?" There was a flash of blue light followed by another and Nai turned up again. "I have asked about this. It would cause too much of time continuum chaos if it set a precedent. But there is a clause that has been taken into consideration. It is something that could have been done before the new law prohibiting it being done is put into place. So I have done it but nobody can ever do it again. Time laws are backdated through time so there isn't a get out clause of going back in time to undo any law.

Code CGH795732, Rennon if you would like to check that the transmitter is working?"

Rennon clicked on his keyboard. "I have a reading from the transmitter. He is in the Xethalon Galaxy."

Nai smiled. "So we finally have a leash on that wild dog but you now have a choice. You can go after the dog and put him down or you can let the dog take you to his master. I would suggest the latter."

Anthorn looked thoughtful. "Difficult choice."

Nai smiled. "Then be glad that it isn't you who has to make it. We're just pieces in this game. It will be up to King Osiris and Queen Isis to make this decision. I will report to Osiris and we will let you know what is decided."

Anathorn raised an eyebrow. "Sometimes you do get a reality check. I forget that we're now just ground troops. I suppose we'd better await our orders then."

A red light flashed on the Prince's console on his desk. He flicked the button under it. "Prince Anathorn, report."

The voice sounded shaky. "This is Kumaris Nis and I am reporting from the Control Room. There is a fleet of unknown craft approaching and they are not responding to my generic hail."

Anathorn jumped up. "I'll be there immediately. Joniel, will you come with me or would you stay with Kyla?"

Joniel smiled. "Aliniel, go and watch over your mother."

Aliniel pouted. "My place is with Anathorn."

Anathorn glared at her. "I am asking you to stay with your mother. We need her protected while she sleeps."

Aliniel frowned then glared at him. "What if I say no?"

Anathorn stood up and pushed past her. "I haven't got time for this." He went into the room where Kyla was resting and picked her up. Joniel held the door open for him and he carried her gently out.

Kyla woke up and cried out as they ran along the corridor. Joniel reached into his pouch around his belt and took out a tiny feathered dart, he took the safety tip off of it. He stepped over to where Anathorn held her and put his hand on her cheek. "Nothing is the matter my love, sleep, it is just a dream." He kissed her, she closed her eyes and then scratched her neck with the dart then put the tip back on it. He shrugged. "They sometimes come in handy. Come on, we've wasted enough time already." He glared at Aliniel who strutted off down the corridor with them. She was very conscious of people looking at her and smiled at them as she went past. Anathorn noticed but he looked away and carried on.

The Command Room was bustling with people. Through the huge window they could see the expanse of space and the fleet but they could also see another fleet which matched them in size coming towards them.

Anathorn gently put Kyla down in an empty seat and strapped her in. "Report please. Are they in weapons range, are their shields up?"

A middle aged woman spoke clearly and slowly. "My Lord they are within weapons range, they have minimal shields up and they appear to be hailing us."

Anathorn sat down in the command chair. "I'll accept their hail."

The screen became opaque and they saw static for a moment then an image of another control room and a purple woman they recognised appeared on the screen. Shantara was looking back at them. She smiled. "Well, did you miss me?"

Rennon smiled. "Good to see you. Well this is a surprise."

The smile fell off of Shantara's face. "Well, not as much as this will be. Shields up, fire all weapons. You abandoned me, this is payback day." Communication was cut.

9

Anathorn screamed. "Shields up full power!" It was too late. The guns had already been manually targeted and there was such a small delay between her giving the command and the guns firing that they could do nothing to get their shields beyond the basic level of protection in time.

Flames burst out all over the fleet and three ships exploded in fireballs. Very little firepower was aimed at the Horus. The shots that did hit were aimed at their guns and their ability to enter the Eion Corridor.

Anathorn shouted. "Damage Report?"

The answer came back from a small blonde haired woman. "We have lost half of our main guns. The Eion Drive has been damaged but it is still functioning. The shield generators have been hit but by rerouting we can maintain sufficient shield to prevent that ship blowing us out of space."

Anathorn hit the communicator. "Report from the Fleet."

Reports came in one by one. Every ship had been targeted and most had lost their ability to jump into the corridor. Nearly every ship had lost its guns and on seven ships the portion of the ship that controlled life support had been targeted. All ships were venting atmosphere and their engineers were struggling to seal up the hull breaches. Two more ships exploded in flames.

Anathorn issued the command. "Fire at will on their command ship with everything you have."

Rennon looked at him in horror. "But Shantara is on there."

Anathorn didn't answer him. He watched as the missiles and energy beams bit into the command ship and it erupted in a ball of flame and sparkling star like lights. "Target the rest of the ships. Fire at will and whenever you have power to do so. Do not wait for further instructions until the enemy fleet is destroyed."

Rennon grabbed his arm. Anathorn looked down at his hand and glared at him. Rennon stared at him open mouthed. "Why? That was Shantara on there?"

Anathorn looked at him and his expression was cold. "Not any more. I did what they didn't expect me to do and the only thing I could do to prevent the greater loss of life. How else would it have gone? She showed her hand. She would have gloated a bit, fired a few more shots and disabled or destroyed more ships and then finally targeted us and it would have gone to a final battle which we may well have won. The result would have been the same."

Aliniel looked horrified. "I don't know you Anathorn. How could you be so cold?" She grabbed his arm and pulled him away from the console. "Look at me when I am speaking to you. Am I not important to you?"

Anathorn turned and faced her. "Because I have to make decisions like that and the decision I make does affect people's lives. It is not all romance being a leader. It is doing the job, taking the responsibility and trying to make the right decisions, not the personally right ones and sometimes not even the morally right ones. You like your position and you like the respect it brings you. That is just a taste of what it really means. If you can stand by me when I make those decisions then you are my partner. If you cannot then you are something else and it is best we part company now."

The room had fallen silent and everyone was watching what was going on in horror. Consoles bleeped, lights flashed but all eyes were on Aliniel and Anathorn.

Aliniel screamed at him. "How dare you berate me in that fashion in front of our men? You…" She didn't finish her statement as Joniel punched her so hard she flew back and landed in an empty chair beside one of the consoles. He marched towards her as she rubbed her jaw. "Don't you ever speak to the Prince like that again. You are acting like a child when he needs a woman. If you want to be with him and if by any vague chance he still wants you after that little outburst then you are going to have to grow up and support him. If not then that is an end of it and I'm ashamed to call you daughter."

Everyone in the room cheered and applauded Joniel before they realised what they had done, fell silent and went back to their work, looking sheepish and casting the occasional glance to watch what would happen next.

Aliniel pouted. "The great Prince Anathorn speaks and Lord Joniel turns into his lap dog. He might as well have a pretty collar round your neck. I am your daughter surely you love me more than him, or is that the problem, you are more than friends. Wait until mother wakes up. She will definitely not be pleased with either of you." She flashed a very wicked smile. "She will understand."

Joniel's gaze was dark and moody. "I very much doubt it." He turned to Anathorn.

Anathorn looked up. The pain in his eyes was obvious. He vaguely nodded and went back to concentrating on the consoles. "Edisal I need you to turn forty degrees to the left and move out into formation. Join with the Eralis and the Keranil and I want the three of you to try to get below that wreckage falling. As it gets to your level I want you to blast with your thrusters, full thrust and put the air brakes on. I need you to blast that wreckage clear of the planet's surface. That is a Class One High Technology Planet with nearly six billion inhabitants. Arista, I want you to move in line with the Searali and use your upward thrusters to keep that ship flying. Destras, keep your course."

He watched as the ships followed his command and got into formation. They blasted the wreckage but it was all too late. The ships crashed down through the atmosphere and landed on the planet. Anathorn looked down as he didn't want to see the ships burst into flames and the corresponding explosions on the planet. His knuckles were white as he gripped the console. He looked about the room at the shocked faces.

Joniel turned on Aliniel. "Those seconds you wasted have just cost those people their lives."

Aliniel burst into tears and ran out of the room. Joniel turned to a guard by the door. "Follow her, make sure she doesn't do anything stupid." The guard turned and ran after her.

Anathorn closed his eyes for a moment and muttered something under his breath. "Right, Jerico, bring the fleet into line. Get those fires out and patch up the hulls. If we can keep everyone flying we'll have to get back to a safe galaxy. If we have ships with no life support set them up with autopilot to follow us and evacuate the crew. Reports please, firepower and damage. Send as a communiqué. Reports please, medical supplies on all ships, not an inventory, I want to know your status."

There was a click and he opened the communiqué. "Euyisa, report, how may we assist you?"

A voice came over the intercom as he put the message on general circulation so the other ships could hear it. "Our Med Bay is hit and vented. All lives lost. We've locked it down but we have no medical supplies. Please help."

A man answered. "Arista, this is the Aranak, we will come alongside and take your wounded."

Anathorn clicked his communicator. "Very good, you have a go."

Three hours later Anathorn handed the comms over to Jerico on the Aurial. He turned to Joniel. "I need to go and read the communiqués. Do you want to go and find Aliniel? I haven't got the time to sort that one out. I'll take Kyla with me if you want to go."

Joniel looked at him, his eyes were cold. "No, she will have to think on this one for a while. We will speak later."

Anathorn smiled. "I am glad. I need you with me my friend." He unbuckled the safety belt and picked Kyla up gently. Joniel made to take her off of him. He hesitated but reluctantly handed her over. They made their way slowly back to the Prince's room, limited by Joniel's limping and found Aliniel sitting in his chair. She smiled so sweetly when he came in. She had brushed her hair and ran to him. Anathorn caught her wrists as she tried to put her arms around him. "No, not now. I will speak with you later."

Aliniel pouted. "By I hurt and I need you. How could you treat me like this? How could you let him treat me like this? He's supposed to be my father and he hit me."

Joniel smiled at her, it was a cold and heartless smile. "You are a big girl and we've sparred enough. Pity that you didn't pay attention when I taught you about peripheral vision."

Anathorn cast a sideways glance at Joniel who very faintly nodded. "Believe me it isn't difficult."

Aliniel screamed at him. "You are a bastard." She then ran out of the room.

Anathorn crossed the carpet and collapsed exhausted in his chair. "She is probably going to go and wreck our room now. Joniel, you are a very lucky man, Kyla has a good head on her shoulders."

Joniel smiled. "I am indeed very fortunate. She also has a great body keeping it there."

Anathorn smiled. "My friend, you can always find a way to cheer me, even in my darkest hours." He stared opening communiqués. "I am glad that you have her and she has you. One day I might find someone to stand by me."

Joniel's smile fell from his face. "I had hoped Aliniel would have been the one. I thought I'd taught her well."

Anathorn looked up and raised an eyebrow. "I know she can be vain and a bit thoughtless but is she acting out of character? Am I misjudging her?"

Joniel looked up in horror. "No!" He ran out of the door just as there was a loud explosion which rocked the ship. Sirens went off and the air became very thin as the life support ceased to function and the air was sucked out of the gaping hole in the side of the Horus. The inertial dampeners were also damaged and the ship began to list.

Anathorn grabbed his desk as the ship tilted and he grabbed the console. "Seal off levels seven to nine, close all bulkheads and lock us down. Get the life support up again someone."

Within half an hour the ship righted itself and the air started to circulate. Anathorn was sitting at his desk and working on messages and trying to come up with a way of moving the ship across the galaxy without it falling apart. The door opened and Aliniel walked in. She stood in the doorway and laughed at him. "I've come to stand with you."

He glared at her. "Back away now." He flicked a switch on his intercom. "Security, here now!"

Aliniel looked confused. "What are you doing that for? Surely you are going to forgive me. I was just shocked that you could do that. I think this has gone a little bit too far."

Anathorn glared at her. "You think that blowing my ship up is a little bit too far?"

Aliniel smiled. "I didn't do that. I think that was Kel. I saw him in a corridor a while back."

Anathorn glared at her. "Don't be stupid. Kel's dead. Why didn't you report what you saw?"

She put her hands behind her back and swivelled on her heels. "Because I had too much other stuff on my mind so I didn't think it was important. Where's father? Don't be silly, Kel's not dead, he was down the corridor on Level 5. So, where's father?"

Anathorn went cold. He looked in horror at Aliniel. "He went looking for you. He hasn't reported back." He softened his voice. "Look I'll talk to you later. Go to our room and I'll be back when I can." She left the room.

As soon as she had gone he called up a scanner and keyed in Joniel's security code. He saw the tracer that Joniel had agreed to wear while on ship moving along a corridor in the general direction of where Anathorn stood and he breathed a heavy sigh. Rennon was still sitting in a chair in the room and was still running diagnostics and assessing damage when Joniel came in.

Anathorn stood up to meet him. "Joniel, that explosion, Aliniel seems to think that Kel caused it." Anathorn again collapsed in his chair and looked exhausted. "When will it ever end?"

Joniel looked around the room. "But Kel's dead."

Anathorn looked even more tired. "I know but his tracking device was still active after he died. They must think he is still alive. So now we know for definite that she has been controlled. She came here and I've asked her kindly to go to our room. Something is very wrong here and I need time to think about how I'm going to deal with it. I have other things to worry about at the moment."

Joniel looked at the floor. "Is there anything I can do?"

Anathorn looked like the weight of the world was on his shoulders. "I don't actually know at the moment. I love that woman but she's impossible. Controlled or not. I've given her everything I've got left in me to give. You know what a step it was for me to risk loving again. I'm playing her stupid games when I should be concentrating and people are suffering. Joniel, what do you think I should do?"

Joniel stared into space. "I can send her back to my ship and my mother will make a good marriage match for her. She can then play as many of her games as she likes in the environment where they are appreciated. I am sorry Anathorn, I had no idea she would turn out like that. I had hoped with Kyla's good sense and our teaching that she would be different. I guess I just have bad blood."

Kyla opened her eyes. "No, you don't, she is just a teenager and as far as she is concerned the world revolves around her. Anathorn, if you still want her start treating her like a child as she isn't yet a woman. She hasn't seen the world and all its pain so how can she hope to understand. If you still want her make her beg. Make her suffer a little before she gets your forgiveness but please be kind about it. Be prepared to give your forgiveness and send her away until this is all over.

She doesn't have bad blood. She just isn't ready for all of this. But give her a few weeks to think on all those deaths she caused and she will be well on her way to developing a conscience and understanding.

If you don't want her anymore then Joniel is right, he should take her to his flagship. Yes I was awake for most of that, you used the wrong dart. That was careless Joniel, that was a paralysis dart, sleep ones are blue, I just couldn't summon the strength to get involved and you both handled it perfectly well without me. Joniel if you ever hit our daughter like that again you will regret it."

Joniel took her hand. "I would never hurt our daughter. I can't believe she didn't duck."

Kyla smiled. "I know, she is getting far too wilful and headstrong to know what is going on about her. I meant slap her, it has much more effect and is less likely to do permanent damage. You nearly broke her jaw you idiot. That kind of lack of concentration could get her killed, as it got Arla killed. We really should have put that sort of thing into their training. She has learnt a weakness in herself and it worked well to get your message across."

The fleet limped through space. Osiris was informed of the situation and they were commanded to return to a safe galaxy where they could undertake repairs.

Anathorn was exhausted. He took a shower in Kyla and Joniel's rooms as he didn't want to return to his own where he knew Aliniel was waiting. He then went to sit with them at the table. Food was brought for all of them and Anathorn arranged for a meal to be sent to Aliniel. He lay back in his chair and looked completely deflated. "Was I wrong in what I said? I pretty much told her that I didn't want a relationship with her. That couldn't be further from the truth."

Kyla smiled kindly. She didn't look much better than Anathorn. "Look at the pressure you are under but she is not likely to understand. We have an assassin about so I would suggest that you don't leave her on her own too long. As she is a distraction rather than support at the moment she will almost certainly be alright. As they think that she is under their influence I doubt they will do anything to harm her. She on the other hand could be up to all manner of mischief. May I suggest that you call her and bring her in here.

I'd put a security detail on Rennon's door as well, but don't disturb him, I hope he's busy and he's very, very quiet. You didn't even notice he was around before did you or when he left? Perhaps some thought for him occasionally might not go amiss. He works very hard and he rarely complains."

Anathorn looked over at Joniel. "Why couldn't your daughter be like her mother?"

Joniel smiled. "I remember when her mother was a wildcat too. We've grown older together. We didn't play games as life never gave us the chance. Aliniel is different. We gave her the peace to grow up and to play. She never had a day's worry and we made sure she was happy."

Anathorn shook his head. "You created a beautiful creature but she's vain and selfish."

Joniel cast a glance at Kyla. "So shall I make her go away? I can take her to my ship."

Anathorn smiled. "You know damn well that I don't want that. You two are just playing games with me. I want her and I need her because I love her. There you've made me say it but you are right Kyla, I need to send her away. She distracts my very soul. That little outburst was not what I wanted the crew to see."

Kyla smiled. "I think that the crew respected you for the way you handled that but you shouldn't have to.

That is just as it should be. I mean that you love her. Joniel, take her back to your mother and tell her to keep her safe."

Joniel looked horrified. "But won't she try to marry her off?"

Kyla looked surprised. "You don't know your mother well do you? If she can secure a marriage to the Royal House do you seriously think she'll go for some noble amongst your people? If you are worried Anathorn, you can swear a life bond with her before she leaves. But there is no way you are getting out of that full state wedding. I need an excuse for a new outfit."

Joniel stared at Kyla wide eyed. "You never stop surprising me. You understand our politics better than I do. You know my grandmother said as much."

Kyla smiled. "Your grandmother is a lovely lady who had to survive in a very harsh world. She gave me this." She pulled a lace handkerchief out of her pocket. She reached out when we were leaving and put it in my hand and smiled at me."

Joniel looked stunned. "That was the handkerchief that my grandfather gave her. She must really like you. This is beyond me, she is a hard and cold woman. Where did that sentiment come from?"

Kyla smiled. "She appears harsh because she has to be. Anathorn, go to our daughter, talk to her now. I know you are tired but she is in a mood to do something stupid."

Anathorn left the room.

Kyla got up and went towards the bathroom. "I'm going for a shower."

Joniel lay back in the chair and relaxed and let all the worries drift away from him. He listened to the water splashing and somehow it was a comforting sound.

In Joniel's dream Kyla come out of the shower, dressed in a towel. She saw him sitting and made herself comfortable in a chair next to him.

The door to their room flew open and Anathorn stormed in. Joniel was on his feet before he realised what was happening. "What is the matter?" He winced and sat back down again.

Anathorn stood in the middle of the room and looked quite helpless. "I can't believe that woman. I go in to bring her back here and she's in my bed with the guard. That's an end to it, I swear it. I love you both like my brother and sister but your child would be the death of me if I carry on with her. Take her back to your ship. I don't want her anymore."

Joniel looked over to Kyla who was looking thoughtful. She spoke gently. "Bring her here, now. Drag her from that man's arms and knock her out if you have to. I am going to make a leap of faith here, I think she's under their influence."

Joniel left the room but he could still see what was going on in the room.

Anathorn sat down, his head in his hands. Kyla put an arm around him to comfort him. He got up and went to the door and locked it.

She looked at him slightly confused as he walked across the room towards her and held his hand out. Electricity ran though her body and she wanted him more than she'd wanted anyone else in her life. She took a step towards him and took his hand. He grabbed her and pulled her towards him, turned around and pushed her up against the door and pulled the towel off of her. She was confused, it felt wrong but it felt right. She tried to pull away but he was too strong and he had her pinned against the door.

It was as if she was in a dream. She could hear Joniel on the other side of the door and her daughter screaming for her father to let her go. She wanted to cry out but she also wanted Anathorn. She wanted him to do what he was doing to her and she could see he wanted it too. In that moment she gave in to it and the energy rose in her and she bit down hard on his neck. Anathorn screamed as she started to drain his blood, she was in kill frenzy and there was nothing she could do about it. Without the restraint of being a healer she couldn't calm the wild energy when the hunger took her.

They both flew forwards as Joniel broke through the door. Kyla screamed and launched herself at him. Her eyes were blood red and her fangs fully extended. He caught her in mid leap and pinned her to the floor, holding her neck to the floor with his hand. "Kyla, listen to me. Hear my voice." She was wild and out of control and couldn't hear him. He grabbed her and carried her screaming and kicking to the bedroom. He shouted. "Anathorn, deal with your woman. I'll deal with mine." He kicked the door shut.

Kyla was struggling and started kicking and punching him. She broke his grip and leapt at him. They fought for nearly an hour, breaking furniture and blood flew in an arc around them. Finally he calculated his strength and with one blow knocked her out, then he bit down on her and drained her blood, replacing it with his.

Joniel lay on the bed with Kyla. She was calm and looked up at him. "What happened?" She looked around the room. The bed was soaked in blood as was the carpet. Most of the furniture was smashed to pieces. Joniel looked exhausted. "Kyla, there was drug in your system. I got it out by draining your blood, all of it. I've given you what I could." He ran the back of his hand down her cheek and pulled her into a hug. "I can handle most things but not that. That was one step too far. Kyla, hold me, tell me you love me and you don't want anyone else."

Kyla held him as tight as she could. "You know I love you and why would I want anyone else?"

He stroked her hair. "You don't remember do you?"

She looked confused. "Remember what?" She screamed and held her stomach in pain. "Help me Joniel, I hurt, I hurt a lot."

He picked her up, wrapped her in a sheet and carried her out of the room. Anathorn was laying on the couch, Aliniel was with him. Without stopping he ran to the Infirmary. He rushed in with her and laid her on the examination table. "She's in pain. Help her." The doctor ran over and began his examination as Kyla screamed and doubled up in pain. "Please leave the room."

Joniel glared at him. "No, I will not. I am her husband, I will not leave her side."

The doctor worked on Kyla for two hours but he couldn't save the baby. He managed to stabilise her and when she was comfortable he analysed the samples he had taken. Joniel sat with Kyla holding her hand as she slept.

The doctor came in. He was carrying a sheet of paper. "Joniel, you aren't going to like this. None of us do.

She's asleep and we're going to keep her that way for a while. I want you to be as calm as you can be. There is a residue of rohypnol in her system. That is a date rape drug. With what has recently happened with her losing her healing ability her body is a mess as it can't clear itself of this sort of thing. Add to that how tired she is, she didn't stand a chance of resisting its effect."

Joniel looked down and sighed. "I just can't bear the thought of someone else touching her, not in that way."

The doctor put a hand on his shoulder. "That is a bit of the good news. He didn't get as far as that. There is no sign of trauma. He didn't touch her in that way. Then she had the best defence ever. I have been treating his torn neck. That is probably enough to put any man off."

Joniel smiled slightly. "Though I wouldn't wish him hurt, I'm glad. I don't know if I could bear it if he had touched her."

The doctor tried to smile. "The rest of the news is worse. I tested some of the blood from your room. There were more drugs in her system. There is no easy way to put this. I haven't spoken to her yet. You brought her in and we've kept her sedated. The drugs in her system were a combination of three abortion instigating drugs. The combination and the strength of the three was more than enough." Jolinel looked down at his hands. He felt anger but it was undirected, he felt lost but there was no Kyla there to hug him and make it right.

The doctor tried to smile. "How do you feel?"

Joniel almost shouted. "How do you think I feel? In one action my wife is nearly raped by my best friend and our baby is murdered. I feel like I want to find the person who did this."

The doctor was checking Kyla's pulse. "Her pulse is weak, something is definitely wrong."

Joniel jumped up and went over to her. The doctor pushed him away as Kyla went into a spasm. The machine that monitored her heart rate showed her flatline and an alarm went off.

Joniel woke up and he was still laid back in the chair in his room. He could hear the sound of water splashing in the shower. It took a moment to work out that it had all been a dream but when he did he felt a real feeling of euphoria and happiness. It was like nothing he'd felt in a long time. It was the sheer relief that it was not real. He got up and opened the bathroom door and after undressing slipped into the shower with Kyla.

Anathorn hesitated outside his bedroom door. He put his hand on the handle, took a deep breath and opened it. Initially he thought the room was empty and then he saw Aliniel in the corner. She was sitting on the floor with her head in her hands.

He crossed the room and stood over her. "Aliniel, stand up."

She stood up but she looked broken, there was none of the fire left in her. She looked up at him and he saw the pain and tears in her eyes. "What have I done? Can you ever forgive me?"

Kyla's words echoed in his mind and he smiled at her gently. "That depends on if you are truly sorry."

Aliniel smiled at him. "Of course I am."

He was watching her carefully and her body language. "You realise that I have a lot of responsibility?"

Aliniel stepped closer to him and he tensed. He had a feeling, something seemed wrong. Her movements were wrong. His mind was racing as she put her arm around his back. He felt her tense and he leapt away, instinct kicking in at the last moment. The knife in her other hand thrust into empty air. "How dare you speak to me like that in front of our men? You humiliated me. I am the daughter of Lord Joniel, nobody talks to me like that."

Anathorn steadied himself, his eyes on the knife as it slashed in an arc towards him. He leapt back and deftly caught her arm. "And you don't treat me like that. I am Prince Anathorn, Commander of Osiris' Fleet. I also happen to love you."

He twisted her arm behind her back, turning her around and just managed to move his stomach out of the way of a vicious thrust back with her elbow. A leg around her unbalanced her and he threw her onto the ground. The knife fell from her hand and he flailed around trying to catch her free hand.

He pressed his body weight down on her and caught her other hand, pulled her hands together behind her back while sitting straddling her and pulled a cable tie out of his inside pocket. "Well, I'm thankful for your father's advice to always carry these. Now I'll put it to good use. I don't know if this is you or the drugs talking Aliniel. For now I'm going to hope that it is the drugs. I'm not going to tell your parents but I am having you taken to the cells for complete examination. I can only hope you have been drugged, if not then you know I will have to treat you as an assassin. You might be your father's daughter but he has served me well over a very long time. Do not presume to trade on our friendship. The good will he has built up is his to use, not yours."

Later Joniel and Kyla sat in their room in thick dressing gowns. Joniel had just told Kyla about his nightmare. There was a knock on the door and Anathorn was there. He backed off to go when he saw them but Joniel invited him in. He came in and sat down.

Anathorn suddenly felt really awkward as Joniel was looking at him strangely and he wondered if he knew what his daughter had done. He turned to Joniel. "What is the matter?"

Joniel looked at Kyla. "Should I tell him?"

Kyla blushed. "I suppose so."

Joniel retold the story of his nightmare and Anathorn looked shocked. "I didn't want to mention it but I had the same dream, from my perspective, the other night."

Kyla looked horrified and grabbed Joniel's hand. He reached over and kissed her. "I'm going to take care of you and our babies, both of them."

Kyla thought about what had been said. "You described how I felt, that doesn't happen in a prophetic dream. However real it may have felt neither of you have the training or the ability as far as I know to see the future. What you are experiencing are the very nasty images being sent by whoever was attacking me."

Joniel and Anathorn looked at each other and relaxed slightly. Joniel still looked slightly upset. He smiled vaguely at Anathorn.

Anathorn smiled. "It was the one thing that would truly put a wedge between us and distract us from what we are supposed to be doing. Joniel, I love Kyla with all my heart but as your wife. If things had been different, who knows as she is a beautiful woman but she is yours. I love your daughter, she is more than enough of a woman for any man. I have spoken to her and she is now contemplating her actions. You might like to give her a day or so to think through what she has done so that she can formulate her own thoughts before you speak to her. Kyla, do you know for certain about the baby?"

Kyla smiled. "When I was in the Infirmary they confirmed it."

Anathorn looked worried. "I want you out of here in the morning. It isn't safe."

Kyla laughed. "Name me a place that is. I will do Isis's bidding. She said that we had this child as a symbol of hope that we were doing this for a good reason not a negative one. That implies that I have to see this through to the end."

Anathorn took her hand and kissed it. "Well then congratulations but I'm keeping you out of the worst of it."

Kyla hadn't stopped laughing. "So you think you can't stop it following me?"

Anathorn stopped to think about it. "You can help all you like but I want all your food and drink to be analysed and safe. Two people dreaming the same dream, that's worrying. Joniel I don't want you leaving Kyla's side not for a minute. Nothing is coming close to her that we don't get analysed first."

Kyla smiled. "That is what they want. We are being distracted from going after them. Look after me." She closed her eyes and lay back.

Joniel moved to sit on the floor beside her though he found it difficult as his leg still hurt although it was healing fast. He didn't touch her. "She's going after whoever is doing this."

Anathorn took one look at Joniel and knew he wasn't happy. "Can we help her?"

Joniel smiled. "Only by making sure the body is comfortable and safe."

Kyla stepped out onto nothing. She was floating in space. All around her there was light and darkness. She could see shadowy images that she recognised as Joniel, Anathorn and a baby. She put white light around them and protected them as best she could. Then she saw something dark in front of her. It rose up like a colossal building, towering over her and making her feel tiny. It arched over her and she smiled. She held up her hand and a tiny grass seed floated up into the air and planted itself in a crack. As the colossus moved the grass seed grew and as it grew it split the stone and the colossus tumbled down to the ground. As it fell more grass grew and it crumbled into pieces. Kyla spiralled the pieces up in a vortex and created a vat of acid beneath them and dropped them into it.

She felt and heard a scream of agony as the pieces dissolved. Then she saw a blade flying through the air. She threw water at it and it rusted to powder and there was another scream.

In the visualisation Kyla reached down into the nothingness and earth created itself around the roots of a tree that started to grow. She became a part of the tree and used it for support. When she felt secure she drew energy up from its roots and threw that energy in a beam at whatever was out there. She focused good intent and everything that she was, all her training, all her love for those she cared about which gave her strength and the stronger that made her the brighter the light became. The scream intensified and went silent and she was thrown back into the room by a vast explosion. Her spirit hit her body at a great velocity. It jolted the body and she came back into it screaming and disorientated.

Joniel grabbed her and put his arms around her. She looked up at him. "I don't know what I've done but it seemed to have quite an effect. I don't think whoever it was expected that. We are on the right track and we have to keep going and not get distracted."

10

All around the ship people were picking themselves up and looking around without the images and confusing information that had been implanted. Rennon had bumped his head slightly when he fell, he was rubbing it and then climbed to his feet and took a look at the project he had been working on. Suddenly it made sense. He had deliberated for hours over it and just couldn't understand it before.

Hours later Rennon grabbed his laptop and headed for Anathorn's office. He knocked loudly on the door and Anathorn opened it as Rennon rushed in and set his laptop down on the Prince's desk. He was out of breath and excited. "I think I've worked it out."

Anathorn went to look at the figures on screen. "Rennon, slow down, what have you worked out?"

Rennon took a breath. "There is more going on than we originally thought. We know that the original infestation came from the pods on the island. I've been analysing that fluid and by what I can see it is a conduit which allows parts of the brain to be activated which we don't usually use. That is how this "entity" is managing to control and confuse us. Those who would normally have been unable to be influenced as they have not trained to access that part of their brain have no defence so they are the easiest for this person to attack. Kel by what I can work out was patient zero. He came into contact with the fluid when he was at their facility. They programmed him and it is likely that he would have been the one who introduced it here. It was cunning as we recycle our water. All they needed was to infect him and then wherever he went the fluid would get into the system. Anyone he infected would do likewise.

I have run tests and it attaches itself to water so it is not filtered out. I have been working on a way of breaking this bond and I think I've found it.

I've been running tests but it has been slow as my mind has been confused. But, hopefully now I'll find a way of getting that stuff out of our water system. Anyone infected is a carrier so wherever they go they spread it.

Anyway, the fluid also interferes with the part of the brain which allows rational decisions. So what I assume happens is that all those base fears, wants and needs come to the forefront of your mind. They then cloud out what you would normally consider important. Literally you will feel every fear and emotion and every want and need without being able to filter them out.

As you and Kyla are less affected I would assume that there is something in your DNA that protects you. Kyla is trained so she hardly had any effect at all. Maran didn't have the DNA so despite her training she was a victim. The DNA doesn't totally protect you, it just lessens the effect. Your shared dream with Joniel is obviously connected to a strong emotion you have towards Kyla which is a bond you share. I'm not saying that you actually physically want her in an inappropriate way but somewhere in your psyche you have thought about it at some point. Or you are worried that you might. Also I'd be careful around Aliniel. Add in teenage hormones and her being trained by Joniel as an assassin and you'll have quite a threat there if she turned on you."

Anathorn looked down. "Aliniel already tried to kill me."

Rennon looked shocked. "You didn't say anything."

Anathorn smiled. "I've had her locked in a cell and I'll deal with that myself. It wasn't her in that room, it was something else and now I know what. I survived without injury. Once you sort out something to counteract the effect we can use it ourselves and we can start introducing it into the water system. I must report this to Osiris. You've done well Rennon, you may well be on your way to saving us again."

Rennon smiled. "Big goddam hero me, ok I'll get back to it."

Anathorn watched him go and smiled. His thoughts were about Aliniel and how she hadn't been responsible for her actions but something else was troubling him, his dream about Kyla. He smiled and accepted it, he had thought about her when they had first met. Now he knew she was Joniel's there was no issue. He sent a communiqué to Osiris and shortly afterwards Osiris' face appeared on screen. Isis was with him.

Anathorn bowed his head. "My Lord, I have much to report."

Osiris smiled kindly. "I have read the report you submitted and I send my condolences for your losses and to the families and friends of those who died. You need make no further comment or explanation if you do not wish to."

Anathorn smiled. "I thank you. I have just had a report from Rennon that the fluid is bonded in our water system and is being passed from infected person to person that way. As we recycle water that was an easy way for us to be effected. As it is likely that Kel was patient zero the infection came through him and was introduced to the base and then as it infected more people they spread it across the fleets when they were transferred. Rennon is working on something that will break the bond so that we can remove the fluid from our system. That is the reason for irrational behaviour, paranoia and many of the attacks we have experienced."

Osiris listened intently. "I will send Rennon any assistance that he requires and I would like to transfer him to our flagship where he will have better facilities. I am moving a fleet in to escort you to a safe haven where you can repair your ships. This is indeed good news."

Anathorn bowed his head. "I thank you."

Isis smiled at him. "You have done well my Prince."

The communiqué cut off and the screen went back to the usual screensaver of a tropical island with a golden sunset.

Within the day Rennon and his assistant Neris were transferred to Osiris' flagship and a fleet moved to escort Anathorn's damaged vessels deep into the Hailis Galaxy where they could be repaired.

Deep in the Rotatian Galaxy Set sat on his black throne. He looked about with dark piercing eyes. The silence of the great chamber echoed around him as he looked first at his hands then the wall again. He sighed and straightened his robes. He ran his fingers through his shoulder length black slightly wavy hair. He looked at his reflection in the black reflective surface of his console and ran his hand over his short goatee beard making sure that it looked just so. Then he waited.

The wall panels were painted as his palaces of old, the hieroglyphs telling the story of his rise to power and greatness. Flames burnt in bowls around the room giving it a shadowy orange ambience. The room smelt of incense, his favourite. He took a deep breath but his expression was troubled.

The door slid open and his Commander walked in. He strode forwards and knelt at his master's feet. He bowed his head, his dark hair was neatly swept up with gel and he sported a day's stubble. His brown eyes were fixed on the floor, his head bowed.

Set glared at him, his eyes glowing red. "You have failed me. I sense that the witch Kyla has managed to defeat you in psychic combat and your powers are now weak. I will not tolerate weakness in any form. If you do not deal with this matter I will deal with you appropriately. You may stand and face me."

Ka stood up and bowed. "I have been beaten this time but I have to report that my control over Maran was complete. She has taken Kyla's healing powers from her. I feel that…." He didn't manage to finish his sentence as Set fixed him in a blood chilling stare.

Set spoke slowly. "I did not give you such an order. Kyla's healing powers were her weakness. If they had not been taken from her she would undoubtedly have destroyed herself. You understand little of those things so you do not comprehend what you have just done. Much as I would not let you kill Joniel when you had the chance. He is her weakness and one day he will be her death because she would die for him."

Ka looked down. "I am sorry Master, I did not realise."

Set sighed. "You do not realise a lot of things but I think it is time that I do give you a little more information, so that we can avoid further mistakes."

Ka looked up, his face looking hopeful. "I thank you Master."

Set relaxed back into his throne. "My war with my brother and sister has gone on for millennia. We are looking beyond the Upper and Lower Kingdom now, we have the galaxies to fight over. I'm not going to lose now, not after all this time and all these sacrifices. So, hear me now and bide my words well. If I cannot torment my sister, I will exact my revenge on her Priestess. Bring her to me.

Their infernal tampering is causing much disruption to my plans. If we do not act they will bring destruction onto the worlds I control. The spread of the virus which is suppressed by the Eltatian Liquid is almost out of control and if they find an antidote to the liquid and immunise people we will have no way of controlling it. Many more of my subjects or prospective subjects will die and many more planets will be destroyed by overuse of resources. They must be stopped at all costs. You may leave now."

Ka marched angrily down the corridor. He pushed guards and other people out of his way and stormed into his room as the doors opened and closed. The room was sparsely furnished and the walls were painted bronze with black swirls intricately laced in a continuous pattern. He sat in the large high backed chair behind his desk and looked at the wall, his eyes tracing the pattern, his mind racing. He then switched on the intercom and keyed in a code. "This is a message to all Legion Heads. Acquire the witch known as Kyla with extreme prejudice." He turned the intercom off.

He smiled to himself. "I'll have that bitch's head on a spike."

He sat down and tried to concentrate but as he reached inside there was nothing there. His visualisation brought back a black and charred wasteland. He could not connect to anything and he felt that there was nothing left out there, even though he knew otherwise. He slammed his gauntleted fist down onto his desk, splintering the wood and stood up. He toppled the desk, throwing it across the room so that it hit the wall and exploded in a shower of splinters and ornately painted timber.

He pulled a private communication device from his robes and flicked it on. "Goyay Yestow, report to my quarters."

He sat back down and waited. There was a knock on the door and a thin man entered. He was dark haired and his eyes were deeply set and shadowy. Beneath his hood his spiky blonde hair could just about be seen. He wore black robes and his hands were incredibly long fingered. "You called for me My Master?"

Ka glared at him. "Indeed I did. You had your orders to eliminate Kyla. Why is she still a thorn in my side? Why are you here and not out there dealing with her? Your failure has cost us dearly. I do not want excuses, I want you to do something about this or your life will be forfeit."

Yestow frowned. "My Master I have not been able to gain access to the Fleet. It has now been taken into a safe harbour and…"

Ka glared even harder. "I do not want excuses. I want that bitch's head. Go and carry out your orders."

Joniel knocked on Anathorn's door and went in. Anathorn was sitting behind his desk and looked slightly nervous as Joniel strode over to him. Joniel smiled. "So you still have her locked up then?"

Anathorn tried to think of what to do and say but settled for the truth. "For now yes, I can't be sure she isn't going to try and stick a knife in me again. Can you guarantee she won't?"

Joniel frowned. "I couldn't guarantee it. All I can say in her favour is that she failed. I am pleased that you are still alive but I would also be very surprised if she truly wanted to kill you."

Anathorn looked shocked. Then he looked at Joniel and saw something cold about him. There was something very different about his friend. "Joniel, what is the matter? You seem different."

Joniel sat down and put his head in his hands. "If we can't count on our skills and abilities what can we count on. I didn't mean it to come out like that. I've always had complete confidence that Aliniel was going to be as good a killer as I ever was. I'm truly glad she isn't but I'm also disappointed. My hope is that her love for you won through and it wasn't a serious attempt. I also don't know what is getting to me. I can't sleep, I can't relax. It can't be any sort of control as that's been wiped now even if it's only a temporary respite."

Anathorn choked slightly. "Well I'm glad she wasn't too. I have information that you need to know as it affects you too. Are you feeling confused?"

Joniel looked up, his eyes looked tired and his face was slightly drawn. "I don't know what I'm thinking these days. Kyla is kicking my butt when we spar to the point that we can't risk that anymore. I can't think straight. I nearly killed her last night."

Anathorn looked shocked. "What happened?"

Joniel looked sheepish. "We had a way that we found to be close and I could give her pleasure without the physical act of making love. It is an assassination technique I learnt in Mystonia where you use nerve centres to cause extreme pain until they cause heart attack and shut down of various organs in the body. Over the years I developed it to give pleasure instead of pain. It is extremely dangerous as if I get it even slightly wrong I can kill her. The last time we tried to make love we nearly killed each other. Neither of us could control our need to feed or kill. I really screwed

311

up last night and nearly killed her, she had a heart attack and I only managed to revive her using drugs."

Anathorn looked horrified. "Joniel, you risked her life. I sometimes cannot believe you. You say you love her so much then you'd put her in a situation like that?"

Joniel looked down. "I know. I'm not in control at the moment and that terrifies me."

Anathorn smiled kindly. "I assume she is alright. I don't have to tell you not to do that again do I? I have some good news for you though. Rennon does have the reason for all this. All he needs to do now is find out what we can do about it. You'll have to be more careful until we can sort something out. I'm keeping Aliniel locked up. Our stronger emotions and passions are what are making us vulnerable. I just hope that Rennon can come up with something fast."

Joniel looked down. "So do I as I don't trust myself anymore."

Anathorn looked up. "I'm suspending all off base missions until we sort this out."

Joniel looked up at him. "Probably a good idea as I passed at least three fights going on in the corridors."

Anathorn frowned. "Rennon said that it was in the water system and it is being spread because the water is recycled and it links to water molecules." Joniel thought about it. "So the more we recycle the water the stronger it is going to get. As a temporary measure why don't we flush our water system and replace it?"

Anathorn smiled. "I'll give the order and we'll give that a try."

The fleet hovered over the planet of Ansliaris, a water based planet on the edge of the Sinnian Galaxy. After ejecting the ship's water into space where it would be harmless the ships restored their water. They tried it out on the Flagship to start with and within three days they noticed a distinct difference. All waste water was discarded and replaced from the planet's surface. The arguments stopped and a general feeling of calm came over the place. Rennon ran tests constantly and finally he was able to present a report to Prince Anathorn that the system was clear of the drug. Anathorn then made his report to Osiris and the information spread through the rest of the fleets.

Prince Anathorn sat in his quarters. There was a knock at the door and two guards brought Aliniel in. They stepped back and left her standing in the middle of the room. The Prince looked up from the papers he was looking at. "You may leave us, wait outside." The guards left. He then turned to Aliniel. "I need to hear it from you. Why did you attack me?"

Aliniel looked down. "At that moment you were everything I hated. Rather than hating myself for being so stupid as to distract you when you were in such a serious situation I reflected it on to you. I couldn't handle it so I struck out in the only way I knew."

Anathorn looked down. "And how do you feel about me now?"

Aliniel tried to smile. "I feel so sorry about what I did. How can you even face seeing me?"

Anathorn smiled. "I have been thinking about that. You were under the influence of the drug and I seriously doubt that Joniel trained you so poorly. If you had wanted to have really killed me I doubt I would have been able to have stopped you. That you didn't is testament to that we still have something between us. Do you still want to be with me?"

Aliniel smiled. "Of course I do. I can only offer the drug as an excuse for what I did. Please don't send me away. I want to be with you."

Anathorn raised an eyebrow. "Then you shall be but hear this if you ever try to kill me again you had better succeed as I will retaliate and I won't fail." His stare was cold and she visibly took a step back. "I am Prince and that is not a title I undertook lightly or acquired easily. I had to fight my way to get to where

I am. Remember that. Yes I am your lover but I am Prince first. I have respect for your father but he earned that. You have my love but you have yet to earn that same respect. Go now and I will speak with you tonight."

She backed away nervously and left the room. As the door closed the door to Anathorn's rest room opened and Joniel stepped out. Anathorn looked up. "Was I menacing enough?"

Joniel smiled. "Not bad, you slipped up a bit by telling her you loved her but in essence I think she got the message. Well hopefully it has given her something to think about."

Anathorn looked up. "Something is troubling me. Do you regret leaving the planet?"

Joniel raised an eyebrow then looked down. "That's a strange thing to ask. There isn't a waking minute that I don't wish that I could be back there with Kyla. The drug has given me such nightmares of losing her and I just want all this to be over so that we can go somewhere and just be together again. I tire of all this Anathorn. The years are weighing heavily on me now and the peace I had there showed me what happiness I could have."

Anathorn smiled kindly. "I value you being here and everything you both do is very much appreciated. I do not underestimate the sacrifice you both made to come back. Aliniel will make me a devoted wife one day."

Joniel looked up. "So when are you going to make her your wife? It would steady her and assure me. I still remember you when you travelled as Thorn."

Anathorn smiled. "I will marry her when she stops trying to assassinate me." They both laughed. "For now I've got to work out what to do next. We know that water systems are being polluted, we can't replace the water system in all of the galaxies so we've got to come up with something that will break down that compound."

Joniel smiled enigmatically. "I have an idea. My old Master might be able to come up with something. Chemicals are his speciality."

Anathorn raised an eyebrow. "I just can't imagine you having a Master."

Joniel laughed. "I had to learn all this somewhere. It's about time I used some of my skills and contacts. Will you look after Kyla for me?"

Anathorn glared at him. "You aren't taking her with you?"

Joniel looked shocked. "To visit a High Master Assassin, you have to be kidding. She's worth too much on the open market. Just make sure that she is ok while I'm away. I don't want to have to worry about her."

Anathorn smiled. "I'll take very good care of her."

Joniel raised an eyebrow. "Not that good I hope."

Anathorn raised an eyebrow and smiled. "I wouldn't stand a chance anyway, she's devoted to you."

Joniel smiled. "I know but I like to remind you. I don't have to mention the barmaid of Xyxveksius 8 do I?"

Anathon laughed. "I would rather you didn't."

Joniel bowed and left Anathorn in deep thought.

Joniel's shuttle touched down in a forest glade. There was dew on the ground and the first rays of morning were breaking through the ancient oaks that surrounded the flat expanse of grass and meadow flowers. He had sent a hail but had no response. Joniel stepped down onto the soft meadow and closed the hangar door and cloaked the shuttle. He pulled his hood up over his head against the morning chill and stepped into the forest.

He was cautious, all his senses were alert and the adrenaline rushed through him. He heard a slight swishing sound to his right and leapt forwards as darts flew through the air he had just occupied. In a smooth movement he caught the branch of a tree and swung up into the branches as he felt the earth giving way under him. Beneath him he saw a pit open, the spikes at its bottom were vicious. He breathed a sigh of relief but it was short lived as he was hit on the side of the head. Dizzy he fell from the branch but caught it and hung, suspended over the pit.

He heard laughing and looked up. A blonde haired man who looked as if he was in his mid-forties with sharp features and short spiked hair looked down at him. "Well Joniel, I guess I win that one. That was careless. I mean really careless. You are better than this. What the hell is wrong with you my friend?"

Joniel pulled himself up onto the branch. "That's the problem Hex. Something is really seriously wrong. You owe me a favour, can I call it in now?"

Hex raised an eyebrow. "Gladly, I can clearly see that something is wrong with you Joniel. This needs sorting out or you aren't going to be breathing much longer. We can't be as careless as that in our line of work, that is if you are still working. Come we will talk."

Joniel and Hex ran along branches and leapt from tree to tree and twice Hex had to grab Joniel as he nearly fell. In the end he slowed down and began telling Joniel what to do and where to walk. Walking and climbing carefully Joniel ended up following exactly in his host's footsteps.

Even then it was slow going. Joniel seemed to tire almost as soon as he started off. His limbs felt like lead and he couldn't concentrate properly. Hex ended up half carrying him.

Hex smiled at him as Joniel rested against a tree. "You are damned lucky that I'm also your friend Joniel. This is one is one situation where I could really cash in on you. There is one hell of a price on your head, put there by the Followers. But of course, nobody in the Brotherhood will take it up."

They came to a cottage in a clearing. The garden was immaculate and filled with an amazing array of flowers. They swung down and approached the gate.

Joniel looked around. "It looks very much the same Hex, you are quite the gardener."

Hex smiled. "Well I do have help." As he spoke an elegantly delicate blonde haired woman emerged from the cottage. She wore an apron tied over a gossamer gown.

She saw Joniel and ran over to him. "Joniel, welcome back. You must have known I was baking today." She leapt the gate and hugged him.

Hex laughed. "Joniel always did know when to turn up. Now, I've heard you have a woman of your own. But, why didn't you bring her?"

Joniel laughed. "I'm not that stupid."

Hex smiled. "Well, I could have hoped, I'd have got a good price for her." He laughed heartily but Joniel looked worried. "You know I wasn't kidding about the price on your head. It is a mighty sum. Did you know about it?"

Joniel's expression turned thundery. "No I didn't know. That complicates matters."

Hex looked worried too. "My friend, I had to tell you that twice, why didn't you react the first time. This is really, really worrying. Your concentration is lousy. Indeed, her price is more than yours, you'll have to keep her at home but I'm sure you'll manage. There are new players out there, Set for one and he's paying big money. He works through his right hand man Ka. He's a bastard even by our standards. So, I know this is not just a social visit as we'll have to sort this out and fast as you won't be totally safe here. Though you are most welcome and you are safer here than most places. Tiatha, please fix us up something to eat and drink, I would talk to my Apprentice." The last word was said with a note of sarcasm.

Hex and Joniel went to sit at a table and chairs in the garden. Hex looked Joniel over. "Something is very wrong with you."

Joniel looked down. He was shivering slightly even though the sun shone down and it was warm. "I know, we have had some real problems with a drug controlling people and people losing control."

Hex got up and walked around the table and lifted Joniel's head by his chin and looked into his eyes. "Something very wrong. We'll analyse your blood and see what we can find out. For now eat something, drink something and relax my friend. You are wired and exhausted. Everything about you is radiating confusion and that is the first thing you got rid of. I had thought it could have been the effect of the healer who is your lover but the good news is that I don't think so. Her way of life is all calm, so she wouldn't create this sort of chaos in your head. This is something else and my money is on it being chemical induced."

Hours later they sat in Hex's laboratory. All around them there were experiments running and Joniel held his arm out for another vial of blood to be drawn. They had put a needle in and were draining from this with a tap. Joniel swayed slightly on his stool and Hex caught him. "We'll have to stop soon, I can't take much more blood off of you. You were weak before you got here."

Joniel shook his head. "I've got to find the answer."

Hex smiled at him. "Then we will. You were always determined, that was one thing I always liked about you. I saw that in you when you were a child. That and your amazing agility and high kill rate. You were one of my better apprentices. I trained Ka as well you know. There was always something about him, something less refined than the rest of us. He enjoyed it all a little too much and lingered too much over the kill. You were always professional and did the job. Remember that if you have to face him, which I think you may well one day."

Joniel's eyelids felt really heavy. "Hex you haven't done anything have you?"

Hex smiled. "In the old days and if I'd have had a price for it I might have done, no I haven't. You are just plain tired boy. Look at you, you look dreadful. I doubt you'll trust me enough to sleep here though and I don't blame you. Taitha, come in here."

Taitha came in carrying hot drinks for them both. Hex smiled kindly at her. "I need you to give Joniel blood. He can't have mine after I was tainted."

Taitha knelt beside Joniel and offered him her wrist. Joniel looked down at her gently. He took her hand with gentle reverence and licked it to anaesthetise it before he bit down on her delicate ivory wrist. Her blood coursed through his veins giving him back his strength. He pulled himself up again and then he felt the anger rise in him. Uncontrolled feral anger that he could not do anything about. His eyes went wild and Hex stepped over calmly and put a hand on his shoulder and Joniel fell unconscious. "Tiatha, I'm so sorry if he frightened you."

She smiled sweetly as he helped her up. "You know I can handle Joniel, even in a feeding frenzy. The poor boy, he's so tired. Shall we let him sleep?"

Hex pulled Joniel's arm away from his body and drew off more blood. "Make him comfortable, he will sleep for hours no doubt, he's that tired. We'll look after him."

Taitha smiled as she laid Joniel comfortably on the floor and brought a pillow for his head. "Are you going to harm him?"

Hex smiled wickedly. "I'd have thought about it a few years ago but not now. They are our only hope, there is no way I'd see any harm come to him. I'm also in contact with Maran, there is no way I'd have hurt Kyla either, but there's no reason for him to think I've gone soft. He needs to sleep, the poor boy is tormenting himself and I doubt he has been resting. He's probably awake most nights watching over her or at least worrying about her. He will be safe with us and when he comes around I might even have an answer for him."

11

Joniel woke up. He felt better than he had in a long time. He opened his eyes and looked around the laboratory. He felt the pillow under his head and realised there was a soft blanket over him. Hex was smiling down at him from his seat at the bench. "So you've decided to join me again have you? Hope you had a good sleep, all nine hours of it. Suffice to say while you've been sleeping some of us have been working. But, good news, I think I've got something. I expect to be paid for this and you might not like what I'm going to ask."

He offered a hand down to Joniel as he got up. Joniel smiled and felt his throat. "Well, that's a turn up, not cut, you must be slipping. We'll discuss the payment now then shall we?"

Hex laughed. "Like you I've changed a lot since I settled down, not that you've settled down. I want Prince Anathorn to grant me a full pardon for all my crimes. And they are many."

Joniel looked wistful. "I did for a while and I know what you mean. I envy you your peace. Kyla and I had 19 years of total blissful peace together so yes, I do understand. I'll send him a communiqué." He pulled out an ornate silver tube from his pocket. The keyboard was a gossamer strip with circles with the letters on it that pulled out from it. The screen another gossamer thin sheet which pulled up onto two ornate hooks. He switched it on and began typing.

Hex was fascinated. "That is beautiful. Where did you get that?"

Joniel smiled. "It was a gift for services rendered to a very beautiful lady on Capricious 9."

Hex raised an eyebrow. "And what did you have to do to get that piece of engineering."

Joniel blushed. "Oh the usual, I removed her love rival and got her the husband she wanted. I did a lot of that work for a while in the Gerhatian Court. You were there for a while weren't you?"

Hex smiled. "I did my duty. I can't say that the extra curricular jobs were that unpleasant either. You sly old dog, I didn't know you were there too. Or were you under covers more often than not?"

Joniel smiled. "I can be honest about it now. No, I did none of that. I did the removals as they were good money and I liked the lifestyle. I was loyal to Kyla, she was all I wanted so it made it very straightforward."

The smile fell from Hex's face. "Now that is something I never thought I'd hear. I am impressed. She must be quite a lady."

Joniel looked wistful. "Oh, she is. But keeping her alive through this is not going to be easy."

Hex looked at his hands and thought for a while. "This isn't breaking the code as I came upon the information. I'm going to tell you something now for free, I owe you anyway for distracting that guard on Efaita. I have spies all over and especially in Set's court now that he's becoming a major player. He has ordered her capture at all costs. What he doesn't know is that Ka has ordered her assassination. It's a very lucrative contract that has only been issued to one man, your rival Goyay Yestow."

Joniel swore. "He's good. That is a problem. He's accepted the contract?"

Hex nodded. "No reason for him not to. He's under exclusive contract to Ka. Don't even think of trying to take out Ka though. He's embedded in Set's court and rarely goes anywhere else. He's got himself a position as Set's Commander. My advice if she was my woman would be to keep her in the fleet and don't let her out of your sight. He's got teleport devices and spook technology, he can move about invisible and silent."

There was a gentle hum and Joniel looked down at the screen. "You've got your pardon if you can give us the answers and the solution."

Hex smiled and sighed. "I didn't think that Thorn would let me down. Well, it's a natural compound which binds with water when it comes into contact with Eion Particles. I've managed to synthesise a catalyst which works with it to turn it back into its basic element and water. What I need to do now is to find something to bind it to so that it doesn't immediately rebind as soon as it comes into contact with other Eion Particles."

Joniel looked mystified. "So how the heck did Set manage to manipulate that?"

Hex smiled. "My guess is that he didn't. It's as much a threat to him as it is to us. I'd guess that his mind control research is to do with controlling those who have come into contact with this, rather than causing it. The infection on your ship was probably more to do with the amount of travelling in and out of the corridors that you have done lately."

Anathorn knocked on Kyla's door. She opened it and jumped slightly so see him there. His voice was gentle. "Can I come in? I wanted to see if you were alright."

She stepped aside and opened the door fully. "You are welcome."

He stepped inside and took a seat that she offered to him. He sat down and looked awkward.

Kyla smiled. "Would you like a drink?"

Anathorn looked up. "I'd love one."

She poured him a glass of an amber liquid and one for herself and sat down opposite him. "Is something the matter?"

Anathorn looked down into his drink. "That dream I had has been troubling me. I can't get it out of my mind. I keep worrying about you and the child."

Kyla smiled. "We are fine, don't worry. It was just an image, something in your mind that was troubling you."

Anathorn looked up. "That worries me more. Why was I even thinking something like that? You are my friend's wife."

Kyla smiled kindly. "We are all close friends as we've been through so much together. That builds a bond between us. There is energy between all of us. The drug just muddied the boundaries and allowed emotions to cross over a little. I am flattered that you would be attracted to me. You didn't physically touch me. Don't let it trouble you or they will have won. Joniel has come to terms with it. He will always be protective and I wouldn't have him any other way. Try to put it out of your mind. You have Aliniel, she is a beautiful woman and she'll give you much to think about over the next few months no doubt."

Anathorn smiled. "It just seemed so real." He shifted in his chair and Kyla looked nervous as he made to stand up. "You see, even you are nervous about me now. I'm beginning to wonder if I can trust myself anymore with this drug going around."

Kyla smiled. "In reality if you'd tried anything like that you would have been the worse for it. I'm perfectly capable of defending myself." She took a drink from the glass and smiled at him. "Don't worry yourself about it, put it out of your mind. I belong to Joniel, I don't want any other man. Why don't you go and spend some time with Aliniel? You need to build your bond with her. I am not upset by what happened so put that worry aside."

They chatted for a while until Anathorn finished his drink and put the glass down on the table. He got up and Kyla walked with him to the door. He turned around and they hugged. He kissed her on the forehead. "Thank you."

She smiled. "Try not to worry."

He left the room and walked down the corridor back to his own room where Aliniel was waiting. She was sitting on the edge of a chair looking very nervous. He opened the door and strode in. She looked up at him and he smiled as he crossed the room to her. He reached down and grabbed her hand and led her to the bedroom. "We could talk for hours about guilt and worry but if we love each other, I know you are sorry, you know I love you. Let's not let anything stand between us."

The Fleet rested for three months while repairs were carried out. This gave the crews a chance to recover and to train new members where they needed replacements. It also gave Rennon and his laboratory technicians an opportunity to work with the new information that Joniel had brought back. Samson had transferred to the Horus and they were preparing for active service again.

In the darkness of Kyla and Joniel's room there was barely a flicker of movement, unseen and silent. The carpet depressed slightly, footfall following footfall. There was a slight ambient light from a glowing bowl in the corner that illuminated the bedroom. It as sparsely furnished, just a bed and a small table on which the bowl of floating candles were the source of the illumination. The air was heavy with the scent of incense and flowers. Kyla and Joniel were asleep, Joniel had his arms around Kyla and her head was resting on his chest. Her hair barely moved as the invisible assailant put a blade to her throat. He savoured the moment, looking down on the sleeping pair. Then he pushed the knife and red blood ran around the blade.

There was a flurry of movement. Joniel awoke and grabbed for his knife and stabbed the seemingly empty air. His blade contacted with flesh and he twisted it, following up to grab the invisible attacker. He felt the bite of pain as an invisible knife plunged into his shoulder. But, he had hold of the attacker and he let his blood lust take him over. He leapt from the bed as Kyla fell back onto the mattress and pinned the attacker to the floor. Again and again he stabbed until the lifeless corpse became visible. Joniel's eyes were blood red as he turned to the bed where he saw Kyla laying in her own blood. She was trying to hold a sheet to her throat to stem the blood as it flowed freely staining everything red. Joniel smelt the blood and fought the bloodlust as it arose in him again. He controlled his emotions and reached for the intercom. His voice reflected his panic. "Samson, I need you here now, Kyla needs you."

Samson rushed into the room barely minutes later. Joniel had Kyla in his arms. She was deathly pale and as he lifted her from Joniel she seemed almost lifeless. He laid her out on the bed and did what he could to stem the flow of blood from her neck. He looked up. "She will live, the cut was deep and any mortal would have died. But our little lady isn't now is she, thanks to you. I think the gift you gave her just saved her life."

Joniel managed a weak smile. "I wasn't much use in stopping it happening though was I?"

Samson was just finishing bandaging Kyla's neck. "Nobody could have protected her any better. You've been her shadow since you got back. We all have to sleep sometime."

Joniel bit his lip. "I'd relaxed, it had been a fantastic evening and somehow I'd come to believe it was alright. I can't believe I was that stupid."

Samson smiled kindly. "You have to sleep sometime. Now I'll take a look at that body on the floor and make sure he's really dead." He turned to go to the body but it had gone. Joniel took a defensive stance and Samson pulled out his bio scanner. He swept the room. "No life signs. He's gone."

Joniel stared wide eyed at Samson. "The amount of damage I did to him, he must have been dead. I can't believe I didn't check."

Samson put a hand on Joniel's shoulder. "I think we had better get a bio scanner wired into an alarm. That way this won't happen again."

Joniel sat on the bed beside Kyla and looked down at her. She was staring up at him with terrified eyes. He put a hand on her forehead and bent down and kissed her. He put a finger on her lips. "Don't try to speak, there will be time enough for talking later."

Samson looked down into his bag. "Yes, you were very lucky, the blade just skimmed over her voice box and missed her vocal chords or you could have had a very quiet wife."

Joniel almost managed a smile. "I suppose some men would dream of that sort of a situation. Thankfully I'm not one of them." He looked down at Kyla and smiled as he saw her glare melt to something more loving. She tried to speak but no sound came out. Her terrified expression was enough to explain to them how she felt.

Samson was drawing off some liquid. "Well I'll leave you two to do what you do. It is soft tissue damage only. I'm sure you can both sort that one out and get her back to her old sweet self."

Joniel smiled. "Thanks Samson. Ok you can watch if you want."

Samson smiled. "Well I might as well just in case you both go mega vamp and rip the ship to pieces."

Joniel offered Kyla his neck and Kyla bit down but choked. She fell back onto the bed and shook her head.

Samson took a deep breath. "I had worried about that. She can't swallow. I'll have to do this direct into her throat below the cut. Sorry Joniel, not as erotic as your usual way but I'm guessing that it is the result that is important."

Joniel tried to smile. "You just wanted to watch. Keep your erotic dreams to yourself mate."

Samson smiled. "Well." He took a transfusion tube and set it up to drain the blood directly into Kyla's throat. He syphoned off some of the blood but it had no effect. He looked at Joniel. "Ok what do we do now?"

Joniel thought about it for a moment. "Can you put a tube into my throat direct to her throat? The only way we can actually take the blood into our system is via an enzyme which is released when we drink. I want to try drinking from myself, that will mix with the enzyme and you can take it from my throat so it will then go into her and be useful."

Samson looked a little worried as he got his equipment from his bag. "Well, I always wondered how it worked. You know, how you could drink blood and it would end up not being digested in the stomach and broken down. Here we go then, I'll give it a try. Lay down beside her."

He set up his equipment and began to syphon the blood off into Kyla. It took a good couple of pints but he could visibly see the wound healing up. He kept going even though Joniel was becoming even paler than he usually was. "I guess you are going to have to feed when you've finished this? Shall I get you a blood bag?"

Joniel smiled. "Well if you fancy a new experience you could always donate some and keep your blood bag for someone who needs it?"

Samson thought about it. "Why not? I've always wondered what it felt like but don't completely vamp out on me will you."

Joniel looked tired. "I won't but I think you'd better stop taking the blood for a while. Let me feed."

Samson closed the valve and the blood stopped flowing from Joniel. He then sat on the bed beside Joniel and offered him his wrist. Joniel lifted it and licked it to administer the anaesthetic and then bit down.

Samson cringed as the teeth sank into his vein and then relaxed. "You know I thought it would hurt like hell but it actually feels ok. I'm not saying it is a pleasurable experience but it isn't bad. Not that I'm planning on taking it up on a regular basis." He looked at Joniel, lifted his eyelid and checked him over. "You are looking better, just a bit more and you should be fine. Now I'm getting worried, time to stop I think."

Joniel pulled back and wiped his mouth with a handkerchief he pulled from his pocket. "Thanks mate, I needed that. Does Kyla need anymore?"

Kyla was sitting up, there was a vague line where the cut had been but she was looking much better. "No, I'm fine thanks. Isn't it time we got back to doing something useful."

They sat around the table in the meeting room. There was a pile of papers on the table. The write on wipe off board was drawn all over. Anathorn was sitting at the head of the table. His water decanter was nearly empty and coffee cups littered the table. There were screwed up pieces of paper all over it and they looked perplexed.

Kyla sat to his left, next to Joniel. "I've been thinking. How do we get rid of the water?"

Rennon looked up from his keyboard. "No idea. Can't jettison it into space so we'll have to find another solution. I've fixed Intendi by the way. He's in my lab at the moment tidying up. Losing the inertial dampeners cause chaos on my shelves and he volunteered. Hope you don't mind?"

Anathorn smiled. "Not at all. But I think we'd better put him to use checking out the fleet pretty soon."

Anathorn's communicator went off and he looked down at it. "Dammit, the same old story, it is all starting up again. They've checked the water, the new water is contaminated."

They all looked at the cups on the table and then each other. Joniel put a protective arm around Kyla. He smiled. "We could all get very paranoid here."

Kyla put her head on Joniel's shoulder. "Don't worry my love, I'm paranoid anyway. Living the life we do it is probably helpful. I am guessing this is something natural that has either been spreading for centuries or something that has been accelerated by something that happened. There is probably no way of knowing but I'm wondering if it is a naturally occurring substance that has come into contact with something unnatural which has sparked it off. Can you get readings? I mean can you find out if some areas have a stronger concentration than others?"

Anathorn looked a little bemused. "I've no idea how we can do that. I can get something set up to analyse the air in the ships. I'm now beginning to wonder if it actually did originate with Kel or whether it is something we just picked up in the corridors."

Rennon looked up. "Probably something we brought back with us from excessive use of the corridors more likely. Something to do with bringing excessive Eion Particles through into this time space."

Joniel was looking at the table and not focusing on the page in front of him. "Something that feeds on Eion Particles?"

Rennon looked up and raised an eyebrow. "Now that's an idea. I'll run some tests. If you will excuse me."

Anathorn nodded and went back to looking at a piece of paper in front of him on the table. It had a very clear coffee cup ring on it but he had just realised that it was very important. His mind was running with too many questions he just didn't have answers to. But he was expected to know and the longer he took, the more people died on the planets. He looked around the faces at the table. He knew every one of them would support him but how could he admit that he had no answers. It wasn't like facing a definite opponent and he wasn't even sure that Set was so much the "bad guy" now. The directive from Osiris that was in front of him was very specific. Cease all offensive against Set's troops until further notice.

Now they were a force without an enemy. The directive was specific, there was still a cause, there was still the possibility that any moment hostilities would commence again. So there wasn't peace either. It was stalemate. But still people were fighting the Followers on the planets and more people were falling prey to the illusive virus or whatever it was. As even that defied definition he was sitting on a ship in a galaxy in space feeling very, very miniscule. This "thing" that had been romantically named the "Morning Star" after some demonised entity that had once been good on earth.

Shadows played around his mind as he grasped for answers. It was as if they were caught in some sort of spell, frozen in space. No way forward and he wasn't even sure that looking back they'd been right either. They hadn't been wrong, given the information but knowing the full picture now in the light of day it was no answer to any prayers either.

Joniel sat at the table and he could see the same look in his face. They were both used to having a definite target, a definite "bad guy" or at least a target. Now, everything was fluid. Now was the time for the scientist and the researchers. Which was driving him nuts.

Rennon of course was in his element. Constantly jumping between a state of the art laboratory on Osiris' flagship and their fleet he seemed to be thriving. He was running with ideas and seemed truly alive. He and his new companion were in the thick of it. Daily they came up with ideas and spent the rest of the day proving they didn't work. Again and again there were hopes that were so soon dashed on the shore of proof.

The thought that actually made him smile was that there were probably similar scientists in Set's fleets trying to do exactly the same thing. Of course even if they solved the Morning Star they would still have Set's plans for Galaxian Domination to deal with.

Even the communiques were silent. Ships were ticking over and looking after their own internal problems. Daily more people were becoming infected and their answer was drugs as well. So were they truly any different? That was one thought that was really biting into his inner calm.

Aliniel was worrying him too. She needed a lover and to be a young woman. His responsibilities were wearing heavily on her and he could feel her distance.

His train of thought was broken as sirens went off all over the ship. There was a voice over the speaker in the room. "Captain, we are under attack from an unknown vessel."

Anathorn's feet hit the ground at a run and he was in the Command Room and seated in his chair by the time the second volley of shot hit their shields. "Open channels and hail them. Who the heck are they? Come on people, stop your panic and do your job. There are protocols. We haven't been hailed and we've been attacked out of hand. Defend for this volley. If they do not respond be ready to fire back with everything we have."

Shiesh, a woman in her mid-twenties with raven hair and a tight fitting uniform which showed off her ample figure looked up. "Captain, they have blocked our hail. I have run diagnostics and they are not of any galaxy that we know of."

Anathorn took a deep breath. "Fire at will, three quarter of the guns and prep the rest. Target weaponry and thrusters. I want them dead in the water. I mean in space."

The lasers cut through space. They looked so insignificant in the blackness. No more than laser lights at any light show but the power they carried had the destructive power which cut into the ship's hull as if it was paper. The ship's shields were not calibrated to defend against lasers. The firing stopped and the ship was left hanging in space.

Anathorn looked stunned. "Open channels and hail them again."

Shiesh flicked switches and pressed buttons. "Sir, I have hailed and run a further diagnostic. It seems that they do not have the capability to pick up our hail. Their system seems extremely basic."

Anathorn looked at Joniel. "Have you seen anything like this before?"

Joniel looked at the ship. "No, well possibly something similar in a book somewhere but I can't remember what it was about. It wasn't a technical manual, I can tell you that. What sort of weaponry were they using? It just bounced off of our shields."

Kreith, a middle aged man with a shock of unruly blonde hair and a struggling waistline piped up. "I've run a diagnostic Sir. It seems that they are firing lead shot at us."

Anathorn looked bemused. "Are you serious? You mean actual lead shot bullets."

Kreith was staring at the screen in disbelief. "I mean actual round, handmade lead shot balls."

Shiesh shouted from her console. "Sir, it seems their ship is venting atmosphere and I can detect life signs failing."

Anathorn turned in his chair. "Place the ship in a force field and protect their atmosphere. Use the tractor beam and pull them in. I think we had better take a close look at what we've caught. Joniel, can you summon Nailindris for me please. I think this may be something he can help with."

As the ship got closer they could see it a lot clearer. It was an actual ship, fashioned to look like an ancient galleon. It had sails and all the attributes of a "Man O War" except that the hull was pressurised or had been until they had shot holes in it. Diagnostics flashed up on the screen. It wasn't made of wood, it was made of some sort of wood substitute and the sails were made of a fabric that resembled canvas.

The ship was elegantly beautiful. It had the Forecastle and all the attributes of a ship all intricately copied. It sported a flag with a skull and cross bones on it.

Anathorn was shaking his head. "Ok, doc you had better check me out. I think the drug is having hallucinatory effects on me. This just can't be real."

There was a small clap of thunder and Nai appeared next to him. "Well it seems your wish is my command again. Will you stop sending me those intriguing." He never finished his sentence as he saw the ship on the console. "Well I will ever be. What the heck is that? That is just impossible and wrong. Well beautiful but wrong. Holy cow, we've screwed up. I am going to get my ancient butt kicked big time for this one."

Anathorn looked at him bemused. "Can you translate what that is all about please? So you have some idea why there is a galleon floating in space?"

Nai grunted. "We screwed up. Somewhere in our tampering with time we have altered the space time continuum."

Anathorn laughed. "Ok, you are having me on, all of you. Big joke. Now can we be sensible about this. You've fooled me, ha ha very funny. Isn't time space continuum some sort of word used in old books to explain why we shouldn't tamper with time?"

Nai lifted an eyebrow. "And?"

The smile fell from Anthorn's face. "You mean that thing is for real? A galleon in space?"

Nai almost smiled. "You can be very stupid sometimes. That is what I'm saying. I'm guessing that in at least one dimension the inhabitants have been introduced to technology far too early. So they have developed it along with their natural progression. Sometimes things leak across, that is why many of the dimensions seem identical. The new technology has overlain the old, so you get a galleon in space. I am guessing that it has come into this dimension from its own as they have developed the ability to enter the corridors. This would indicate that the original source was Fey in nature. So someone has right royally screwed up and as it was likely one of my people I'm guessing that I'm going to be the one who has to carry the male furry rodent for this one.

Problem is what to do with a ship full of people who have seen far too much. I'm guessing you aren't going to let me blow them out of existence."

Anathorn leant back in his chair. He was smiling. Not out of seeing Nai in a quandary but just because it was such a strange situation that he really didn't know what else to do.

Nai was leaning against a console and looking at the ship held in space in the blue of the force field and tractor beam. "Well, this one baffles me. Kyla, have you got any ideas?"

Kyla thought for a while. "Can you turn the clock back on their world and take out the influence? Would the Taliesinians let you?"

Nai smiled at her. "They might if this is the only incursion and we can neatly turn the clock back without any other anomalies. I'll ask them." He disappeared.

Anathorn sighed. "Ok, so we're left holding the rather out of place galleon floating in space then. I hope he doesn't take long as I would imagine our Inter Dimensional Tourists are probably getting a little tired of the view by now."

Kyla frowned. "Well I'm more worried about what he's going to do with them when he gets back. I'd like to come up with a plan if I could but I think going over there is only going to compound the problem. I'm wondering if he could convince them that they had had some sort of drug induced hallucination?"

Anathorn looked up at her hopefully. "Well as if we don't have enough problems without the possibility of deviations from other planets' histories turning up to add colour to our day."

Rennon was looking at the ship intently. "Well I think it is pretty darned marvellous that they managed to get that vessel to fly through space. It is quite a feat of engineering and really something quite amazing. I'd love to meet them and find out more. But, I'm guessing you aren't going to let me just nip over and have a chat now are you?"

Anathorn shook his head.

Rennon sighed. "Oh well, it was worth a try."

Nailindris appeared back in the room. He looked exhausted and as if he had the weight of the worlds on his shoulders. "Well that didn't exactly go well. There is good news and bad news. Well isn't there always."

There was silence in the room.

Nailindris sat down. "Well the good news is that we have permission to go back and sort this one out. I'm saying "we" as I'm going to need your help. If we can find out who, what and when this happened we can put it right. Your ship is going to have to stay here and hold the galleon in the tractor beam and protect it with the shield. If it disappears then we've succeeded. If it doesn't and we fail then us and anyone who has noticed that ship is going to be eliminated. The ship will be eliminated as well in order to preserve the time and space continuum. So I think that is enough incentive for you to try to help me."

Joniel laughed ironically. "I would guess that it is. So, where or should I say when do we start?"

Nai looked down at his hands. "That is the problem, I have no clue as to where or when and the powers that be aren't being much help either. I am guessing that the people on that ship are many generations after whoever was involved in the original sin. If they have computers we can extract a world history. If we see a vast jump forward in technology then we can pinpoint the mess up. Then we can see if we can get a specific location. Rennon, is this one for you?"

Rennon half smiled. "As usual, yes. A few sleepless nights should solve it. Oh well, make sure there is enough coffee delivered to my lab and I'll get onto it."

Kyla stood on the observation platform looking out over the vastness of space. Stars twinkled and planets cast their light across the void. The deep blue of the nothingness seemed to swallow her up and her thoughts were racing between trying to find answers and trying to find an inner peace. The latter was proving just as hard as the former.

In the stillness she could feel something. It was like a velvet touch of a lover, gossamer gentle, fleeting but repeated again and again. She closed her eyes and felt as though she was falling. She opened them again and she was exactly where she had been. She looked at the metal of the window and realised that it seemed closer and then further away. Colours seemed to alter and as she turned she felt very light headed. Then she remembered or rather she couldn't remember when she had last been to sleep. This lack of sleep was clouding her senses. She was having stupid accidents. Her hand ached after she'd caught it in a door. Her leg was bruised from hitting a table she had passed a hundred times before. She needed to sleep, she knew that but somehow sleep evaded her. She would lay down but a million worries would jump unbidden into her mind and she would lay there thinking over the same old problem.

She yawned involuntarily and all answers just seemed so far from her grasp. She also felt so alone. One call to the outside world, one question and drawing their attention to the galleon would make anyone she spoke to liable to be taken out of existence as well. So much as she was desperate to contact others, particularly Maran for help, she could not. They were alone in this, they had to come up with the answers and if they didn't well that was an end to it all.

This was another fight without a known enemy and in defining the enemy they would be on their way to finding a solution. She shook her head, her eyelids were so heavy and she ached all over.

She felt a gentle touch on her neck and turned as Joniel pulled her hair back from her face and licked her neck. He gently ran his teeth down her neck and kissed her shoulder. "My love, stop worrying, we'll find the answer. We'll have long enough to do it. Nailindris has taken us out of time. So now there is no deadline. We just have to stay here until we can come up with a solution.

She turned around and laid her head on his chest as he wrapped his arms around her. "Kyla my love, you are worrying too much. Worry will drive the answers away. You need a clear head. Come, we will sleep and when we wake we will find our answers. In your dreams you may find the answers as well." He put a strong arm around her and led her to their room.

She lay in his arms for nearly an hour before the worries subsided and she drifted into a much needed sleep. The velvet darkness of oblivion shrouded her worries and the floated in the warmth of her dreams. They came almost immediately, blissful memories transformed into current times, people long gone walked again and those she loved were around her.

The mist swirled around a woodland glade. The light, filtered by the swirling vapours gave it a mystical air. The air felt chilled against her face, her hair damp, grass beneath her bare feet wet, springy and soft. The air smelt of loam and wood, flowers and damp vegetation. Step by step she entered the glade through the trees. Their ancient solid structures stood sentinel around the open vibrant green. As she passed from darkness to light she heard something. She turned and from the other side of the glade a solitary creature stepped from between the trees. The body of a pure white horse, a single silver horn protruding from his noble head. His hooves huge and feathered, his shoulders standing a good eighteen hands high from which his strong and muscular neck arched as he proudly stepped into the misty sunlight.

He approached her and bowed his noble head. She reached up and touched his soft and velvety nose as he snuffled and smelt her, his ears one forward, one back, listening and waiting. His eyes were watching her intently, his back hoof at rest showing he was relaxed.

He tensed and in that moment she realised that something else was in the glade. A small dark creature with pointed ears and a long pointed nose crept from the trees and cautiously stepped into the sun. It cowered nervously, it sought cover and moved stealthily although it was very easy to spot. Its withered skin was sunken and dried out, its clothing mere rags. It reached out with long spindly fingers, touching the leaves and moving them aside as it crept. Scrawny limbs climbed over the plants that got in its way. Its eyes darted about, left and right, left and right. It scuttled slightly sideways, spooked by a brilliantly coloured butterfly as it took flight. With a howl it sought sanctuary behind a small boulder, its spindly arms over its head to protect itself from the ferocious beast.

The butterfly nonchalantly fluttered off, oblivious to the fear it had caused in the small one. It had seen a flower. That was all it was interested in. Determined to fulfil its destiny it fluttered off leaving the creature cowering. The creature looked up, looked around, sniffed the air and cowered again. It waited, looked and sniffed again. Satisfied that it was no longer in danger it stepped out from behind the rock. Cautiously, step by step.

There was a flutter of feathers as the hawk seemingly came from nowhere. It dropped like a stone from above. Vicious talons bit deep into the creature.

Green blood blossomed from where the talons impaled its fragile skin. It gave a shriek but that was its last as the sharp beak bit into its neck, severing its vocal chords and its life thread. It hung in the talons as the hawk took flight, what had been life was now meat, born up into the heavens to the uppermost branches where a nest and babies were hungrily waiting.

The unicorn spooked at the shriek and bolted for cover then all was still in the glade. Birds were singing, the sun was shining and Kyla was left standing alone beneath the arching trees at the edge of the clearing.

She woke up at that point. The room was dark and she could feel the comforting warmth of Joniel beside her. He was still asleep, all strain was gone from his face and she couldn't help thinking how angelic he looked when he was sleeping.

Now her mind truly was racing and trying to decide if it was just a dream or if there was some hidden meaning in it. If there was then it was very obscure. She got up and wrapped her gown around her and went to the bathroom. She closed the door and put on the light. Its yellow glow driving the physical darkness away but it did nothing for the darkness and confusion in her mind. Somehow the creature's death had disturbed her. But, then it was a natural death, the circle of life. It had fed the babies who would then grow because they had food. It was only horrific to her as she had seen it happen when no doubt things like that happened every day. What was more worrying was why she had dreamed it? What was her psyche trying to tell her? Or was there something really glaringly obvious that they were missing? Well obviously they were missing something or they would have their answer by now. So, she thought it through. Someone or something had gone back in time, gone to a planet and left something behind or taught the people there something that had given them the advantage.

She felt a slight chill and pulled her gown closer around her. This was where she was missing something. Why? Why would something like this happen? To what purpose would someone go somewhere and do something like that? With time travel it would have to be someone from Nailindris' realm. If it was then with all the evil and twisted individuals there it could just have been on a whim. If it was then how could they pinpoint it? If they just dived into that planet they could well cause even more problems.

She thought about all the places they had been and what they had done. They had never thought for one moment that they were interfering on anyone's world but that was because they were doing it all in their same time dimension. Then the thought came into her mind that it could have been some sort of temporal accident. If it was then they were truly stuck as it would be a totally random event.

Silently she slipped back into the bedroom and climbed back into bed. Joniel rolled over and put his arms around her and she felt wonderfully reassured that everything was alright. Then somehow he always had that effect on her. She lay there in the dark just enjoying feeling him next to her. The moments slipped to minutes, the minutes into hours and still she let her mind run over the ideas and everything she knew about the situation.

Her pager went off and both she and Joniel leapt out of bed and into their clothes to answer the call to go to the meeting room.

When they were assembled Anathorn addressed them. His voice was formal and that in itself was unnerving. "I have been asked to inform you that the Taliesinians have decided to give us a day's deadline to sort this problem out. It is proving impossible to keep that portion of space free of any scanning or visitation. So it seems that we now have forty eight hours to solve this."

Something struck Kyla, the hawk and the creature. "We have been going about our business but we haven't been looking at possible other things that the Followers could be up to. Do you think this might be something more than a coincidence? Is it possible that while we've been worrying about the problems that were obvious we have missed their master plan? This is a pretty effective way to take us all out of the equation isn't it? Is it possible that some of the things we have seen on various planets have just be natural progressions and possibly accidents? Is there something specific about this piece of space?"

Rennon looked completely bemused. "I really can't see what you are getting at with this? Are you saying that we have been set up to see this galleon and to be in this situation?"

Kyla smiled. "I'm saying exactly that. What has happened to us so far has got us jumping at shadows and reacting to everything. We've been so tied up with that that we missed their master plan. Which was to catch us in this very situation and leave it to the Taliesinians to take us out of existence."

Rennon smiled. "Kyla, I think you are letting your conspiracy theory worries get the better of you."

Kyla glared at him. "Well humour me then. Do a check. Is this the perfect place for us to see something like this without fear of anyone else becoming involved?"

Rennon raised an eyebrow and entered the co-ordinates into his laptop and instigated a search. He waited a second and then a puzzled expression came over his face. "Well I never. You are quite right. Taking into consideration trade routes, corridors, planets and other systems, this is one of the few pieces of actually empty space where what is happening cannot be viewed from any planet or star system. I think you may have something here."

Nai looked bemused. "Well, how do we sort this one out then?"

Kyla smiled. "Erm… well I don't know that but at least we know it is a set up and I would guess that there is no progression that we can track back to find out when exactly the problem started."

Joniel frowned. "Great, so that is an even worse situation. It gets better and better. Just tell me who I have to eliminate and I'll go do it."

Anthorn smiled. "Oh that it was that easy?"

Kyla looked intently at Joniel. "Well, it could be. We just need to know who. There has to be a limit to the number of creatures who can tinker with time and space. Even amongst your people Nai."

Nai thought about it. "There is but with artifacts and other things, who knows."

Kyla looked thoughtful. "Did you say a while back that you'd lost your ability to travel in time?"

Joniel smiled. "Sorry dear, that was me. I lost the ship that could do that."

Kyla looked at him intently. "How did you lose it?"

Joniel sat down and lay back in the chair. "Well it got badly damaged and we had to abandon ship just before it exploded. We'd been attacked by the Juxtaha Thiathons. A small matter of their leader's second in command coming down with a very swift fatal illness caused by a knife across the throat. I underestimated their firepower."

Kyla thought about it. "Did you actually see the ship blow up?"

Joniel smiled. "Well not exactly. I was too busy trying to land the shuttle while being fired at and then surviving on a less than hospitable planet."

Kyla smiled. "Did your ship have any sort of a tracking device that you could locate it now?"

Joniel frowned. "That ship was history."

Kyla glared at him. "You so certain? Do you have a tracker?"

Joniel sighed. "I do and you aren't going to let this one go are you. You should have been there. The whole place was blown to bits. Shields were down. Life support was damaged and the engines had suffered a direct hit."

Kyla smiled. "Humour me darling. Or so your instruments told you. What if someone was on that ship and had rigged the instruments."

Joniel laughed. "You have got to be kidding me. Well ok, here Rennon let me use your laptop. I'll put the code into your tracker."

Rennon logged onto the page and Joniel tapped in a twelve figure code and hit send. The screen showed a count up of the systems it had searched and then it flashed green and showed a location.

Joniel looked totally stunned. "I really don't believe that. You mean that I abandoned a perfectly good ship to spend nearly three months in that hell hole? Someone is going to die horribly for this."

Kyla smiled. "I somehow feel that you aren't kidding here. Well my love, shall we go and get you your ship back and find out where it has been and more importantly when it has been?"

Joniel looked down. "Yes dear."

Anathorn smiled to himself and looked around the assembled faces. "Well I guess we have our action at last. I'm guessing that the ship is going to be armed and there is a very strong possibility that if we went in there all guns blazing that they'd use the self destruct. So, Nai, are you willing to take a small group of us on board so we can access the computer, find out what it has been up to and then to see if we can sort out reclaiming Joniel's lost property?"

Joniel looked at the floor. "I can see I'm going to get the full blame for this one."

Anathorn laughed. "It was your ship mate."

Joniel smiled wickedly and shook his head. "Stories, stories, so many stories."

Anathorn looked slightly worried until he saw Joniel smiling. "Ok, so we all make mistakes. Let us just get the ship back and right the problem. We could use another ship in the fleet."

Kyla was watching them both and their body language. "You two miscreants, I bet you had a wild old time back in the day."

Joniel raised an eyebrow. "Yes, I bet we did. And no I'm not going to elaborate. Some things are better left unsaid."

Kyla smiled as she saw both Joniel and Anathorn looking awkward. "I'll find out one day."

Joniel whispered so only Anathorn could hear him. "Well I certainly hope not." Then he smiled and spoke for everyone to hear. "So who is going and what is the plan. I would suggest that I actually do this one on my own. I know the ship and I can move faster on my own."

Anathorn saw Kyla's look of anger and cut in before she could speak. "Well it would be the most practical solution. You are the stealth assassin after all."

Joniel looked down. "Retired, sort of, and I'm not just a hired killer."

Anathorn smiled. "Yes I know but we aren't going into all those stories now are we." His eyes twinkled as Kyla looked intrigued and Joniel looked worried. "I think the mission would stand more chance of success but I also think that Nai should go with you. I would put money on him being stealthy and if you get a chance to solve the time travelling mystery you might need to do something straight away before they notice what you are up to."

Nai smiled. "Well I can be remarkably stealthy if I have to be and don't worry Joniel, I have a way that I won't cramp your style. Shall we?"

Joniel looked at Kyla. "You mean right now?"

Nai smiled at them both. "I mean that now that we know it is better just to go and do this. So, do you want to go and get changed and kit yourself out with all those nasty stealthy little devices and darts you are so fond of?"

Joniel smiled. "Well yes of course. Sorry Kyla, no time for long goodbyes but keep the thought."

Anathorn blushed. "Oh, well, ermm, well."

Kyla laughed. "Don't worry, you two are so funny sometimes. I can just imagine you both drunk in some brothel by the riverside."

Anthorn flushed a darker shade of red. His mouth opened and closed.

Kyla smiled. "Don't worry, your secret is safe with me."

Both Joniel and Anthorn stared at Kyla who winked at Joniel. "You see, it is annoying isn't it when someone implies something and doesn't give you all the answer. Now go on Joniel, go pack your pointy things."

Joniel turned and put his arms around her and kissed her. "Ok darling but I don't like the idea of going without you."

Kyla smiled. "I don't like the idea of you going but I can see the logic of it."

Joniel took a deep breath and turned and went. As the door shut Anathorn looked around them. "It really is the best thing to do. With his teleport device he can move in there without a trace and hopefully get what we want and get out. I know what that man can do. Don't worry Kyla, he'll be fine."

Kyla smiled. "Don't say that. I've seen enough films to know that when you say something like that generally something really bad happens. Just leave it that he's going off to do another job." There were tears in her eyes and they could all see how worried she was. "I'm just worried that he'll lose his edge because he has too much to lose now. Before when he was a free agent we loved each other but it was an impossible thing. Now we both know the value of what we have. It would be a bitch to have to go on without him."

Anathorn smiled. "This is Joniel we're talking about. He'll be fine."

Joniel was in the bedroom and he pulled out a bag that he had kept in the wardrobe. He unzipped it and started lovingly taking out the contents which mostly consisted of different types of devices, daggers and darts. He began secreting them about his person. It took him a good hour but he then zipped up the empty bag and put it back in the wardrobe. He looked at himself in the mirror, checking to see that nothing showed and he then checked his wrist teleport device.

He took a look around the room and pressed his teleport device. He appeared moments later on a planet many thousands of light years away. The planet was tranquil and serene. Wild flowers added spectacular colour to the meadow and the trees were in full leaf. He stood beside a cottage. The garden was immaculate, roses were blooming in full majesty. He reached over the fence, took out his dagger and cut a single red perfect bloom. Then he put his dagger away and pressed his wrist device and returned to the room.

He laid the rose on the pillow and left the room.

When he returned to the meeting room everyone was waiting. They had papers out on the table. He took a quick look and recognised the plans for his ship. "Decent vessel isn't she. I'd quite like her back. Shall we go?"

Nai nodded. "Oh, before you go teleporting I think I'll hitch a lift". Nai spoke words that they could hear yet they couldn't. They knew he was saying something but somehow the words wouldn't register with their mind. Everyone was watching him as a blue glow seemed to surround him. He began to shrink until he was only three inches tall. Gossamer wings fluttered behind his delicate body. His hair was longer and his tiny hands had impossibly long fingers. "Now that's better." His voice was in no way miniscule and definitely did not match his now small stature. "Well I wouldn't want to cramp your style Joniel, I'm sure in your pocket I won't get in the way." He fluttered his wings and took to the air and clambered into Joniel's pocket.

Joniel looked stunned. "Well now that is a neat trick. Well if everyone is ok about this I'll go see if I can get my ship back." He held out a hand to Kyla who took it. He kissed the back of her hand. "My love, I'll see you soon. Don't worry. Anthorn, look after her while I'm gone. Nai, if you are ready." He pressed his wrist communicator and disappeared.

Joniel appeared in a metal room. It was grey and had a single table in the middle of it with a computer terminal on it. There were no doors or windows.

"Ok Nai, you can come out now."

Nai fluttered out of his pocket and enlarged to full size. "What? No sneaking?"

Joniel laughed. "This was my ship. I had it built for me and I'm the only one who knows everything about it. This room they don't know about. I had it designed so I could run the ship without anyone else interfering when I was on covert missions. I'd set the crew down on a planet for a bit of a rest and then I'd take the ship off on my own. I can run the whole ship from here. Now, let us take a look at what they have been up to."

He tapped his passcode into the computer and the screen jumped to life with start up codes. When it steadied itself a hologram which looked an awful lot like Kyla appeared in front of Joniel. "My Lord, what do you wish of me?"

Joniel smiled as Nai looked stunned. Nai walked around the hologram. "Remarkable, quite remarkable."

Joniel smiled and looked at the hologram. "My lady, I would like you to download any time travel that this ship has done since I last gave you a command into this communicator device." He picked up a hand held communicator.

The hologram bowed slightly. "That is a simple task my lord, there has only been one trip."

Joniel looked at the screen and showed Nai. Nai smiled. "We've got them. We have the precise co-ordinates."

Joniel smiled, his eyes were cold. "My lady, is there anyone on this ship who was part of my crew before I left?"

The hologram thought for a moment. "All crew members other than Justus Crieik abandoned ship with you."

Joniel frowned. "What did Justus do after we abandoned ship?"

The hologram thought for a moment. "He removed the programming he had inserted into my memory banks and took the ship into the space corridor. He met with the Akillian Sheraktor and a new crew was taken on board."

Joniel smiled but it was a cold smile. "Were the people who were taken on board Follower believers?"

The hologram thought for a moment. "All of them were."

Joniel thought for a moment. "Are they still on the ship? Is everyone who was on this ship when it travelled in time still on this ship now? Has anyone joined the ship since?"

The hologram thought for a moment. "They are. Yes. Nobody has joined this ship since."

Joniel took a deep breath. "My lady I want you to initiate the green A4563879 canisters in Mid Level 34, Sub Section 45. My access code is XER8793E. Await orders."

The hologram bowed. "Very good my lord."

Joniel turned to Nai. "I am going to take this ship back in time to just before they caused the time flux. I am going to do this cloaked so that nobody in that time zone can see us. I'm then going to eliminate everyone on this ship."

Nai raised an eyebrow. "Nice idea but it won't work. The ship has already been back in time so taking it back earlier isn't going to help. Get the time co-ordinates and we'll go back to this ship just before it went back."

Joniel thought about it. "You are right. Ok, here are the time co-ordinates. My lady, you may stand down on that last order. Tell me what actions this ship has carried out since it took the trip."

The hologram thought for a moment. "It has rested here in space awaiting orders. It has communicated once with the Follower High Command. Other than day to day maintenance duties no other actions have been recorded."

Nai looked at the screen and typed the co-ordinates into his wrist device. He then grabbed Joniel and they felt a slight tingling sensation. The hologram disappeared but everything else in the room seemed the same.

Joniel typed into the keyboard again. He checked the time, date and dimensional information was correct and the hologram appeared. "My lady I want you to initiate the green A4563879 canisters in Mid Level 34, Sub Section 45. My access code is XER8793E. Preserve our life in this room but eliminate everyone else on the ship."

The hologram bowed. "Very good my lord." The hologram hesitated for a moment. "Your orders have been carried out."

Joniel smiled. "Well that has hopefully sorted out the problem."

Nai looked shocked. "How many people were on the ship?"

Joniel looked serious. "My lady, what was the total number on the crew manifest excluding us two."

The hologram bowed slightly. "One thousand, two hundred and fifty six."

Joniel looked at Nai who was staring wide eyed at him. Nai opened his mouth to speak and couldn't. He swallowed hard. "Joniel, you just killed all those people."

Joniel looked down. "Of course I did. It was the only way to stop them going back and carrying out the plan. They hadn't left the ship in between so it was the only way to eliminate the time distortion. Everyone on this ship had to die."

Nai looked at the screen on the table. "Now I know why you don't want Kyla to know about your past. You didn't show any remorse there at all. I thought us fey were cold."

Joniel smiled but there was no warmth in it. "I feel remorse, probably more than you'll ever know. I just don't let it cloud my judgment. Well, it seems I have a ship. Shall we bring it into the present and take it home?"

Nai nodded, he was looking away as if he couldn't face to look at Joniel.

Joniel keyed in the time and space co-ordinates and they felt a shudder as the ship phased out of that time zone and into the new one but to a location near to the fleet headed by the Horus. Joniel keyed in his hailing code and sent it to the Horus. It was picked up, acknowledged and he was invited to dock.

Joniel took a deep breath. "Well that was successful. Oh My Lady, please deal with the corpses on board. I would like them sent to AX56734 Code GHDEC effective immediately."

Nai looked up. "I don't think I even want to know what that meant."

Joniel half smiled. "No you don't. But it was an ecologically sound solution."

Nai shook his head. "Well you'd better be getting back to being the family man then. I think this Universe will be a little safer knowing that you are. I'm just glad you never took up a contract with my name on it."

Joniel smiled. "Back to my well-earned retirement."

Nai smiled back. "Oh yes? I think you've just made up for your time off."

Joniel looked quite serious. "It was necessary."

Nai sighed. "That is the problem, it was. You didn't hesitate. I'm actually glad that it was you dealing with it as I would have had a whole world of problems up here in my head if it had been me."

Joniel looked down. "And what makes you think I don't?"

Nai looked a little shocked. "I just assumed."

Joniel looked up at him. "Well don't ever presume to know me. I do what has to be done and I've done it well over the years. That time at least it was the right thing to do. Now if you don't mind I would like to get back to my wife."

Nai put a hand on his shoulder and Joniel looked up at him. Nai just smiled and they went back to the Horus.

12

A solitary ship floated gracefully through the blackness of space. It was unmarked and slipped silently into the galaxy where the Horus and the rest of the fleet were stationed awaiting orders. As it entered the galaxy it cloaked, the miniscule amount of time that it was visible on any radar lost in time and space.

On board a solitary creature checked the dials and calculated the ship's every move. His long green fingers tipped with black claws clacked slightly on the dials and knobs as he made minute adjustments to his course.

When he was within a hundred yards of the Horus he sent a hail. "Greetings to the Horus. Code X45THARE."

Anathorn was in the command chair when the hail arrived and he nearly jumped out of his seat. "Rennon, I think this may interest you. There is someone here giving almost an identical code to your security code."

Rennon walked over and looked at the screen. "Well I never, I wouldn't let that miscreant on board if I were you, that's my brother!"

Anathorn smiled. "You mean there was another one like you at home?"

Rennon smiled back. "What is so unusual about that? Three more actually and a sister. My parents liked a big family. Well you'd better let him on board."

Anthorn raised an eyebrow and typed in the acceptance code. The ship decloaked and came in to dock.

Rennon strode to the docking port with purpose. He had left his laptop in his lab and his hands were free. He stopped for a moment and adjusted his clothing using the reflection in a window. He smoothed down his hair but it jumped back up again and he took a deep breath. He then continued and went to the port where his brother was just coming through the security scanner.

He walked down the corridor like a gunslinger facing a showdown. His stomach was full of butterflies and somehow now, as always, he felt somewhat inadequate. His brother always made him feel that way. He was taller, stronger and in so many things he was so much better than Rennon. He would even have to share his name if they chose to call him by his surname. There he was, dressed in his smart space suit, his twinkling blue eyes alert and keen. His physique toned from hours spent in the gym. He walked down the hallway towards Rennon and the two embraced.

Rennon cleared his throat. "Good to see you Athane."

Athane nodded. "Good to see you too. I thought I'd pay you a visit but this is not all pleasure. I need to talk to Prince Anathorn."

Rennon smiled. "Well that can be arranged. How long are you staying? We have a room for you if you need it."

Athane looked around. "It looks like a nice place you have here. I'd like to stay a day or two if that is alright. Well depending on how my meeting with Prince Anathorn goes. I can't tell you anything until I've spoken to him obviously. Afterwards we can discuss things. I'd value your help little brother, you were always the bright one."

Rennon almost stopped in his tracks to hear his brother talk like that. Memories of the years of his brother always beating him at everything came to mind. He raised an eyebrow and as his brother turned to look at a viewing platform that gave him a view out of the expanse of space Rennon scanned him. All scans appeared normal. He scanned again.

Athane caught the reflection of what Rennon was doing and smiled. "Little brother, you won't find anything there. I've already been through your security scanners. But I expect after all you've been through it would make you a little nervous. Mother is very proud of you by the way."

Rennon looked bemused.

Athane laughed. "Well you little brother are a bit of a legend these days. Who would have thought it eh, my brother! You really don't know do you? How in the Universes can you stay so modest? Don't you think that the tales of what you and your friends have done haven't become the stuff of legend? In every bar on every planet I would guess that someone knows your name." Athane shook his head in disbelief. "My little brother, working with the Prince, rubbing shoulders with King Nailindris. Who would have believed it?"

Rennon looked down but secretly smiled to himself. "I haven't really had a chance to think about it. These are just my friends and we did what needed to be done."

Athane smiled and patted his brother on the back. "Only you could be so matter of fact about something so huge as what you and your friends have done. It is quite remarkable."

They walked together down the corridor as Rennon keyed in that Athane requested an audience with Anathorn. Anathorn responded immediately and they went to the meeting room.

Anathorn was sitting at the head of the meeting table when Athane was shown in. Rennon came in with him but let him go ahead.

Athane stepped forward, bowed and waited for the Prince to speak.

Anathorn looked him over. He was indeed half a foot taller than Rennon. His hair was slightly longer, his face broader and his jaw was stronger. He was a bull of a man, his chest was solid and obviously toned. Where Rennon was the Scientist his brother was the warrior. "Welcome to the Horus. May I ask if this is a social visit to pay your respects to your brother or do you have business here as well."

Athane looked up. "I have come on behalf of the Hakasinian Embassy on Derakalos 9. Since the start of the hostilities we have been unable to safely travel the trade routes between the outer planets and Hakasin. It was only via a very complicated route that we managed to get a message from the Galaxy. It seems that the whole area has been shut down by the Followers. We know that our people are starving as they are refusing to bow to the Followers' will. Everywhere else in the galaxies the Followers are decimated and an ineffectual force. I am here to ask that the force that they have in that galaxy is similarly wiped out.

We have put a request to King Osiris but we have received no answer. I have been sent here to ask for your help. Our people are starving and they need to be liberated. Would you be able to help me?"

Anathorn looked down at his hands on the table. "I will consider the matter and I will let you know what I have decided later today. You are welcome to spend some time with your brother while I make my decision."

Athane looked disappointed. He bowed grudgingly, turned on his heels and left the room, followed by Rennon.

Anathorn looked at his screen. His fingers hovered but somehow he didn't feel comfortable about the whole situation. It had been a short conversation but something about Athane made him nervous, set him on edge. Or was it the situation in general. If Osiris hadn't responded then there was most likely a very good reason. To ask him again would possibly cause problems.

He leant back in his chair and put his hands on his lap. It was a quiet moment amongst the chaos of the day. The communiques kept flickering up on screen but he let them. He stared at the ceiling, not least to be able to look at a blank nothing for a moment. Thoughts, problems and questions crowded his overtired mind and forced out any possibility of finding an easy answer. He longed for a quiet moment.

The door opened and Aliniel walked in. He loved her, he knew that but he longed for her to just want to be quiet with him.

She strode across the room. "Anathorn, I have received a communication from my grandmother and she has invited us to a Grand Ball on her ship. Are we going to be able to attend?"

Anathorn was screaming inside. He wanted her to just walk in, walk over to him and put her arms around him. To kiss him and to tell him that everything was alright. To be soft and gentle with him like only she could.

He reached out his hand for her to take it, which she did but she had him caught in one of her "you had better answer this" stares. He didn't want to. A trip to the Grandmother Ship at the moment was the last thing he wanted to do. He wanted her to understand that what he was doing was important. If he made a mistake people died. She made a mistake and it was a fashion disaster and in truth nobody on the Horus was in any way interested. He did love her but she was pushing that love to the boundaries that he couldn't take it.

She smiled sweetly at him, sat on his lap and pushed the laptop lid down. That angered him even more as he had an unfinished communique sitting there that had taken him nearly an hour to get right. She put her arms around him and she had that look on her face that he knew all too well, the "give me what I want" look. She put on her purring voice and spoke gently in his ear. "Anathorn, we could really do with some time away from all this. I need some of your special attention."

Electric shocks ran down his spine and confused his thoughts. At that point he just wanted to forget about everything and take her where she wanted to go. He was torn between duty and love, well lust, he did know the difference. What he felt for her was a good mixture of all three. The sort of emotions that should have cemented their love and made them a rock for each other to lean on in times of trouble, even if her advice was never really all that useful and usually involved the showiest approach. Thankfully he could remember when he was a lot like that, so he was able to forgive her, humour her and take enough of her advice that she believed she was in control. As, deep down he'd always known she wanted to be and recently he had admitted to himself that control was her main goal. She wanted to be the power behind the throne. Something he had no objection to really except that her judgment was poor and her ideas based on vanity and a selfish need to express that part of her nature.

He couldn't help looking at her and wondering what life would have been like if he'd met her mother before Joniel had. Joniel was right, there was a lot in her that reminded him of Kyla but that in itself didn't help. He was with the daughter, not the mother. The mother was support, wisdom and all the things that he needed. Her daughter was a selfish brat who had done everything she could to drive his love into the deepest recesses of his mind on occasion. Where Kyla was prepared to devote herself to the matter in hand and had beliefs, Aliniel was prepared to devote herself to looking good. He shook himself out of his vicious thoughts as she kissed him passionately. He kissed her back, he couldn't help it, he wanted to but he also knew he had a million other things that he would have liked to have been able to discuss with her and then perhaps when they were a little more solved in his mind enjoyed what he knew would come next.

That part of him could not ignore her pert breasts and suggestive movements, the way she sat on his lap and the way she stroked his hair and ran her fingers down his spine.

Joniel and Kyla were in the training room. Joniel had just finished developing a new move and was picking her up off of the floor. She rubbed her bruised arm and laughed. "Well that was pretty effective. I like that one but I think it depends more on your strength and height. It isn't one I could do successfully."

He saw the bruise developing on her arm and put his hand gently on it and looked down at her. "I'm so sorry, I got a bit carried away there."

She smiled. "Not to worry, only another bruise, it will heal quickly and not as bad as the one I got last night." She showed him a purple welt on her shoulder.

Joniel looked confused.

Kyla laughed. "So last night was so unmemorable for you?"

Joniel hadn't forgotten and smirked when he remembered how she had got the bruise.

Rennon was sitting talking to Athane. The conversation was going around in circles about Anathorn offering help to his planet. Rennon was slightly distracted after the third hour of the same speculation and the conversation going between planning what they would do if Anathorn said yes and the deep despair of what would happen if he said no. Rennon was distracted because his woman was on a research mission to Osiris' ship and picking up supplies for him. He never liked it when she was away and this time particularly he wished she was there. He wanted to show Athane, he wanted to prove to him that he did actually have someone in his life now. He shook the thought from his mind and focused back on the conversation before Athane required any answers that he actually needed to be concentrating on.

Aliniel walked down the corridor towards the room that she had demanded so that she could have a private dressing room when Anathorn was being boring and ignoring her. She had seen it as a major victory when she had got it but now somehow she felt it was a room he could exile her to. She strode down the corridor, catching her reflection in any chrome surface that was smooth enough. She stopped for a moment and straightened her hair and then smiled as a group of new recruits smiled at her as she strode past them.

She was convinced that a tall and good looking man in a pilot's uniform she passed was watching her. She smiled at him and looked down shyly.

Her heart raced as he looked at her and she felt really good about herself. He carried a box and looked like he was going somewhere but as soon as he saw her he changed direction and followed her.

Down corridor after corridor he tailed her but of course she noticed him and pretended that she didn't. She got to her room and keyed in the code. As she was about to enter he stepped forwards.

His voice was deep, it resonated inside her somehow. "I am so sorry for this rudeness but I couldn't help but follow you to find out who you are."

She stepped inside. "You had better come in and I'll tell you."

He stepped inside. He was tall, imposing, muscular and he took her breath away. His emerald green eyes seemed to reach into her very soul and his very presence excited her. She was almost breathless as he stepped aside to let him pass and closed the door. All fear had gone, all caution thrown to the wind. Her mind was racing and all she could think about was him and to wonder why she hadn't noticed him before.

He smiled and pointed to a chair. "May I sit?"

She nodded. "Who are you? I don't think I've seen you around here before. Which crew are you on?"

The stranger smiled. "I am Daks. You wouldn't have noticed me, I'm just a pilot. But I noticed you and you looked sad but so beautiful so I thought I'd see if you were alright."

It went out of her head that she had just locked herself in with a total stranger. It didn't occur to her that someone as good looking as him would have stood out without question. She wasn't questioning anything, any training had gone. She smiled at him. "I'm forgetting my manners, may I pour you a drink?" It totally went out of her mind that it was four in the afternoon. "What would you like?"

He got up and followed her to the table. "You choose for me, I'll have what you are having."

She poured a drink and passed it to him. As their hands touched she felt an electric shock that tingled down her spine. It was exciting and confused her. Her hand seemed to go numb and she dropped the glass which shattered on the hard floor and without thinking she bent to pick it up as did Daks. She was too busy looking at him and didn't see the glass shard that he pushed at her so that she cut her finger.

The now too familiar stranger smiled and met her eye to eye. She was too busy watching him to notice that he slipped a cloth from his pocket. She was too entranced to smell the vague aroma that resembled cloves. As she looked deep into his eyes she didn't realise he was wrapping the cloth around her cut hand. She felt it was soothing, both the pain and the pain in her mind, the confusion was gone. She was no longer questioning everything, all she wanted was to hear what Daks had to say.

Daks cupped her injured hand between his, one hand above, one below.

He was holding the cloth close to the wound to make sure that the liquid soaked in and floated off in her bloodstream. He smiled and spoke, the words seemed to embed themselves in her very soul. "You poor thing. You are so beautiful and so wise. He doesn't appreciate you but you know that. He is too busy dancing to the King's tune and improving his own political situation. You aren't important to him anymore, neither is the child that you carry. He is laughing at you and your father. I can see it in your eyes. You know don't you? You know that he's in love with your mother."

She looked stunned and tilted her head on the side. "But I'm not pregnant."

Daks smiled. "Oh, I'm sorry, I thought you were, I can usually tell things like that. I must apologise."

Aliniel smiled. "An easy mistake to make as anyone would assume that such a seemingly loving couple would have ensured that sort of thing by now. But sadly affairs of state seem to keep my lover from my bed on far too many lonely nights."

Daks clasped her hand tighter. "That is awful, the man is a fool. A beautiful woman such as you should not be left on her own. Nothing should be more important to him than you. You are a precious jewel that he does not deserve."

Aliniel jumped slightly. "Is there a woman in your life?" She didn't know why she was asking. It was like she was two people. One was screaming "no", the other wanted him so badly it physically hurt.

Daks looked sad. "There was once but sadly she died. She was a rare beauty, very like you. That was why I felt bold enough to come and speak to you. You remind me of her."

Aliniel blushed slightly and looked down. "You honour me too greatly. I am sure that your wife was a rare beauty. You must miss her very much."

While she was looking down Daks pulled a small vial from his pocket and inhaled from it. By the time she looked up his eyes were watering and tears rolled down his cheeks. "My dear, I miss her so much."

She stepped close, pulled her hand away from his hands and put her arms around him and held him close. "You poor, poor man. Well you won't be alone any more, we will be firm friends."

Daks stroked her hair with his hand. "You are a wonderful person. I do hope that we will. But now I must go, I have duties I must carry out. I hope that I may visit you again. But if the Prince knew I was talking with you he would probably forbid it and I might just disappear. I know what that man was once like. But be careful my love. If you know his secret then you will know why."

Aliniel's face brightened up. "You know about Anathorn? Tell me please. He won't tell me anything of his past."

Daks smiled. "My dear, it is not a tale a woman such as you should hear and he is a man with a good many secrets, especially now. Believe me you are better off not knowing. If he wanted to tell you he would tell you himself. Or perhaps you should ask your mother. I'm sure he's told her but then I suppose she'd keep his confidence, whoever was asking. I must go, I fear him, he is a cold blooded killer and I would not be caught here if he did not wish it. Promise me you will not tell him I have visited. He would kill me if he found out."

Aliniel smiled. "Of course I won't tell him."

In the pilot's quarters a man lay dead. He would have been tall, muscular, imposing. His dark hair and neatly trimmed beard were matted with blood. He had been tortured and savagely beaten. His shift didn't start until the next day so he lay there in his room, alone, on a ship, in the cold expanse of space as what looked like his duplicate walked down the corridors until he came to an empty room, touched his wrist device and disappeared.

Anathorn was reading his communiques and trying to remember the wording of the one he had lost. The words were still there, hanging in space but somehow revisited they didn't seem to go together the same way. He could get the general idea but not the way he had conveyed it the first time. His concentration was shot, all he could think about was Aliniel and what they had just experienced together. He shook his head and opened another message. It was basic admin but it needed his attention, they all did and there were only so many hours in the day.

The minutes slipped into hours, the hours into the next day. Night came and went without him noticing. There was no sun or moon to remind him, just the blackness of space perforated by a million sparkling diamonds that were eternally bright, impossibly far away and some of them not even there anymore.

He was hungry and tired when he finally managed to get the wording right and signed off on the message. He sent it into the virtual ether to find its intended recipient. He felt insecure, he was unsure about it but it had to be written. It was mundane, just admin but to the person who had expressed their concerns it was their employment, their life. They had taken the time to point out to him a defect in the system that ran Keronikos 5, an air cooling machine. It had been a genuine offer of information. He just hoped that his very carefully written message that could say no more than they didn't have the parts would be enough to calm the man's fears that they were about to be simultaneously put into orbit in a hundred pieces. The importance of the wording being that a supplies vessel had not arrived and that was something he really didn't want to reveal to anyone who didn't need to know. It didn't take much to realise that that could be the portent for more trouble to come. A supply vessel didn't simply not arrive, it usually meant that someone had intercepted it and soon they would feel the gap left by the supplies they now didn't have.

Rennon sat in the observation window with his brother. They both had a glass of whisky which Athane had brought with him. It was from Earth and rare outside the Milky Way, a single malt and one that Rennon particularly liked. They had talked into the early hours. To start with things had been fine but gradually the cracks had begun to show.

Athane took a sip of his whisky. "So, you are a friend of the Great Prince Anathorn. What do you think of his decisions? Do you always agree with him?"

Rennon looked up surprised. "Well that was direct. I think that the Prince works excessively hard. He asks for advice of those who know a situation before making a decision and when he makes a decision it is usually very well informed. Don't worry, if he is able I'm sure that the Prince will help you."

Athane looked down. "I'm not so sure. There is no power in it for him. Haven't you noticed that he's looking for the glory that he lost when King Osiris stepped in and took Anathorn's position? He would have been king."

Rennon smiled. "You don't know him well enough yet. He might have had a difficult past but he's every bit a Prince now."

Athane shook his head. "You were always a devoted follower Rennon. Even back at home. I suppose that comes of being the legitimate one and the one with everything offered to him. Some of us had to work harder for appreciation."

Rennon's smile faded from his face. "Father treated us both equally well. We were the same, but different. My studies were more something that he could understand. He wasn't martial."

Athane looked down. "Pity that he hadn't been or he may have been able to defend himself that night."

Rennon raised an eyebrow. "You mean when he died. But that was an accident."

Athane smiled but a dark shadow came over him. "For someone so enquiring you sure did accept our father's death easily. Didn't you ever question what happened? A man as brilliant as our father mixing two explosive chemicals and then heating them up? Is that really what happened?"

Rennon looked down into his drink.

Athane laughed. "You see, you didn't question it and our father's killer got away with his murder. Well I did question it and I found the man. Justice was served but I had to serve my time for it as well. The jury said there was no proof he had killed father." He rolled up his sleeve and showed Rennon the tattoo on his arm which was the symbol for Tangarasura, a high security prison on the Partehanon Planet. "That was how much I loved that man even though he wasn't my father. What did you do?"

Rennon went to stand up. "I had no idea."

Athane laughed. "Of course you didn't. You were always protected and allowed to get on with your wonderful work. You never had to do the dishes, or the housework or anything. All you did was sit in your corner at your desk and work. Well I hope it was worth it. You broke mother's heart when you went."

Rennon opened his mouth but closed it again. "I had no idea."

Athane took a large mouthful of his whisky. "Well, of course you didn't. The precious one should never be disturbed from his great work. And now you are working for the Vain Prince. Can't you see how he flounces around the Universe? Osiris' pet. You luxuriate here while the rest of us live in poverty. Yes you might be destroying the Followers but their pockets of resistance are destroying people's livelihoods. People are still being killed. You sit here in your ivory tower and look down on the rest of us ants. I bet we're just an ever growing death toll to you. Or is it just another chance for you to solve problems and bask in the glory?"

Rennon stood up. "Athane, I think you have had too much to drink. It has been a pleasure to see you again. Please do not spoil it by letting the alcohol speak for you."

Athane got up and swayed, he spun and knocked a decanter over. It spun out of control across the table and Rennon stared helplessly as the whisky spilled across his precious laptop which immediately went cold and dead. Athane tried to catch the decanter but moments after it had done its damage. He then put his finger to his lips as he swayed badly. "Oh, oops, did I break it. Well I'm sure that your Lord and Master will give you another and better one. I'm off to bed now and I'll see what his Flouciness has to say in the morning as to whether he is going to let all my people die." He swayed and staggered off to the door and down the corridor.

Rennon spent hours trying to dry and salvage the computer. At first feverishly desperate, at times just sitting and holding a cloth to soaked parts. Finally he grabbed it and threw it across the room. The pain of what his brother had said hit home. It was his laptop but did it matter, all his work was on the mainframe anyway.

He drank various glasses of water as he stared into the blackness of space. Somewhere out there was someone who truly did understand and he really missed her. His brother's words had cut him but how could he be blamed for something he didn't know about? Should he have questioned it? But at the time he was so lost, so lonely he just wanted to honour his father's memory.

The hours ticked away for him. He sat in the near darkness looking at the broken pieces of his beloved laptop laying against the wall. They had been so far together, he'd done so much good work on that machine. But, it was just a machine, cold, metal and plastic, it had no heart, no soul, no life. So why did he feel like he was mourning the loss of an old friend?

The morning must be bright somewhere Kyla thought. She stood at the window, her silk kimono showing her curves that were not lost on Joniel who sat up in bed watching her. Kyla was lost in thought. She had slept well but she felt tired, drained. It was like the happiness had been sucked out of everything. The thought came into her mind that terrified her. What if he was gone? She turned, walked back to bed, kissed him and slipped out of her robe. He smiled, slightly confused but happy enough to accept the situation as he cupped his hand around the back of her head and pulled her to him for a passionate kiss.

Set sat on his throne in an empty throne room. He had dismissed his servants and all the hangers on. He just wanted a bit of peace and quiet. The worries of the worlds were bearing down heavily on him. His desk in his private chamber was piled high with reports, none of them good. Most of his fleets had been wiped out, most of his soldiers were dead. His elbow rested on the ornate gold arm of the throne, his brow was resting in his palm. It didn't make him feel any better, nothing did. Ideas were evading him, he reached out to touch them and they scampered and slithered off to the furthermost reaches of his consciousness.

He screamed to the empty air. "It was not supposed to be like this!"

The silence was only momentarily broken and it closed up after his words, slamming shut on his moment of frustration. He looked around the room and felt the impossibility of his situation. He knew he could not build his fleets again, he didn't have the heart to do it. He knew that the virus would gradually take over, the madness would reach everyone. Now he could neither use it nor control it. It had been a huge and wonderful resource that out of control would now tear the worlds apart. The question had to be asked and he asked himself. Would it be without him or would he still get involved? There was no chance of total domination but could be broker a deal and be a part of all this?

In his mind he ran through the inventory of what was left. There was precious little in the grand scale of what there had been. He thought on the worlds he had controlled and all he had achieved and he felt at a loss. Why had they done this? Were they so keen to succumb to the madness? Did they really want to see families torn apart and people fighting out of sheer paranoia? How could they want this? Then the truth came to him, they more than likely didn't know. Only now at the end of it all he realised it. He had known the truth but perhaps they didn't.

Set smiled to himself. There was his power now, he knew and knowledge is power. He had a choice, he could become a small dark force and probably be hunted down fairly quickly. Or he could abandon his plans for total domination and settle for trying to be a part of the future and see where that would lead him.

Was their battle of eons worth all this? He'd seen the reports. Planets slashed and burnt by those who sought to rebuild. They call him evil, they blacken the name of his troops but they are the ones who are destroying the ordered communities he had sought to create. He had all the reports, they were stealing from other planets to build their own, paying the locals a fraction of the worth of what they were taking or not paying them at all. Great cities being repaired and rebuilt and they were calling it progress.

The lunatic that had started it all, he was still out there. But where? He had sent out scouting missions and listened for a whisper of the individual. That creature of carapace, that heartless, soulless monster who infected everyone and everything it touched. He was impotent against that creature now. It would wander, he would wander, he didn't even know what to call it, was it still a him? Did it still think? Or was it just wandering the realities infecting and screaming in madness?

Set pressed a button and a mechanical arm brought a keyboard in front of him. He pulled back his dark hood and spoke. "Lights".

Immediately the room filled with a myriad of sparkling lights which reflected on all of the black and chrome surfaces. The room shimmered and sparkled. Set didn't notice, he was too busy with the keyboard in front of him. His fingers flashing across the keyboard, backtracking, then typing some more.

"My dear brother and sister,

I must congratulate you on your success and I realise that it has been many eons since we last communicated. It is because of this that I feel that it is imperative that I contact you now as I feel that you have misunderstood the situation.

Over the eons our feud has been infinitely destructive and it has not served any of us. Now that you are reunited it is possibly time for all of us siblings to set aside our old enmity and to move forwards for the good of the galaxies.

I have invaluable information that, if we work together, may provide a solution to our current problem. All three of us after all are merely interested in the survival of the galaxies. There is nothing to gain from spending eternity wandering past dead worlds.

I offer the brotherly hand of friendship and I await your response."

He smiled and sat back, hands on the arms of his throne as he read back the message he had typed. He rubbed his chin, thought about it and then hit send.

Printed in Great Britain
by Amazon